MW00489766

Print ISBN: 978-0-6483246-6-9

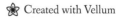 Created with Vellum

KERI ARTHUR

Demon's Dance

A LIZZIE GRACE NOVEL

With thanks to:

The Lulus
Indigo Chick Designs
Hot Tree Editing
Robyn E.
Julianne P.
Marjorie A.
The lovely ladies from Central Vic Writers
Lori from Cover Reveal Designs for the fab cover

ONE

The phone rang sharply, a shrill sound that made me jump and drew an obscenity from my lips. I opened one eye and studied the old-fashioned clock on the bedside table. The numbers did a somewhat blurry dance before revealing it was three in the morning. I'd been asleep for a whole two hours.

The warm body lying next to me echoed my obscenity as he groped for the phone. He hit the answer button and then said, voice husky with sleep, "Ranger Aiden O'Connor speaking—how may I help you?"

Though I couldn't make out exactly what was being said, I could hear the woman's tone—it was shrill. Horror-filled.

I turned and peered over Aiden's bare shoulder. The number displayed on the screen was the ranger station's; it had been diverted to Aiden's phone because he was on call for the next couple of nights. While there were seven rangers within the Faelan Werewolf Reservation, Aiden was head ranger and seemed to believe it was his duty to take the majority of night calls. His dedication to his job was one of the many things I admired about the man, but it was at times like this I couldn't help wishing he'd share the shift around a bit more.

Of course, it wouldn't be such a problem if the two of us actually went to sleep at a sensible hour.

"Ms. Jenkins, you need to calm down—"

The woman's screech was so loud that even I heard it, and it had Aiden yanking the phone away from his ear.

"Don't tell me to fucking calm down," she said, "I've just walked into the house to discover my goddamn boyfriend is dead—"

"I heard, Ms. Jenkins," he said patiently. "But I can't do anything until you give me your address."

She rattled it off and then said, "Do you think it'll be safe for me to remain here?"

Aiden hesitated. "Have you a neighbor you could go to? Just in case?"

"Yes. I'm sure Mrs. Potts won't mind."

I wondered if *her* Mrs. Potts was the same one who'd founded the Castle Rock gossip brigade. They'd recently declared the café I owned and ran with my best friend and fellow witch, Belle Kent, their "venue of choice" after I'd helped Mrs. Potts find her errant husband and, in the process, two grandchildren she never thought she'd have. If it *was* the same woman, then I was sure she wouldn't mind looking after the fraught Ms. Jenkins, if only because it would give the brigade something juicy to ruminate over.

"I'll have someone there in ten minutes," Aiden said.

"You can't get here any sooner?"

"I'm sorry, no."

She grunted and hung up. Aiden immediately dialed

both Byron—who lived closest to Castle Rock—and then his sister, Ciara, who was the reservation's coroner.

Once both were organized, he turned, gathered me in his warm arms, and kissed me. "I think you'd better get dressed."

I blinked. "Why? From what I heard, it's a simple murder—"

"Except it may not be. She mentioned bite marks, so we're either dealing with a murderer with a weird fetish, or we have another vampire on our hands."

I doubted it'd be a vampire, if only because Maelle Defour—the woman who owned and ran the Émigré night-club in Castle Rock—happened to be a blood sucker, and certainly *wouldn't* appreciate another vamp stepping into her territory. While she'd promised the council not to take blood from the unwilling in exchange for secrecy about her presence within the reservation, it was a promise that wouldn't hold if another vampire had set up shop here. Vamps did *not* like competition.

But I couldn't say any of that to Aiden, as the council hadn't yet seen fit to advise the rangers about Maelle. I certainly wasn't going to—I'd promised not to, and there was no way known I'd go back on that. The bitch was scary.

"I never thought I'd say this, but I'll be glad when the new witch gets here. At least he'll be in charge of all super-natural investigations, and I might be able to get some solid sleep."

Which didn't mean I wouldn't be involved. Aside from the fact the psychic part of my soul—the part attuned to evil and that kept tossing prophetic dreams of doom and disaster my way—kept suggesting this reservation was mine to look after, there was the whole wild magic factor to consider. Or

3

rather, the fact that it had somehow become a part of me—a part of my very DNA.

"You've only yourself to blame for tonight's lack of sleep." Aiden sounded far too cheerful for someone who was sleep deprived. "You were the one who insisted we watch the end of *The Two Towers* rather than going to bed."

"Because it's the best of the three movies and can't be watched piecemeal."

"I'll argue about the first part of that statement later. Right now, we need to get moving. Up, lazybones."

He threw the sheet off and got out of bed. Like most werewolves, he was on the lean side, but his body was well proportioned and nicely muscled, and he did have a rather nice backside.

I stretched the kinks out of my body, then wearily climbed out of bed and started getting dressed.

"I really wish you could be the reservation witch—it'd make more sense now that you're linked with the wild magic." He held up a hand to stall my almost instinctive response. "And yes, I know you've never been through accreditation or whatever you call it, and would therefore never be government approved."

Accreditation—or lack thereof—was certainly a good enough reason for never becoming a reservation witch, right alongside my decided lack of knowledge and training when it came to spell craft. But the *true* reason was the fact that the reservation witch was basically the government's mouthpiece and was expected to remain in regular contact with the high witch council. Given I was on the run from my parents, I had no intention of doing anything that might have them looking too closely at this place.

Of course, Castle Rock had now been without a proper witch for well over a year, and it had placed the entire reservation in a dangerous situation thanks to the presence of a large wellspring that had been left unguarded for entirely *too* long. Wild magic was neither good nor bad, but it would *always* draw the darker forces of the world if left in a raw, unprotected state. While *that* was no longer the case thanks to the spells both Ashworth—who'd been sent here by the Regional Witch Association to chase down a soul stealer, and who'd then stepped into the reservation position temporarily—and I had placed around it, the repercussions of leaving it unguarded would be felt for years to come.

In many respects, we were lucky the situation wasn't even worse, as there was a second wellspring here—one that Canberra didn't as yet know about. But both the ghost of the reservation's previous witch—Gabe Watson—and the soul of his werewolf wife—Katie, who also happened to be Aiden's younger sister—protected that one.

"Neither you nor I nor anyone else should be relying on my link with the wild magic, Aiden, because I shouldn't even have it." My voice held the slightest edge, one that was based on trepidation of a future possibility I could see coming and didn't want. "I have no idea if it'll even last. This reservation deserves someone who knows a hell of a lot more about spelling than me."

And if I put that statement out there in the universe often enough, maybe it'd listen.

"And I think you're downplaying your role and your magic far too much, Liz." He sat and pulled his boots on. "It wasn't the RWA witches or the heretic hunter who took out the various evil entities that have hit us in recent months. It was you—"

"It was *never* just me," I cut in curtly. "And there was always a high degree of luck involved. Sooner or later, that luck *will* run out."

5

His gaze met mine. Though his expression gave little away, I knew he sensed my fear. Knew he understood that it didn't come from the possibility of death, but rather discovery.

I took a deep breath and changed the subject. "I doubt we're dealing with a vampire—they generally don't leave bodies littered with bite marks."

Something flickered through his blue eyes—annoyance or disappointment or maybe even both—but all he said was, "If it's not a vampire, then what else could it be?"

"There's all manner of supernatural beasties that don't mind taking a bite or two out of humans." I paused, and then, in an attempt to lighten the mood, added, "And apparently a few werewolves who don't mind the odd nip or two, either."

The smile that tugged at his lips didn't quite dispel the annoyance in his expression. The confrontation I feared—the one where I either told the truth about myself or walked away—was looming ever closer.

"Only when begged. Which you did—and rather loudly."

Which was certainly true. But then, he did do some of his best work with teeth and tongue. I grabbed a tie and swept my hair into a ponytail, then shoved my feet into sandals and slung my purse over my shoulder. While I didn't have much in the way of witch paraphernalia with me, I'd gotten into the habit of keeping a small, bubble-wrapped bottle of holy water in an inside purse pocket. There weren't very many situations in which it wouldn't provide at least some protection, even if it was something as simple as forming a protective circle over which evil could not cross.

He swept his keys, phone, and wallet from the bedside table and then said, "Ready?"

I nodded and headed for the stairs. His house was a lovely two-story, cedar-clad building situated on the curving shoreline of the Argyle Lake and, aside from the two en suite bedrooms upstairs, had a ground floor that was a combined kitchen, dining and living area. Light poured in through the wall of glass that dominated the end overlooking the lake, and though the moon was currently in a waning phase, her power sang through my veins. It was a force all witches could feel, and one that could greatly amplify the strength of spells.

I crossed mental fingers and hoped that I didn't have to use her tonight. That whatever had caused the death of Ms. Jenkins's boyfriend *wasn't* supernatural but rather a simple murder—an affair gone wrong, perhaps. After a couple of tumultuous months dealing with vampires, soul-sucking spirits, and a heretic witch determined to claim the larger wellspring as his own, we really deserved a few months of peace.

But that rather annoying prophetic part of my soul said a month was all we were ever likely to get. That peace wouldn't be ours until the whispers of an unguarded wellspring finally stopped echoing through the darker places of the world.

Aiden's truck was parked out the front of the building; the lights flashed as he hit the remote, flaring briefly across the lake's dark but still water. He didn't switch on the siren until we were out of the park and on the main highway.

It took us just under thirty minutes to get to Castle Rock. Aiden sped through the main part of town, then swung right and drove through a number of dark side streets until we were up near the secondary college.

After a final turn, he pulled up beside the two green-and-white ranger SUVs already parked there. The house was a simple double-fronted, fibro-cement building that was painted in what could only be described as baby-shit yellow. The roof tiles and the front door were dark brown, and there were cream-and-brown-striped canvas awnings pulled halfway down over the only two windows in the front of the building. At the far end of the long drive was a carport; parked inside were two vehicles—a Mercedes and a new-looking four-wheel drive. The house might be modest, but the occupants obviously weren't struggling for a buck.

The front door opened, and a familiar figure strode toward us. Like most Marin werewolves, Byron was tall, with dark amber eyes, brown skin, and brown hair that had a slight tinge of red. Surprise flitted across his expression when he saw me, but all he said was, "There's no sign of intruders or a break-in, and all the doors were locked from the inside. Whoever did this was invited in. Ciara's inside examining the body."

"Have we got an ID yet?"

Byron nodded. "According to his driver's license, our victim is Kyle Jacobson, and he's twenty-nine."

"Wolf or human?"

"Human. There's no indication of a struggle and no obvious sign of death, although the body is riddled with bite marks."

"Of the vampire variety?" I asked.

"The only vampire bite I've seen was on the neck of that teenager, and she didn't have the same sort of bruising as this bloke." Byron shrugged. "I guess it depends on whether every vampire has a different style of feeding."

"They tend not to," I said. "While the length of their canines can vary—and some of the older ones even have the ability to retract them totally—the incisions generally have the same look. Unless, of course, they simply tear at the throat, and that's usually the province of newly created vamps who haven't gotten control over their blood lust."

Byron blinked. "I think that's more information about vampires and their teeth than I ever wanted."

"Let's just hope that's *not* what we're dealing with here," Aiden said. "Have you talked to Ms. Jenkins yet?"

"No, but Mrs. Potts came out when I first arrived to admonish me for the time it took to get here. I dare say we'll be getting a bad rap around their gossip table."

So it *was* the same Mrs. Potts. I had no doubt she was already aware of my presence here, and that I'd be quizzed about it on Tuesday when we opened again. "There won't be anything bad said—not if they want their usual coffee and cake."

"I suspect the decision as to whether they prefer gossip over your cakes will be a very tough one for them to make." Byron returned his gaze to Aiden. "You want me to dare the lioness's den and grab a statement from Ms. Jenkins?"

Aiden shook his head. "I'll do it once I talk to Ciara. Head home, and I'll update you tomorrow."

"Thanks, boss." He nodded at me and then walked away, whistling softly as he headed for his car.

Aiden glanced at me. "Ready to confront whatever mess lies inside?"

"Whatever lies inside is *not* going to be anywhere near as stomach churning as a wolf that's been skinned."

"Which is something I'd really like to believe, but after the events of the last couple of months, I'm not sure we'll *ever* be able to say that with certainty."

"We will. It'll just take a couple of years before the

darker forces realize the wellspring is protected and there's no point coming here."

"A statement I *don't* find comforting."

He led the way across the parched-looking lawn. Once we'd put on the disposable shoe protectors either Byron or Ciara had dumped near the door, we entered the house. It was as basic on the inside as it was on the outside—there was a central hall off which there were a number of rooms, and what appeared to be a combined kitchen-living area at the far end. The air ran with hints of lavender and orange and was almost too warm, but there was no immediate sense of evil or death. Which didn't mean anything—there were plenty of supernatural beings clever enough to conceal their presence from psychics like me. But I had no sense of a ghost, either, and that meant this death had been ordained. Unless, of course, said ghost hovered over his body. Many of them did in those initial few hours—some because they couldn't accept what had happened, others because the manner of their death confined them to a certain area. Despite what many non-witch textbooks might say, there really were no set rules when it came to either ghosts or shades.

Aiden walked into the second room on the right. Ciara was examining a wound on the victim's arm but glanced up as we entered. Like Aiden, she was tall and rangy in build, with short blonde hair that gleamed silver under the room's rather bright light, and eyes that were a deep blue rather than the usual amber of a werewolf. But then, the O'Connor pack were gray wolves, a color that tended to be somewhat rare amongst Australian packs. Most were brown, red, or black; the O'Connors ran the full gamut from silvery white to a blond so dark it was almost brown.

The bedroom was basic and rather unromantic,

although the patches in the plasterwork suggested they'd been in the process of doing it up. Aside from the queen-sized bed, there were two rather ratty-looking bedside tables —one of which was stacked high with romance novels—and a couple of freestanding wooden wardrobes that had also seen better days. The air here was even hotter than in the hall, and it had my "other" senses prickling. That heat *wasn't* the result of a long week of above-average temperatures, of that I was sure. There was something to be found here—maybe not in this room, but definitely in the house itself.

"What have we got?" Aiden stopped at the end of the bed. "Aside from a naked and very dead male?"

Ciara grimaced. "Multiple bruising and puncture marks, but no other wounds and no immediately obvious reason for death."

"Do you think we're dealing with a vampire?"

"Hard to say without opening him up and seeing the size and location of the lividity—which," she added, with a glance my way, "is where any blood remaining in the body after the heart stops pumping will settle in direct response to gravity."

"Ah." I stopped beside Aiden and studied the man on the bed. He had a shock of vivid red hair, dark stubble around his chin, and pubic hair that was black, which suggested red wasn't his natural color. There were multiple blue-black marks on both his arms and his inner thighs, and all of them rather weirdly resembled love bites. If this *was* a vampire attack, then he or she was acting outside known norms.

I ignored the growing sense of trepidation and returned my gaze to Ciara. "Which of the bruises have puncture wounds?"

"All of them."

"Is it okay if I look at one?"

"Sure—do you want gloves?"

I shook my head. "I have no intention of touching him."

I moved around the bed and bent to examine an arm wound. It wasn't hard to see the bite marks, and they certainly *did* appear vampiric in nature. And yet, doubt stirred, if only because most vamps didn't leave this type of bruising behind.

But it wasn't like I was an expert when it came to vampires. My experience was limited to what I'd read in the books Belle had inherited from her gran and the bits and pieces I'd learned during my encounters with both Maelle and the vampire witch who'd come to the reservation seeking revenge.

"The wounds are definitely penetrative," I said, "but vamps aren't the only supernatural creatures who dine on their victims' blood."

"I'm not sure I really want an answer to this," Ciara said. "But what sort of creatures are we talking about?"

"Off the top of my head, there's the lamia, a type of demon who takes on human form to seduce men and then drain them when they're asleep. There's also a Scottish fairy that's a cross between a succubus and a vampire." I hesitated. "But if he didn't die of blood loss, then we could be dealing with something like Kitsune—they don't actually take blood, but rather their victim's life force."

"How likely is it to be the latter?" she asked.

My gaze swept Jacobson's body again. Despite the bruising, he still very much looked like a man in his late twenties. "Unlikely. Everything I've read about them suggests the process seriously ages the victim."

"If the autopsy can't pin down a cause of death," Aiden

asked, "is there any way to reveal what type of supernatural creature we're dealing with?"

"I can't sense his ghost in the house, so other than asking Belle to make contact with his soul, no," I said. "There's certainly nothing within this room to suggest what might have done this."

Aiden's gaze narrowed. "Does that mean you're sensing something elsewhere?"

"Maybe." I hesitated. "It's the heat, more than anything. It just seems rather unusual."

"We're in the midst of a heat wave," Ciara commented, "and these old places don't have much in the way of insulation."

"I know, it's just—" I shrugged. "Something feels off, that's all."

"In what way?" Aiden asked.

"If I knew *that*, I'd say."

"Do you want to look around?"

"It may be nothing—"

"Or it might be something," he cut in. "I don't think any of us would dare discount your concerns after the last few months. Yell if you find anything."

"Of course."

But I didn't immediately leave the room. Instead, I walked around, skimming a hand above the various surfaces and items. Prophetic dreams and an odd ability to sense evil weren't my only psychic talents—I was also gifted with psychometry. On a surface level, the talent let me trace misplaced items and sense emotions via touch. But on a deeper level, I could track missing people or slip into the mind of whoever owned the item I was holding, allowing me to see and experience whatever was happening to them at the time.

The latter was *not* something I did very often—I'd heard too many tales of psychics losing themselves in the minds of others, and I wasn't about to risk anything like that.

I did have one advantage over most other psychics, though—Belle. She wasn't only a witch, but also my familiar. It was a situation that had caused great consternation to my powerful blueblood parents—not only did I have the audacity to be severely underpowered, but I also had the temerity to have a lower-powered witch as a familiar rather than the far more acceptable cat or spirit—even though *that* was something I had no control over.

But Belle's presence in my life had saved it more than once—she was, in fact, the best thing that had ever happened to me.

And here I was thinking that award went to Aiden.

Belle's thought whispered into my mind, her mental tone soft enough to suggest she wasn't entirely awake. While telepathy was one of her psychic skills rather than mine, the ability to share thoughts was one of the many benefits that came with her being my familiar. *He falls into the "best thing right now" category. What are you doing up? It's four in the morning.*

I had to pee. What's your excuse?

Aiden was called in on a murder.

And he's dragged you along to the crime scene? Why?

Suspicious bite marks.

A groan ran down the mental lines. *Don't tell me we've another vampire.*

That I can't say for sure as they're not exactly traditional bite marks.

At least the new witch arrives today. He can deal with the damn problem.

Hopefully.

Hopefully? I'm not liking the sound of that.

It's that whole thing about counting chickens. I just don't want to jinx things.

I finished the sweep of the room and headed for the door. There was nothing untoward here—nothing other than the heat, anyway. Which should have been a relief but instead only ramped up the trepidation.

You can hardly jinx something that's already a signed and sealed deal, Belle said.

But the witch isn't yet here. Until he is, I'll continue worrying.

And about more than his arrival. I had little doubt he'd get here; it was more the possibility it'd be someone we knew that worried me. There were a lot of witch families in Canberra, and the chances of that happening were remote. *Extremely* remote. And yet, I couldn't escape the notion that that's exactly what we were about to face.

Belle's concern ran down the line. *Is this another of your premonitions? Do I need to start packing?*

I'm not running anymore, Belle. I hesitated. *I'm not entirely sure it'd even be possible.*

Her concern increased. *Because of the wild magic?*

For whatever reason, I've developed an affinity with the power of this place—and it's an affinity that's growing. I don't think it'll let me leave.

But you've been beyond the boundaries of the reservation more than a few times with both Aiden and me.

Yes, but none of them were permanent. The wild magic—or at least the portion controlled by Katie—would have been aware of that. I hesitated again. *Of course, it's possible these fears are nothing more than my natural instinct to expect the worse.*

She snorted, the sound reverberating loudly through my

brain. *Given the wild magic has somehow mixed itself with your DNA, I doubt it. Besides, your instincts haven't led you astray very often of late.*

No, they hadn't—and that in itself was somewhat scary. My instincts had been hit and miss my entire life—right up until the point we'd entered this reservation, in fact. I had no idea if the change was due to the wild magic or whether something stranger was happening.

I walked down the hall, discovering two more bedrooms, a bathroom, and a laundry but no real source for the growing certainty something *other* than a vampire had been in this house.

I'll keep all bits crossed that it's wrong this time—at least when it comes to the new witch, she said. *Especially if it turns out this place* is *the end of the line for us.*

Would you be upset about that if it was?

Warmth and a mental hug briefly filled the link. *Hell no. I love the café, I love this area, and I'm more than ready to settle down.*

And finally have a real life somewhere. She didn't add that bit, but we'd been friends for so long now that she didn't need to. Guilt slithered through me; it'd been Belle who'd paid the greater price when we'd run from Canberra. Her entire family was very close, but the situation I'd run from had been so extreme that even her mother—one of the few people we'd actually confided in—had said it would be better if we stayed out of contact.

You didn't force me to go with you, Belle chided softly. *I might be your familiar, but I still had the choice. I did it because I wanted to.*

I took a deep, somewhat shuddery breath and released it slowly. *One of these days, I'll make it up to you. I swear.*

Her amusement swam around me. *Can you really*

imagine me in Canberra? How long do you think it would have been before I said or did something inappropriate and ended up in the adjustment center for magical delinquents? Or worse, fall to the dark side and become just another witch on the Heretic Investigations Center's hit list?

I snorted softly. *Yeah, your mom would really have let that happen.*

Maybe not, but you get the point. She yawned, a sound that echoed down the line. *Do you need anything else? Because otherwise, I'm off back to bed.*

Go for it. I'll fill you in on events later this morning.

As her thoughts left mine, I paused and studied the rear living area. The kitchen to my left was brand-new, and yet it looked like something straight out of the sixties—the cabinets were canary yellow with round, white plastic knobs that matched the color of the counters; the tiles were a mix of both. Even the large fridge was yellow; in fact, the only modern-looking appliance was the freestanding stainless steel cooker. The rest of the room was L-shaped, with a dining area immediately in front of the kitchen and the living area to the right. Folding glass doors ran the full width of the room.

I walked over. The doors were all locked and there was absolutely no indication of physical, magical, *or* supernatural interference.

I frowned, but nevertheless did a full circuit of the room. Again, there was nothing that even remotely stirred my psychic or magical senses—nothing other than the fact it was noticeably cooler here than in either the hall or the master bedroom. But that might well be a result of there being such a large expanse of glass in the room—it not only let heat leach in, but also the cooler night air.

I spun and backtracked to the laundry. Byron had said

there was no sign of a break-in, but he would have meant *physical* evidence rather than the other kind.

I stopped again just inside the doorway, and couldn't help but note the sudden rise in air temperature. It was even hotter in here than in the hall or bedroom, and it had me wondering if we were dealing with some sort of fire spirit. It would certainly explain the abrupt variations in temperature.

I grabbed a pen out of my handbag and used it to flick on the light. While I doubted Kyle Jacobson's killer would have been stupid enough to leave any prints behind—presuming, of course, he or she even had fingers—it was still better to avoid spoiling evidence or adding mine to the mix.

The laundry was large and surprisingly modern, with a lot of built-in storage as well as all the usual appliance paraphernalia. There were two doors—one to my left led into a toilet, and one directly ahead that led out to what looked to be the side driveway. Beside this was a small window, through which I could see the fence that divided this house from Mrs. Potts's. My gaze returned to the door and its handle, and a prickle went down my spine.

It was the source of the wrongness.

Or, rather, the keyhole underneath it.

And yet, both the door and the keyhole looked untouched, and there was nothing to suggest it had been magically interfered with.

I stepped closer and reached for—but didn't quite touch —the keyhole. I didn't need to. The closer my fingers got, the more they itched and burned; whatever had killed Kyle Jacobson had left via the keyhole. And *that* very much ruled out vampires. Despite what Hollywood and fiction might have people believe, they couldn't change shape or become nothing more than mist and shadow. If a vampire disappeared before your eyes, it was because they were in your mind altering your perceptions rather than changing their shape.

I headed back to the bedroom. Ciara glanced up as I appeared.

"Aiden's gone next door to take the girlfriend's statement. He said you're to take his truck home, and he'll drop by in the morning to collect it."

"Keys?"

"In it."

"Good." I hesitated. "Would I be able to take a couple of photos of the wounds? We've a number of illustrative books that discuss different type of demons, and I'd like to see if I can match the bite to the creature."

She waved a hand toward the body. "Let it be noted that I find it rather disturbing you possess such books."

I grinned. "Technically, I don't. Belle inherited them from her grandmother, who was something of an authority on spirits, demons, and all things that go bump in the night."

"I don't find that comforting."

"You should. It was those books that gave us the means of tracking down the soul sucker."

She grunted, but her expression remained dubious. "Did you find anything else in the rest of the house?"

I pulled out my phone and opened the camera app. "Whatever did this left through the keyhole in the laundry door. Combine that with the heat in the three rooms, and I think we could be dealing with some sort of fire spirit."

"Great," she muttered. "Just what we need in the middle of a very hot summer."

"Yeah."

I took several photos of the wounds on his arms, then quickly snapped one of his face. After saying goodbye, I headed outside. Part of me hoped Aiden would appear to kiss me goodnight, even though I knew he had a job to do and wouldn't ever jeopardize a case by running out to say goodbye to his latest bedmate.

I climbed into his truck, adjusted the seat, and then drove off. But I didn't immediately head home. Maelle was the only person currently within the reservation who could immediately confirm whether we were dealing with a vamp or not; she was also our one chance of hunting the vamp down quickly if we were.

I found parking in a side street close to Émigré and walked back. It was a rather strange-looking building, and definitely not something you'd expect to find in the middle of the Victorian countryside. The matte-black walls were decorated with weird, alien-looking, biomechanical forms, and the strategically placed green and purple lights gave the entire building a surreal feel. In fact, it looked like something that belonged in a science fiction movie.

The bouncers standing in the front of the airlock-shaped doors opened them the minute they saw me. Roger, who was Maelle's servant—or thrall, as they were more commonly known—had ordered I be allowed inside no matter what the time *or* the inappropriateness of my dress. The jeans, T-shirt, and sandals I currently wore definitely *weren't* on the club's suitable attire list.

Roger had obviously been advised of my presence, because I'd barely stepped into the main room when he appeared out of the shadows and stopped in front of me.

"Lizzie Grace," he said, all effervescence and warmth. "What a delightful surprise."

He was a tall, thin man with pale skin, paler hair, and eyes that were a weird milky white. I wasn't entirely sure if the coloring was natural or something that had happened after he'd become Maelle's thrall—a process I really didn't know a whole lot about aside from the fact it involved magic and the consumption of her flesh, and basically gave him eternal life.

"You're in a rather good mood tonight," I commented. "I take it your mistress has recently fed?"

I didn't bother lowering my voice. The music was loud enough here that even if there *had* been someone near, they probably wouldn't have heard the comment. Maelle didn't encourage conversation; she wanted her patrons dancing and drinking.

Which, given the number currently on the dance floor, plenty were willing to do.

"Indeed she has," he said. "The replacement feeders have worked out better than we'd hoped."

A shudder I couldn't quite control ran through me at the thought of willingly becoming a vampire's meal ticket. Maelle might be a generous benefactor—as far as I'd seen, anyway—when it came to her feeders, but I was sure there were plenty of others who weren't. I'd been bitten only once in my life—by the vamp who'd come here seeking revenge—and I had no intention of ever repeating the experience. Maelle could assure me her bite would be utterly different as much as she wanted, but it was never going to happen.

The amusement briefly glinting in Roger's eyes suggested he'd caught the shudder, but all he said was, "I take it—given your attire—that this is a formal visit rather than a pleasurable one?"

"I'm afraid so."

"Then my mistress will be down in a few minutes. In the meantime, allow me to get you a drink."

He turned and led me toward the bar. The crowd parted silently before him, though I doubted they were even aware of it. It made me wonder if there was some sort of psychic ability or even magic involved. Just because I couldn't feel either didn't mean it wasn't happening. Maelle was capable of magic—she'd admitted that more than once—so it was totally possible her creature was similarly gifted. Or perhaps—given she could see and speak through him if she so desired—it was more a case of her allowing him to use some of her mind tricks and magic.

I turned my gaze to the vast room. The inside area had been painted battleship gray rather than black, but biomechanical and alien forms still adorned the multi-arched ceiling. At the point where they all met, Maelle had built a dark glass and metal room that—despite the strobe lighting—was all but invisible. Only the occasional glimmer of light across its dark surface gave its position away. The room wasn't only Maelle's lair—a place from which she could keep an eye on everything happening within her small kingdom—but also her safe place.

Few people were invited into it.

I rather suspected the uninvited never got out of it.

Roger motioned me to one of two spare chairs in front of the bar—a vast twisted metal and glass construction that dominated this side of the upper tier. As I sat on the alien-themed barstool, a bartender appeared and gave me a bright smile.

"What can I get for you?"

"Just a sparkling water, thanks."

"That's a rather staid choice given it's on the house," Roger commented.

"Yes, but I'm driving, so better safe than sorry."

A smile twitched his lips. "I'm thinking one drink would not tip you over and, even if it did, our ranger would not charge you."

"Then your thinking would be wrong."

Awareness prickled my spine, and I turned to see Maelle approaching. She was wearing a dark green riding habit—the sort women in the Jane Austen era might have worn—and her rich chestnut hair had been plaited and curled around the top of her head. Under the bar's cool lighting, it looked rather crown-like. Her porcelain skin was perfect and her lips a deep, ruby red—a sign of just *how* recently she'd fed. There were no lines on her face and absolutely no indication that she was, in fact, centuries old.

If not older.

"I tend to agree with you, young Elizabeth." Her softly accented voice carried easily over the noise. "The ranger is nothing if not a stickler for the rules."

"He has a job to do," I said, somehow managing to keep the surge of annoyance out of my voice. "It's not about being a stickler, more about keeping this reservation—and everyone within it—safe."

She perched on the vacant seat beside me, her movements oddly regal. "I would think the true guardian of this reservation is not a ranger, but rather a certain witch."

The bartender appeared with my drink. I gave him a nod of thanks and tried to ignore the sliver of alarm that ran through me. Not so much because of *what* she said, but because it oddly matched my own nebulous but nevertheless strengthening feeling.

"I rather think this reservation deserves far more than an underpowered witch."

She studied me for a moment, the pale depths of her eyes giving very little away. "As I have said before, this reservation seems to have other ideas."

"This land—and the magic within it—isn't sentient, Maelle. It can't decide anything."

Which wasn't exactly the truth—not now that Katie's soul was part of the wild magic. And if anyone was the protector of this place, then it was Katie. It was, after all, the reason she'd given up what was left of her life.

Maelle's smile held little in the way of warmth or belief. But then, given her ability to both sense and create magic—even if it was the darker kind—she'd have to be more than a little aware of what was happening in this reservation.

And it made me wonder if magic was the reason why she'd come here. She might have already denied it, might have made no play to use the wild magic in any way, but I still doubted it was a coincidence.

"Roger said you visit for business rather than pleasure," she said. "So what is it you desire?"

I hesitated. "A man was murdered tonight, and the rangers suspect it might be a vampire."

Something flared in her eyes. Something that was dark and *very* dangerous.

"I hope you're not here to accuse." Her tone hadn't changed, but chills nevertheless raced down my spine. "Because *that* would be very unwise."

I resisted the urge to rub my arms. Or, better yet, run. "I wouldn't have come here so unprepared if I'd intended to do something as stupid as *that*."

A smile twitched her lips, though it didn't ease the coldness in her eyes. "Then what is it you wish?"

"I have some photos of the wounds. I was wondering if you'd look at them and tell me if they're vampiric or not."

She studied me for a moment, not moving but very much reminding me of a snake ready to strike. "You don't think they are?"

"No, but I'm not the vampire expert here."

That smile got stronger, and the shroud of dangerousness that had so easily fallen around her faded. It by no means meant I *was* any safer, but at least it felt that way.

"Show me," she said.

I opened up the photo file on my phone. She plucked it from my hand, her fingers briefly touching mine. Though I was well guarded against the sensory hits that came with psychometry, images still flowed; a blonde-haired woman who looked far too young to be a vampire's meal ticket, the flash of a golden crown in her hair, the deep red of the velvet chair behind her. Only it wasn't a chair, but rather a throne.

Not recent images, but older. *Far* older.

Which was puzzling. Generally when images or emotions *did* get past the shields I'd developed over the years to protect my sanity, it was because I'd been caught unprepared or they were simply too strong. So either Maelle had been seriously dwelling on a past conquest, or that prophetic part of me was trying to tell me something about her.

"These are not the bite of a vampire," she said. "Our bite doesn't leave bruise marks such as this."

"That's what I figured." I hesitated. "I don't suppose you have any idea what sort of demon or spirit *does* leave that sort of bruising?"

She shook her head. "I've not come across anything like this in my many years alive, and I've crossed swords with more than a few demons or spirits in that time."

"Figuratively or literally?"

"Literally, of course." Her tone was cool, but amusement glinted in her pale eyes. "I was not always as refined and ladylike as I am today, and a long sword made of blessed silver is a *very* satisfying method of banishing demons, let me tell you."

I nodded. Witches often used blessed silver knives for the exact same reason, and a sword did have one advantage over a knife—reach. "Isn't it a little dangerous for a vampire to be picking up a weapon of blessed silver?"

"Not if one is old enough or wearing the appropriate protection."

Which meant gloves, obviously. Still, it was good to know that blessed items of *any* kind weren't as big as a deterrent against vampires as many believed them to be.

"Anything else?" she asked.

I hesitated again. "I don't suppose you'd know if a man by the name of Kyle Jacobson was here tonight?"

"Is he the victim?"

"Yes. There's a photo of him at the front of those other pics."

She flicked back through until she'd found the hastily snapped one of Jacobson. "He's not someone I've noticed. Roger?"

He stepped closer and peered at the screen for several seconds. "He does frequent the club, but I can't recall him being here tonight. Which, of course, doesn't mean he wasn't. I could check the security cams, if you'd like."

"If you could, that would be great." I retrieved my phone and shoved it back into my purse. "If the being that did this to him had come into the club, would you have sensed it?"

"I'd think it unlikely given I'm not attuned to such forces, only those of my own kind." She rose elegantly. "You know where to find me if you have further questions, Elizabeth."

And with that, she disappeared into the darkness. I blinked and glanced at Roger. "That was rather sudden, wasn't it?"

"A problem has arisen in one of the private rooms that needs attending to."

I hadn't known there were private rooms, and I had absolutely no desire to uncover what they might be used for. I quickly finished my drink then followed Roger through the room and left.

It was close to dawn by the time I got home. I parked Aiden's truck beside the old Ford wagon Belle and I owned, and then slipped inside the café through the rear door. Shadows filled the hallway but pale light filtered through the windows in the main dining area, highlighting various bits of mismatched furniture and the small teapots of flowers that decorated each table. The air was warm and rich with the scents of cinnamon and chocolate, and magic caressed my skin. Its source was the multiple layers of protection spells we'd placed around the building. No one intending us harm would ever get in here easily; not even, I suspected, the strongest of witches. While I hadn't intended it, the wild magic was layered through the spells that protected us. It gave us an edge—one that had already saved our butts.

Of course, it was also something of a liability given any witch who came into the café and started looking a little too closely at our spell network would notice the presence of the wild magic; it was something that would raise questions I couldn't—and wouldn't—answer.

Trepidation stirred anew, but I did my best to ignore it and ran up the stairs to my room, where I stripped off and climbed into bed. I was asleep almost as soon as my head hit the pillow; if I dreamed, I didn't remember it.

It was close to ten by the time I rattled down to the café. Belle had left a note saying she'd gone for a run, and I discovered a text on my phone from Aiden stating he was heading home to sleep, and that he'd drop by to get the keys in the after-noon, just before he started his shift. I made myself some break-fast and then started decorating the cakes Belle had baked last night. Normally it was an activity that soothed my mind, but I found myself constantly looking at the nearby clock to check the time. The trepidation that had stirred last night was not only back, but increasing in intensity the closer it got to twelve thirty—the time the new witch was supposed to arrive.

Belle reappeared just before that. She was a little over six feet tall and had the physique of an athlete—something she was proud of and worked hard on. She was a Sarr witch by birth, so had their ebony skin, long, silky black hair—which was currently swept up into a ponytail and dripping sweat onto the floor—and eyes that were a gray so pale they shone silver in even the dullest of light.

I was almost her polar opposite, possessing the crimson red hair of the blueblood lines, pale skin, and a smattering of golden freckles across my nose and cheeks. The one thing I would never be described as, however, was athletic. I tended to be a little more generously curved, and my exercise was no more strenuous than walking and yoga.

I pulled out the revitalization brew we kept in the fridge and poured her a glass.

She gulped it down and then said, "I needed that."

"Apparently so," I replied, amused. "And now you'd better go shower, because Ashworth and Eli will be here with the new witch soon."

Eli was Ashworth's partner and a retired RWA witch. While the two of them were currently living in temporary accommodation, they'd recently decided to move to Castle Rock permanently. Not only because they liked life in the reservation, but because Ashworth was apparently fascinated with the "conundrum" Belle and I presented. According to him, our magical abilities combined in a way no one had thought possible. We'd long been able to draw on each other's strength, but neither of us had—until he'd mentioned it—been aware the merging was deeper than that.

"I'm not sure why he's bothering," she said. "He knows we want as little to do with the man as possible."

"He really hasn't got a choice—our magic is helping to protect the wellspring, and we'll need to be involved in dismantling it so the new witch can weave his own spells around it."

"There's no guarantee the new witch's protection net will be any stronger than the one you and Ashworth have woven around it."

"Except for the fact that even Ashworth has stated his knowledge of recent spell developments is seriously lacking, and his power will not be enough to counter any major entities that head this way."

"I guess." She dumped the empty glass in the nearby sink. "Just don't give them the fresh cakes—not until we know if this new fellow is worthy of them."

I snorted and, as she headed upstairs, walked around the counter to set up the coffee machine.

One o'clock came and went. I did more prep for tomorrow, but it did little to ease the gathering tension.

I wished I knew why. Wished I knew what it was about *this* witch that my psychic senses were picking up and fearing.

"Ashworth's just pulled up outside," Belle said as she came down the stairs.

"And the witch?"

"With him, obviously." Her gaze narrowed slightly. "I can't read him."

The tension became alarm. "Why not?"

She hesitated. "I think he's wearing one of those devices that stop telepathic intrusion."

"Why on earth would he be wearing one of those?"

"Maybe he was forewarned about us." She frowned. "I could probably get past it, but it'll take some effort."

"It might be worth attempting to do so. All we know about him is his name, and Frederick is a very common name in the various branches of the Ashworth tree. It doesn't tell us anything."

It certainly didn't tell us if he was related to the Marlowe branch of the witch tree, which did have Ashworths scattered right through its bloodline.

"True." Belle's expression became somewhat distracted as she began breaking through the electronic shield protecting the other witch's mind. "It's interesting *our* Ashworth didn't know him, though."

"Not really." I walked over to the sink and washed my hands. "I wouldn't recognize most of the witches in the Marlowe family tree, even if I passed them in the street."

"And we've been running from the ones you *would* recognize."

A smile touched my lips. "True."

The small bell above the café's front door chimed merrily and then a familiar voice said, "Lizzie? You here?"

Ira Ashworth, not the mysterious Frederick.

"In the kitchen." I hastily dried my hands on a tea towel, and then headed out into the café.

Three men came through the door—Ashworth, Eli, and the man who was the new reservation witch.

He was tall and well built, and looked to be around the

same age as Belle and me. His crimson hair gleamed like dark fire in the sunlight streaming in through the windows, and his features could at best be described as pleasant.

Pleasant *and* familiar.

This man was Fredrick *Montague* Ashworth.

Otherwise known as Monty.

My cousin.

TWO

A wide grin split his features. "Lizzie! What the hell are *you* doing here?"

Ashworth's gaze went from us to Monty and back. Surprise, and perhaps a hint of understanding, touched his expression. "You know each other?"

Energy surged, a force as fierce as a gathering summer storm. Belle, pulling out all stops to break through Monty's shield and prevent the words that would give away our real identities.

"Hell, yeah." Monty tossed his bag on the nearby table and strode toward me. "We went to school together. We're actually—"

The rest of that statement never made it past his lips. His eyes went wide and he stopped abruptly. "What the fuck?"

His gaze slipped from me to the door into the kitchen—he might not be able to see Belle, but he certainly knew she was in there—and anger stirred in the silver depths of his eyes. But he didn't say anything. He *couldn't*.

As Belle hastily wound some preventative measures

through his mind, I forced a grin, stepped up, and threw my arms around him.

"Monty," I said, with a bravado I certainly wasn't feeling. "Why the hell have you accepted the position here? Isn't it a little less than fitting for an Ashworth heir?"

Monty's father—another Frederick—had come from England to marry my aunt. While he wasn't as powerful as my father, he nevertheless held a seat on the high council—a position that usually passed on to the firstborn child, thanks to the fact blueblood witches generally only married into a family with similar magical strength. In the distant past, that had sometimes meant cousins and even siblings marrying. The net result had, of course, been an increasingly higher rate of congenital and inherited disorders. It was one of the reasons why the witch lines were now so heavily monitored, and why arranged marriages had come into existence. And the law had no problem with such arrangements —unless, of course, one or both parties were coerced or even forced into the marriage.

Monty grabbed my arms and thrust me away. For several seconds, multiple emotions crossed his face—anger, frustration, and confusion—before he said, "I had very little choice in the matter—it was either this or remain in the spell records department."

I frowned. "Why would someone of your stature be shoved sideways into a cataloging position? Isn't that usually reserved for second-tier witches?"

And Monty certainly wasn't *that*.

His brief smile held more than a little bitterness. "When I went through accreditation, it was revealed I didn't have the expected magical strength."

"That still doesn't explain—"

"Let's just say my parents were so damn disappointed

that I accepted the first available job and got the hell away from them." His gaze narrowed. "What's your excuse?"

I knew he wasn't referring to the reasons we were here, but with Ashworth and Eli here, I wasn't about to answer that truthfully.

"We left for a very similar reason."

"At sixteen, and well before you ever went through accreditation."

"Which wasn't exactly necessary, was it?" Not when all of Canberra had known not only my status as an utter disappointment to my parents, but also the fact that my father held me responsible for the death of my sister. She'd been the family's star, possessing so much magical depth that she outshone even my parents and, at the age of nineteen, had been named successor to my father's seat on the high council. But none of that had saved her when a dark sorcerer had come calling.

I'd tried to. And failed.

"No," Monty said, "but given how furious your father was in the weeks that followed your disappearance, it's very much a story I want to hear."

I could well imagine my father's fury—after all, I'd not only managed to circumvent his plans for me, but also tarnished his good name.

The only story he actually wants to hear, Belle said, her mental tones weary, *is how—and why—his speech has suddenly been restricted.*

Which we can't explain until we're alone. And maybe not even then. I pushed some strength her way, and then said, *You'd better sit before you fall.*

I'd rather keep out of his way, she said. *I'll cut up the cake while you make the coffee. I can lean on the counter afterward without it appearing too suspicious.*

"That's a story we *all* want to hear," Ashworth said, his tone dry. "But one I suspect will be some time in coming."

My gaze finally returned to his. He was bald, with a well-tanned face full of wrinkles and eyes that were muddy silver in color. The power that rolled off him was fierce, but it was little more than the flicker of a candle when compared to Monty's output. And *he'd* been classified as not being strong enough to fill his father's shoes.

"You already know far more than most," I said. "Would you like a coffee? And cake?"

"Nice redirect, but one that will always work." He slapped Monty on the shoulder with his good hand—his right arm was still in a cast after he'd broken it during our efforts to stop the dark witch—then pulled out a chair and sat down. "If you're a true foodie, this is the place to be—they make the most amazing cakes."

"A statement I'll certainly test the merits of." *At least until he'd gotten some answers*, his expression seemed to add.

"What would you like to drink, Monty?" I walked over to the counter.

"I'll have a short black, thanks." He sat down and crossed his arms, anger vibrating from every inch. "A strong one. How long have you been living here?"

"We arrived a few months before Christmas." I started making coffee. "The place simply felt right."

"And the wild magic entwined within the protections you've layered around the café?"

Fuck, he sensed that quickly, Belle commented, as she began plating up thick slices of black forest cake.

He's a couple steps up the power ladder from either Ashworth or Eli, so that's not really surprising. I'm just glad he isn't sensing it on me.

I daresay he is, she said. *But he won't be able to comment on it until we're alone.*

Oh. Good.

"It would appear Liz has something of an affinity to the wild magic here," Ashworth said, his gaze on me. There was a warning there—one that said I dare not stray too far from the truth if I wanted to keep my deeper secrets. "It's bolstered a couple of her spells over the last few months."

Monty studied me through slightly narrowed eyes. "That's not possible."

A statement that very easily could have been a reply to Ashworth's comment, but one I rather suspected was actually aimed at what he was sensing in my magical output. It might still be the output of a low-powered witch, but there were now wisps of wild magic evident if you looked closely enough.

And he was.

"So we'd believed until we witnessed it ourselves," Eli said. He was a handsome, well-built man in his late sixties, with neatly cut salt-and-pepper hair and eyes that were bright blue. "But the spells here are evidence to the fact that it's not."

Monty didn't reply, but I could see the questions in his eyes even from where I stood. I put all the coffee mugs onto a tray and carried them over. Belle followed me with the cakes, then retreated to the counter.

Once seated, I said, "It's just as well you arrived today. We've another situation the rangers will want help with."

"Supernatural?" Ashworth immediately said.

I nodded, even as I wondered if he'd remember he was no longer the acting reservation witch. "I think we're dealing with some sort of fire spirit."

Monty frowned. "They're rather rare in areas like this.

They tend to prefer big cities, where it's not as easy to sense and track their heat spoors."

A statement that not only emphasized my lack of knowledge, but why I could never be this reservation's defender.

"What makes you think it might be a fire spirit?" Eli asked.

I gave them the details and then showed them the images on my phone.

"This definitely isn't the work of a vampire," Monty said. "But there are a number of demons and spirits who leave marks similar to this. I wouldn't mind seeing the body myself—it's rather hard to get any true sense of the wound from a photo."

"I'm sure Aiden will arrange that once the autopsy has been performed," Ashworth said.

Monty grunted and scooped up some cake. Whether he liked it or not was hard to say, because his gaze kept sending daggers my way.

"You haven't sensed anything along the psychic lines?" Ashworth asked.

I shook my head. "But that's not entirely unusual. I only sensed the soul sucker because of the bell that tolled when it killed."

Which wasn't exactly the truth, but Monty already had enough questions about Belle and me. I didn't want to add to them.

"Your psychic powers always were more powerful than your magic," Monty said, "or, at least, they used to be."

"Still are." I sipped my coffee and tried to ignore the continuing trepidation. "Where are you staying?"

"The council have set me up in a place along Lyttleton Road. Nothing flash, but it'll do for now."

I raised an eyebrow. "Meaning you'll be looking for a grander place once you've had a chance to look around?"

"Indeed." A faint smile touched his lips despite the annoyance still evident in his eyes. "I always did have high-brow tastes, remember?"

"I can certainly remember the Armani suit you turned up in for the Year Ten formal," Belle commented.

He raised an eyebrow. "I wasn't the only one wearing Armani."

"No, but you were the only one who paired it with a Kermit the Frog tie."

"Which caused less of a stir than it should have," he murmured. "That honor went to the two of you."

Yeah, because they hadn't expected an underpowered witch and her Sarr familiar would have the courage to turn up at an event designed to commemorate achievements in a year in which they'd had none.

"You should come for dinner once you've settled in," I said. "We can catch up on everything that's happened since we last saw each other."

"How does tonight sound?" he said. "Saves me worrying about a meal."

And gave him the answers he wanted so much sooner.

"Sure." I glanced past him as the bell over the door chimed and a middle-aged woman stepped inside. Her gaze quickly swept the five of us then shot back to me. She was a tall woman with brown hair and eyes, and an aura that ran with swirls of muddy gray—the color of fear. She was also human rather than wolf. While I vaguely recognized her, I couldn't recall her name.

She hesitated and then said, "I know you're closed today and I'm sorry to interrupt, but I'm in desperate need of help and I don't know where else to turn."

I frowned. "The rangers—"

"I've talked to the rangers. They suggested I come here."

"And if that doesn't speak of a complete turnaround in attitude when it comes to witches," Ashworth murmured, "I don't know what does."

"There's been a problem between rangers and witches?" Monty asked.

"You could say that," I replied, and then returned my gaze to the woman near the door. Aside from the color of her aura, my "other" senses weren't picking up too much in the way of information, but that might have simply been because she was standing too far away.

"What kind of help do you need? A reading? Or something else?"

She hesitated again, her gaze sweeping the three men and her expression uncertain. She didn't want to air her troubles in public, I suspected.

"Would you like to come into the reading room and discuss it more privately?" I said.

Relief crossed her expression. "Yes."

Great, Belle said. *Leave me to entertain Monty, why don't you.*

Well, he did fancy you when he was a teenager. Maybe you could rekindle the feeling.

Her mental snort ran down the line, loud and derisive. *Rekindling is not on the cards. The only thing he wants to do right now is to strangle me.*

Obviously, black forest cake is not a path into his good books. We need to try something else next time.

A statement that suggests we'll be making a habit of annoying him.

I rather suspect we might. I picked up my coffee and rose. "Would you like a cup of tea or coffee, Mrs.—?"

"Dale. Alice Dale. And no, thank you."

I motioned toward the reading room at the rear of the café, then glanced at Monty. "I'll see you tonight—around seven?"

He nodded, his gaze suggesting I had better come up with some answers at that point or there'd be big trouble.

But trouble was going to hit either way—of that I was sure.

I turned and followed Alice. The reading room was the dedicated space we used for psychic readings; we also created the various charms we sold within the café—and the stronger ones both Belle and I now wore full-time—within it. While the café as a whole was fully protected against magical attack, the spells surrounding this room had been specifically designed to stop arcane forces from entering without permission, or attempting an attack during a spirit reading. Not all the souls Belle talked to were benign.

The air sparkled briefly as I entered, a sure indication the spells were active and ready. A simple wooden table sat in the center of the small room, and around it were four mismatched but comfortable wooden chairs. A large rug covered the floor, and bright lengths of material were draped across the ceiling. They not only provided the otherwise drab room with some color, but also hid the spell work etched into both. I motioned Mrs. Dale to the nearest chair, then lit a candle, closed the door, and sat down opposite her.

The flickering light lent the other woman's features a warmth they didn't otherwise have. I crossed my arms and leaned my forearms on the table—a position that protected my hands from accidental touch. "What would you like me to do, Mrs. Dale?"

"It's Miss, but please call me Alice. Mrs. Dale is my mother's preferred address." A sob escaped. She drew in a deep, somewhat shuddering breath, and then added, "She— Mom—said she'd call me back last night, but I haven't heard from her and it's not like her to do that. I just *know* something is wrong."

"I take it you've been over to her house?"

She nodded. "I have a key, just in case. She wasn't there, and her purse and car are missing."

"Is it possible she's gone out again and has simply forgotten to call you?"

Alice began shaking her head before I'd even finished. "As I said, she wouldn't do that."

I frowned. "Did she mention going anywhere the last time you spoke to her?"

The rangers had undoubtedly already asked all these questions, but it didn't hurt to repeat them, if only for my own peace of mind. Plus, the more information I had, the greater my chance of filtering out the muck and getting to the nitty-gritty when I tried tracking her mother.

"She said an old friend had rung out of the blue and that she was meeting her for dinner. She didn't say where and I have no idea who the friend was, other than her name was Marilyn." Tears glistened in the flickering light. "Please, you have to help me. Something has happened to her, I'm sure of it."

"I'm more than happy to try, but there's no guarantee I'll succeed. Psychometry isn't always exact—"

"I know," she cut in. "But I just need you to try. I can't— won't—sit around and do nothing."

A sentiment I could certainly understand given it was the exact same one that had driven my attempt to rescue my sister.

41

I just had to hope that *this* search wasn't similarly doomed.

"I'll need something of hers," I said. "Something she kept close to her skin."

"I brought the necklace she wore most days—she only ever took it off when she was going somewhere fancy. Would that be okay?" When I nodded, she opened her bag and then pulled out a blue velvet jewelry box and offered it to me.

I flexed my fingers and then carefully took it. The minute my fingers touched the box, the psi part of me began to stir.

And not in a good way.

I took a deep breath in an effort to calm the gathering trepidation and then opened the box. Inside was a delicate silver chain on which hung a plain silver wedding ring.

"It was my dad's," Alice murmured. "He died just on a year ago."

"It must have been a hard time for you both."

It was a statement rather than a question—even without touching the necklace I could feel grief emanating from it. What I couldn't immediately feel was any sense of life, and I really hoped that was due to the fact I wasn't yet holding it. I very much doubted Alice would cope with the loss of a second parent.

"Yes." A tear tracked down her cheek. "I don't know what I'd do—"

I reached with my free hand and squeezed hers. Her fear and grief washed over me, a wave that would have been overwhelming had I not been prepared.

"There may be a simple explanation for all this." I kept my voice soft—soothing. "You may be stressing over nothing."

She nodded, even though her expression suggested she didn't agree with me in the least. I half wondered if she had undiagnosed psi powers; I couldn't see anything in her aura to suggest it, but that might just be because her fear and grief were overwhelming everything else. "Are you getting anything from the necklace?"

"A little." I carefully freed it from the box. The grief increased in intensity, but the pulse of life remained absent. It really *wasn't* a good sign.

I returned my gaze to Alice. "If you could just sit silently for a few minutes, I'll see what I can get."

She nodded and hastily dabbed her eyes with a tissue. Despite the growing sense that this would not end well, I closed my eyes and reached down to where my second sight lay leashed and waiting.

But there was absolutely nothing on this necklace for it to latch on to—no pulse, no hint of life. The only thing I could pick up were shadows and grief—and while it very much suggested death had already claimed Alice's mom, it did at least mean there was still a chance I could find her remains. But only if I hurried—emotions rarely clung to such items for very long after death.

Which was *not* something I could say to Alice. Not until I was absolutely sure. I opened my eyes.

"Well?" she immediately asked.

I hesitated. "I couldn't pick up much more than the lingering veil of her grief over your dad's death, but that might just be enough to track her down."

She thrust to her feet. "Can we go now?"

"I'll go, but it'd be better if you—"

"I can't stay behind," she cut in fiercely. "I *need* to know she's okay."

"Ms. Dale," I said, keeping my voice conciliatory as

possible. "For tracking via psychometry to work, I need airspace untainted by deeper emotions. I'm afraid your fear will likely disrupt the signal."

"Oh."

"If you'd give me your phone number, I'll call you the minute I discover anything."

"You'll do it now?"

"Yes."

"Thank you." She hesitated, and then said, "And payment? I know it's your day off, so would double—"

"Just the normal finding fee will be fine." Especially if what I sensed in the necklace did indeed mean the worst. I gave her the figure and then said, "Belle will take your phone number and the payment now, if you'd like, while I get ready."

She nodded and headed out. I carefully put the necklace back in its box and then walked across to the full-height bookcase lining the wall to the right of the door. After moving an ornate pottery fairy, I placed my hand against the bookcase's wooden back. Energy immediately crawled across it and, a heartbeat later, the wooden panel slipped aside to reveal an eight-inch-deep compartment. It wasn't the only hidden compartment in the bookcase—there was one behind every shelf. A witch could never be too careful when it came to protecting magical items and potions.

I grabbed my spell stones—or warding stones, as some witches preferred to call them—and a couple of general purpose potions to ward off evil, and then carefully secured them all in the nearby backpack. Once I'd picked up the blue velvet box and tucked it into my pocket, I blew out the candle and slung the pack over my shoulder as I walked out.

Alice was still in the café, but the three men had gone.

They left not long after you went in the room, Belle said.

Had Monty cooled down any?

Nope. It's going to be an interesting evening.

As my relatives go, he's fairly reasonable. Or he used to be.

Which isn't saying much, Belle cut in dryly. *Although he did at least have a sense of humor back then—a trait that's certainly absent in most of your family.*

He's a side branch and not a Marlowe. They do tend to be more—

Human? Belle cut in, amusement heavy in her mental tone.

Alice handed me a scrap of paper with her phone number on it. "You'll call me as soon as you know anything?"

"Yes." I didn't offer anything else. Didn't say it would be all right. It wouldn't be. Not if the shadows on the necklace were anything to go by.

"Thank you." She accepted the coffee Belle handed her with a wan smile. "I'll head home and wait."

"Do," I said. "And try not to worry."

She nodded and left. Belle's gaze met mine. "You don't think her mom's alive, do you?"

"No. But I could be wrong."

"Given your psychometry skills are more reliable than your prophetic ones—and even your prophetic ones have been pretty damn accurate of late—I'd say the chances of that are between zero and none." She slid my purse and a coffee cup across the counter. "I added some herbs to the coffee to help keep you awake. I don't think Aiden would appreciate finding you asleep in the mangled wreck of our car."

I snorted softly. "I slept until ten so I'm not really sleep deprived. Besides, you're coming with me."

She raised her eyebrows. "Meaning the sensations rolling from the necklace have a distant feel?"

"Yeah, and they're also fading. I don't really want to drive while trying to keep a strong enough grip on them to find her."

"Give me five, then."

As Belle dashed upstairs to grab some shoes, I walked through the café to lock the front door. Once she was back down, I tossed her the car keys and then headed down the rear hall to the back door.

"Where to?" she said, as we pulled out onto the main street.

I tucked my coffee mug into the center holder and then tugged the blue box from my pocket. The necklace felt cold and dark in my palm. I wrapped my fingers around it and, after a moment, said, "Right at Barker Street."

We headed out of Castle Rock. I sipped my coffee but, even with the herbs, felt no more awake for it. Tiredness was a pulse that beat through me with gathering speed; I might have slept until ten, but it definitely *wasn't* enough. It was probably just as well Monty was coming around tonight, as it basically stopped me from going back to Aiden's where I'd risk worsening the sleep deprivation.

Because there was no doubt that I would. Sleep wasn't really a priority when it came to that man.

"Are we heading onto the freeway?" Belle asked as we approached the ramp. "Or onto the overpass?"

I hesitated, briefly tightening my grip on the necklace. The silver wedding ring remained cold and inert against my palm, and the shadows and grief pulsing from the chain were fading at a faster rate. We only had a few minutes before I lost the trail. "Over."

I guided Belle through a maze of tree-lined streets until

we were on a single-lane road on the outskirts of a small town known as Hank's Mill.

"We're close," I said. "You'd better slow down."

"There's nothing around here but farmlets—why would she be meeting someone for dinner here?"

"Maybe the friend owns one of the farmlets."

She glanced at me. "You don't believe that."

The smile that twisted my lips held little in the way of amusement. "No, but mainly because Alice said she only took the necklace off when she was going somewhere fancy."

And there was nothing fancy about any of these old places.

As we started up a long incline, a number of large farm sheds came into sight at the top. Just for an instant, the remaining shadows within the necklace pulsed strongly, a signal that suggested those buildings were our destination. Then the emotions faded, and the chain became as inert as the wedding ring.

"We need to stop at the cluster of buildings ahead." I tucked the necklace back into the box and secured it in the backpack's pocket.

Belle pulled off the road and into the stone driveway. There were three buildings in the immediate area; the one farthest away looked like a storage unit while the closer one had "office" emblazoned on its side. The largest was— according to the sign above the double-width doorway—a cold store.

"You know," Belle said. "It might be wise to call the rangers. We both know this search will probably lead to a body, which means we'll end up calling them anyway."

I hesitated, torn between the need to do the sensible thing and the desire not to call them out until we had something more concrete than the tenuous feeling of death that had been radiating from the chain. But of all my abilities, psychometry was my strongest; if it said death was waiting, then it certainly was.

Belle stopped the car and then reached around to grab the backpack. As we both climbed out, I made a quick call, catching Maggie, the station's receptionist and a ranger in training. "It's Lizzie Grace, Maggie, and I'm afraid—"

"That you've found a body," she finished heavily. "It's the only reason you ever ring when you know Aiden isn't here."

"We haven't *actually* found it yet, but all the vibes I'm getting are saying the woman I'm tracking is dead. I just thought I'd make the call early for a change. Sorry."

"It's hardly your fault this place seems to have become a haven for murderers of late. Where are you?" Once I'd given her the address, she added, "I'll inform Tala straight away, but Jaz is on her way back from Readsdale, so she'll probably be sent straight across. Ciara will take longer to get there."

"Thanks, Maggie."

"No worries."

She hung up.

I shoved the phone away and then looked around. The wind stirred, caressing my skin with heat but bringing little in the way of sound beyond the nearby gentle rattle of loose roofing tin. There were no lights on in any of the buildings and the cold store's doors were padlocked.

"The cold store looks far newer than either of the other buildings," Belle said. "The office has definitely seen better days."

"Maybe they've moved all their operations into the

newer building," I said. "You've got longer legs, so I'll check the office and you can check the other one."

She snorted softly but nevertheless walked away. I went to the front of the old office building and strode up the ramp. The wood bounced and cracked under my feet, more evidence of just how bad a state the building was in. The door was locked but a faded "hours of business" sign said the place was closed Sunday to Tuesday. The nearby window was caked with grime, but I created a clean spot and peered inside. There were multiple stacks of unmade boxes, a number of old filing cabinets, several desks that had seen better days, and some chair remnants. The thick layer of dust that lay on both the boxes and the desks suggested no one had entered the room in some time.

I walked back down the ramp and waited for Belle.

"There's nothing more than junk in the other one," she said.

"Same with the office." I studied the cold store for a second. "And we're not going to get through that chain in any sort of hurry."

"It's likely the rest of the place is locked down as tightly."

"Probably, but we still have to look." If only because a cold store was the perfect place to hide a body, especially given it had been closed the day Alice's mom had gone missing. "I'll go left, you go right."

There were a number of allocated parking spaces out the front of the cold store and, on the building itself, two more signs—one saying "office" with an arrow pointing to the left, and the other saying "pick-up and deliveries" with an arrow pointing right.

The office was one of those freestanding portable buildings. I walked up the steps and peered into the nearest window. There were newish-looking desks, filing cabinets, and chairs in the main room, with two doors leading off it—one was a kitchen, the other a bathroom. The front door was locked and showed no signs of being tampered with.

I continued on. There were no windows on this side of the building, which I guessed was no surprise given it was a cold storage facility. I walked to the end and turned the corner. About halfway down there was what looked to be a large loading bay. To my left were four large dumpsters, and to my right a door. I tested the handle; like the rest of them, it was locked.

Belle appeared at the far end of the building as I headed over to the first dumpster. *Anything?*

Two locked doors but little else. Any luck on your side?

Not a goddamn thing.

We might have to just call it quits and handball it back to the rangers.

Let me check these dumpsters first.

If there was a body in any of them, you'd have smelled it by now, given the heat of the last couple of days.

I still want to check—I owe Alice that much. I grabbed the first lid, but it was heavier than it looked. I used both hands to shove it up and then peered inside. It was empty.

I let the lid go and, as the clang of metal rang out, moved over to the next one. This one had a few boxes down the bottom but little else. The third was jammed full with both boxes and plastics.

There's no way of getting inside from the loading bay, Belle said. *All the doors and roller shutters are locked down tight.*

Without the damn necklace to give us directions, we're basically looking for a needle in a haystack. I walked toward the final bin. *No matter how much Aiden might trust my instincts, I doubt any judge is going to issue a warrant to search this place on something as vague as a witch's say so.*

Werewolves have an advantage over us—they can check a person's location via scent. And do they actually need a warrant? It's not like he's actually gotten one for any of the other crimes we've gotten involved in.

Good point. I grabbed the lid and thrust it up.

And was hit by a smell so bad that I gagged, dropped the lid, and jumped backward. For several seconds, I did nothing more than suck in air and stare at the last bin with trepidation.

I had to open it again. Had to find out whether or not we'd just found our needle.

"You could just call the rangers," Belle said, as she stopped beside me.

"And what if it's a dead cat or something?"

"You don't think it is." She tugged a couple of tissues from her handbag and handed them to me. "Shove them up your nose. They're lavender scented, so it should counter at least a little of the smell."

I folded the tissues, shoved the end of each one into a nostril then took a final breath of clean air and quickly stepped forward. The smell was just as gut-wrenching but at least this time I was prepared for it.

I reached inside and shifted a couple of the torn-down boxes sitting on top, and found the source of the smell.

It wasn't a cat. It was a human.

A woman.

And she'd been completely and utterly skinned.

THREE

I let the lid drop again and bolted for the grassy area behind the bin, where I violently lost everything I'd eaten.

Belle silently handed me a bottle of water once I was done. I rinsed the bitter taste of bile from my mouth and wished I could so easily wash the images from my mind.

"God," I muttered, my gaze on the rusty blue dumpster. "I really hope that's *not* Alice's mom."

"Yeah." Belle rubbed her arms, her usually bright aura shadowed and swirling with horror. She might not have physically seen the body, but she'd caught a glimpse of it through our connection before she'd shut it down. "At least we saved some time by calling the rangers early."

"Yes." I hesitated. "It's making the call to Alice that worries me."

"You can't contact her—not until we know for sure who it is in there."

"She's going to think the worst has happened if I don't."

"True." Belle scrubbed a hand across her eyes and swore softly. "I wonder if this is the work of another group of hunters after wolf pelts? It would certainly explain her skinned state."

A shudder went through me and my stomach heaved again. "Except if it *is* Alice's mom in there, she's human rather than wolf, and I doubt there's a black market for human pelts."

"Also true." She hesitated. "I don't know if there're many demons who go to the trouble of skinning their victims, though."

"It's not like either of us are experts on the matter, although I daresay your grandmother has it noted somewhere in one of her books if there is."

She raised an eyebrow. "And why would we even be looking for them? Monty's here now, remember?"

"I don't think our participation in these matters will end just because he's here."

I motioned toward the building. "We'd better wait out the front."

"It's certainly better than waiting here." Belle fell in step beside me. "I'm sure it won't comfort Alice at all, but her mom's ghost doesn't linger. She's moved on, which means this death was ordained."

"I can't help but wonder what the fuck she did to deserve such a horrible death."

"It's an unfortunate fact of life that not all deaths can be pleasant."

"I know, but being skinned—" Horror once again shuddered through me. "I just hope she was dead when it happened."

"Surely someone would have heard her screams if she wasn't. There are houses close enough to have done so."

"That's *if* she was killed here rather than just dumped

after the fact. Were there any vehicles around your side of the building?"

"No."

"So either her car has been dumped elsewhere, or the killer now has it." Although if we *were* dealing with a dark spirit of any kind, I couldn't imagine the latter would apply. After all, why would a demon or spirit bother driving his victim's car away from the scene of his crime?

"There *are* some capable of taking human shape," Belle said. "So it *is* theoretically possible for at least some of them to be capable of driving."

"Except most demons don't like the feel of metal."

"And most cars these days are more plastic than metal."

"True." I threw the pack onto the wagon's back seat, then grabbed my coffee and leaned back against the door to drink it. And wondered just how well it would sit with my still churning stomach. "Do you think it's a coincidence that we've two dark entities on the reservation? Or could they actually be connected?"

"A question we could pose to Monty once he's finished ranting at us tonight."

I smiled. "I still think rants could be avoided if you threw a little charm his way."

She snorted. "Don't take this personally, but I'd rather avoid getting involved in *any* way with someone who has *any* connection to your family tree—even one that's an Ashworth sub-branch."

A sentiment I agreed with, but not one we could do much about. Monty had been appointed here, and that meant we were stuck with him—unless, of course, he decided the job wasn't for him, and given what he'd said about Canberra and his dad, that seemed very unlikely.

Jaz arrived ten minutes later. She was a brown-haired,

brown-skinned wolf who'd come here from a New South Wales reservation and married into the Marin pack.

"I'd say it's nice to see you both again, but considering the circumstances, it doesn't seem appropriate. What have we got?"

"A body. A *skinned* body."

"Fuck." She thrust her hand through her hair. "Any idea if it's a wolf?"

"Human." I hesitated. "We think it might be Alice Dale's mom. Alice came into the café today convinced something had happened to her, and asked me to find her. She said the rangers had suggested it."

"We did. Or rather, *I* did. We put out an alert, but there wasn't much more we could do given there was no sign of trouble at her house." She studied the buildings for a moment. "Where is the body?"

"In the blue dumpster at the rear of the cold store. The heat of the last few days has made it... unpleasant."

"I can imagine." She grimaced and got out her phone. "I'll take your statements now while we're waiting for Ciara and Tala to turn up. That way, you can leave."

She started with me and then moved on to Belle. Once both recordings had been done, she put her phone away and glanced around at the sound of approaching sirens. "Have you made any further contact with Alice?"

"No, but I said I'd call her if I found anything, and I feel obliged to at least tell her something."

"Don't tell her you found a body—not until we've confirmed ID."

I nodded, even as relief stirred. It might mean lying, but it also meant I didn't have to be the one to give her the bad news.

Another SUV pulled up beside Jaz's. Tala Sinclair—

Aiden's second-in-command and a straight-talking, no-nonsense wolf—climbed out. "Don't take this the wrong way, but I'm really *not* happy to see you both right now."

A smile tugged my lips. "Trust me when I say we'd rather *not* be here right now."

Something close to amusement briefly touched her otherwise stern expression. "How nasty is it?"

"Breathing mask nasty."

"Ah." She glanced at Jaz. "Have you taken their statements?"

"Yes, but I haven't checked the crime scene yet."

Tala grunted. "I'll do that while you wait for Ciara. She should be only five or so minutes away now." Her gaze returned to us. "You two can go, if you'd like."

"Thanks." I hesitated. "If the body does belong to Alice Dale's mom, could you not tell her we were the ones who found it?"

"That shouldn't be a problem, but why not?"

"Because I promised her I'd call if I found her—"

"And *none* of us have any idea if you have," she cut in sharply.

"I know, but she'll be looking for someone to blame for her mother's death, and her anger will fall on me if she learns I've withheld information, even if under orders. I'd rather avoid that situation."

"*That* I can understand."

She moved around to the back of her truck and started getting her kit out. We climbed into our wagon and got the hell out of there. It wasn't until we got back to the café that I finally called Alice.

"Hello? Is that you, Lizzie?" she immediately said, with far too much hope in her voice.

I closed my eyes and silently cursed whatever gods were listening for doing this to her.

"Did you find my mom?" she added.

"I'm afraid the vibrations coming from the necklace completely faded before we could." I said it as evenly as I was able. "But we got a general location and the rangers are up there now looking for her."

She was silent for a moment, and then said, a catch in her voice. "Did you find her SUV? It's a gray Hyundai—"

"There were no vehicles like that in the area that we could see."

"Where did the trail end?"

"Up the back of Hank's Mill. I'm sure the rangers will be in contact the minute they find anything. You need to relax—"

"Would you?" she cut in, her voice a mix of anger and desperation.

"No." I hesitated again. "I'm sorry we couldn't be of more help, Alice."

"At least you've pinned down a location," she said. "That's more than we had before."

"Yes, it is."

She sighed. "I guess I'll just have to wait. But thanks for trying."

"No problem—and I'll keep my fingers crossed for you both."

She hung up. I blew out a breath, then flashed a smile Belle's way as she handed me a whiskey. "I know it's very early to start drinking, but I figure we'd need the fortification to get through the night."

"And you only half filled the glass? What, is there a drought on or something?"

She chuckled and immediately topped the glass up.

The whiskey did its job, though, because I was able to get through the rest of the afternoon without stressing too much over the upcoming confrontation.

My phone rang just after four; the chime told me it was Aiden. I all but danced across the room to grab it, then hit the answer button and said, "Good afternoon, gorgeous."

There was a long moment of silence, and then he said, with something close to amusement in his tone, "Have you been drinking?"

"Only a little. The new witch is dropping by for dinner, and I needed the fortification." I hesitated. "It's my goddamn cousin, Aiden."

He swore softly. "Are you okay? Do you need me there?"

"I'd love you here, but I think it better if we just hash things out between the three of us first."

"In other words, there are truths you still don't want me to know." His tone was neutral, but I nevertheless heard the annoyance behind it.

"And you know why, Aiden."

"I don't accept or understand those reasons, Liz. Not when it's pretty damn obvious to even the blindest of fools that I'd never do anything to hurt you."

But you will, I wanted to say, *because you're a werewolf and I'm not*. And that meant we could only ever be as we now were—lovers and friends but never anything more. Until I found that "more"—until I found the man I would spend the rest of my life with—then the deeper truths about my past would remain mine.

"If the situation was different, if you weren't a werewolf —" I hesitated. "But we can't change what or who we are, Aiden."

He was silent for altogether too long—perhaps digesting not so much what I'd said, but what I *hadn't*.

I used the moment to change the subject. "Are you dropping by to pick up your truck this afternoon?"

"It won't be until much later. We've just received word of an abandoned SUV that matches the make and model of Mrs. Dale's, so Tala is picking me up and we're heading out there now."

"I may have already crashed if you're back too late. Do you want me to leave your keys somewhere?"

He hesitated. "No. If we're late getting back, I'll ask Tala to drop me home and then pick it up in the morning."

"Are you coming for breakfast?"

"If it's being offered, most certainly." The smile in his voice didn't defuse the anger still evident. "I'll see you tomorrow, Liz."

When we'll talk some more. He didn't say that, but it nevertheless seemed to shimmer down the phone line.

"You will." I hung up and silently cursed fate and anyone else who might be listening for putting me in this position—even if, in truth, I had no one to blame but myself, my fears, and my inability to fully trust anyone but Belle.

"You've got good reason *not* to trust after being betrayed by your own goddamn father," Belle said. "But if you're right—if Castle Rock *is* our end destination—then I think you need to come clean with Aiden."

I wrinkled my nose. "Even if I do, it doesn't change the situation between us."

"No, but it will at least end the lies." Belle hesitated. "And if your premonitions *are* right—if your dad does discover and come after us—then we're going to need him in our corner."

I snorted softly. "Do you really think either my father or Clayton will take any goddamn notice of a ranger?"

"No, but I doubt Aiden will be the only one in our corner. I rather suspect Katie and the wild magic will be too, and not even your father can do much about the latter. Your mom certainly proved that strength and breeding don't matter when it comes to wild magic."

Which was true enough. I didn't really know the exact details, as it had happened in the months before I was born, but I did know her efforts to channel and control had almost resulted in her death.

Was *that* the reason I could do what she couldn't? Had her close call with the wild magic somehow made me more attuned to it?

It was possible. *Very* possible.

I threw my phone back into my bag and went back into the kitchen to finish preparations for the evening meal. Sunlight was still streaming into the café by the time seven rolled around. Monty arrived at five past and rapped loudly on the door.

"Ready?" I said, with a glance at Belle.

"Yeah. But he can't actually ask any questions until I release his thoughts, so expect a thick wave of anger and frustration."

"Great." I shored up my defenses, then walked across to the door and opened it.

He strode in, his face thunderous and his body practically vibrating. "You had better damn well explain—"

"Monty, sit down, shut the fuck up, and we will," I said. "But please believe we had a very good reason for stopping you blurting out our real identities to all and sundry."

He glanced at me, eyes narrowed and expression unconvinced. But, after a moment, he moved across the room and threw his coat over the back of the chair at the table we'd set for dinner. Belle silently handed him a glass of red and then sat down opposite him.

I perched between the two of them and wrapped my hands around my whiskey glass. "You know how you said earlier that you had to get out of Canberra because your dad was angry accreditation had uncovered the fact you were less than expected?"

His nod was a short, sharp movement.

I glanced at Belle.

Don't look at me. He can speak—he just doesn't want to.

Oh. I returned my gaze to Monty. "Imagine how much worse it would have been if you'd not only been declared underpowered, but were also held responsible for the death of a sibling who *did* meet your father's expectations? A sibling who was the shining light in your father's eyes?"

He frowned. "Why would your father hold you responsible for Catherine's death? She was killed by a dark sorcerer, and while she might have been the last victim, she was by no means the only one."

"Because," I said, my voice holding an edge of bitterness I couldn't quite control. "I tried to save her, and I failed."

His confusion deepened. "I take it you tried to do so alone?"

"Yes."

"But why on earth would you do that? Why didn't you talk to your parents?"

I raised my eyebrows. "Would you have listened to someone you considered a failure as a witch?"

He hesitated. Belle's snort filled the silence. "*That* right there is your answer."

"That might be true enough," he said, his expression losing some of its anger. "But surely after five other deaths, they would have at least been willing to entertain your information."

"Except the information didn't come via magic. It came to me as a prophetic dream." One that had taken me entirely too long to understand. By the time that I had, it had been too late to save Cat.

"Ah."

"Yeah," Belle said. "We all know just how highly blue-bloods value psi powers."

"That's because most of them are of little true use." He paused. "Which I guess is your point."

"Yes." I took a drink, but the fiery liquid did little to check the rush of images that pressed at my mind—the grimy abandoned warehouse where Cat had met her doom, the bloody parts of her body within the black pentagram, the sorcerer's face smeared with her blood. The force of his energy hurtling me backward and then smashing me into one wall after another, until my body was almost as broken and bloody as Cat's. The desperate, last-minute spell I'd cast that had set him alight and broken bones even as Belle raised the spirit world and sent them riding to my rescue.

I probably should have died that day, right alongside my sister. It was only thanks to Belle that I hadn't. To this day, I had no idea what had happened to the sorcerer who'd killed Cat and the other witches. His body had never been found; the general consensus in Canberra was that the dark spirits he'd dealt with had claimed both his flesh and his soul on death.

My prophetic dreams believed otherwise.

I gulped down the rest of my drink. "My parents held me accountable for her death. It didn't matter that they wouldn't have believed me, didn't matter that she was already dead by the time I got there. Their golden child was gone, and they *had* to blame someone. I was the easiest target."

He was silent for a moment, his gaze on my face. It was something I felt rather than saw, simply because I didn't dare look at him. It might have all happened just over twelve years ago now, but the pain and the deep sense of betrayal still hurt as fiercely now as it had back then.

"Why did you run?" he asked eventually.

I grimaced. "Because my father decided the best way to deal with a problem was to get rid of it."

He blinked. "You're not saying he tried to kill you—"

"No. But sometimes there are worse things than death."

And Clayton had certainly been one of those things.

A shudder ran through me. Belle silently filled my glass again and I hastily gulped it down. At this rate, I'd be drunk before dinner was even served.

"So what has any of this got to do with you shutting down my ability to say your names?"

"You *can* say our real surnames," Belle said. "Just not when you're in the company of anyone else but us."

He didn't look relieved by this statement. "Why the restriction?"

"Because we legally changed our surnames to Grace and Kent to ensure my parents could never track either of us down."

"If they'd wanted to find you, they would have by now." His voice was dry. "Tracing spells are very proficient at such things."

"Yes, but there are also spells to counter them."

"Which you don't have the magical strength to perform." He studied the two of us for a second. "Or, at least, you didn't back then."

"But I *did* have a large inheritance from my grandfather.

It's amazing what money can buy if you apply it in the right areas."

"Which you—as a sixteen-year-old—should not have known."

"The three low witch houses are not as finicky in their friends as the three blueblood," Belle murmured. "And sometimes that very much plays to their advantage."

"Is that why your mother was taken into custody and questioned?" Monty asked.

Belle leaned forward at that, her expression alarmed. "Did they harm her?"

"Not as far as I heard—and I heard quite a lot given I was still my father's shining light at that stage." He hesitated. "They would have spelled her to speak what she knew, though."

"Which wouldn't have revealed anything," I said. "She might have been the one who advised us to run, but we never told her our plans or what we intended."

"And haven't contacted her since, I'm guessing," he said.

"Yes." I frowned. "Why?"

His smile held a bitter edge. "You really have to ask that?"

I stared at him for a second, then swore softly. "They placed a spell on her so that she'd inform them if and when she heard from us?"

"So my father said." He glanced at Belle. "But it's doubtful the spell would have lasted much longer than a few weeks, so you're probably safe to contact her now if you wanted."

An almost wistful smile touched her lips. "As much as I'd love to, I don't really think we can take the chance."

He shook his head, disbelief evident. "I hate to be blunt about this, Liz, but it's been twelve years—do you really think Edward has any remaining interest in you? He has grandchildren now—four of them."

"Juli has *children*?" I said, even as Belle said, *Well, hell, there's a scary thought.*

Extremely. My brother had been a conceited twit barely able to look after himself, let alone four kids of this own....

"Yes, and he dotes on them," Monty said. "He has no need to chase after someone who doesn't want to be found."

Meaning he *didn't* know the whole story. And if he didn't, how many others wouldn't? Of course, a lack of knowledge didn't make me safer, as not even my father could make legally signed and submitted documents go away. Nor could Clayton move on until I'd been found and the documents voided.

Though I doubted moving on was what Clayton would want, even now. Not given the fool I'd made out of him.

I raised an eyebrow and tried to ignore the renewed churning in my gut. "You worked in Canberra, and you certainly know my parents. Does my father seem the type to forgive and forget to you?"

He frowned. "Well, no, but—"

"This isn't just about my sister's death, Monty. While he certainly held me accountable for that, my bigger crime was the fact I embarrassed him. Me—an underpowered nobody—made him look like a fool in front of a man who wasn't only a good friend but a powerful member of the council. He won't ever forget that."

Neither of them would ever forget that.

Monty's confusion increased. "I certainly can't remember anything along those lines being spoken about—"

"And probably never will. My father is not one to air his dirty laundry, even amongst his own family."

He leaned back in his chair and eyed me for a moment. "Let's do a deal."

Belle and I glanced at each other; though her expression gave little away, I could feel her uncertainty as strongly as my own.

"What sort of deal?" she asked warily.

"For a start," he said, "you stay out of my goddamn head."

"And?" I said, because there *was* obviously more.

"You tell the truth about the wild magic. In exchange, I won't mention your presence here in the reservation in any of my reports back to Canberra."

"That by default means you can't mention the wild magic in any of them."

"Why the hell not? There are certainly traces of it both in your spell work and in your energy output, but the former, at least, isn't particularly unusual in a reservation all but awash with the stuff."

"But the latter *is*," I replied. "So if you want the truth then you have to agree to not mention the wild magic."

"Except I'm not *only* here as the government's representative but to investigate the rumors of the wild magic's unusual pattern of behavior."

So someone *had* read Ashworth's report and had been curious enough about his comments to word Monty up. "What exactly were you told about it?"

He shrugged. "Just that it appeared to have gained some sort of sentience and was, in some instances, acting with intent."

Which was certainly true, and not just because of Katie's presence. The wild magic had woven itself through my spells long before I'd become aware of its presence, and the café was nowhere near the main wellspring. And while the long strands of its power hovered over the reservation's wilder regions, it was very rarely found anywhere near Castle Rock.

"What about a compromise? You can mention the wild magic but can't mention the truth of this place." I hesitated. "And it's not just because of me and Belle."

"I'm not entirely sure that's—"

"Monty, there are some secrets—just as there are some magics—that are too dangerous for general consumption."

"We're talking about the high council here. I don't think—"

"You don't yet know the truth," I said. "It's not what you think."

His gaze narrowed for several seconds, then he glanced across at Belle. "I suppose if I don't agree, you'll just make sure I can't say or send anything about this place to the council."

A smile touched her lips but she didn't bother replying.

He swore and then held out his hand. Energy sparkled across his fingertips. "Fine. A deal then."

I clasped his hand, and my magic merged with his. Except it wasn't *just* my magic. "A deal sworn on the power of this place is a deal that cannot be broken," I said softly. "Do so at your own peril, Monty."

Something flashed through his expression—something that was both fear and understanding. "Ashworth was wrong. It's more than just an affinity with this place, isn't it?"

I hesitated. "I actually don't know what it is. I just know that I can use the wild magic—and not just in spells. I can call it to me—and aside from the change in my eye color, it's had no real effect."

"Apart from being drained to the point of insensibility

and coming close to death," Belle commented, voice dry. A timer went off in the kitchen and she rose. "I hope you still like lasagna, Monty, because that's what we've made."

"Perfect." He watched her walk into the kitchen and then said, "Define what you mean by use if you don't mean in spells?"

"I can draw it into my body and direct its energy."

"No," he said, almost automatically. "That's not possible. You wouldn't be alive if you did something like that."

"Except that I have—and a number of times now."

"Fuck." He swept a hand through his longish hair. "How?"

"Again, I don't know." I grimaced. "But I will say it almost feels as if the wild magic is a part of my soul—a part of my very DNA."

"No wonder you didn't want Canberra here," he muttered. "They'd study you as thoroughly as a bug under a microscope."

"Yeah, and this is one bug who has no intention of ever letting that happen."

"Understandable. But there is a bigger question here—"

"Why would someone so notoriously underpowered as myself even be capable of using wild magic?"

A smile twitched his lips. "Yeah."

"Again, I have no idea. We've only been here for a few months, and this is all very much a new development."

"Huh." He glanced around as Belle returned with the tray of lasagna. "There's enough there to feed a goddamn army."

"You did have quite an appetite, if I remember correctly," I said.

"Still do."

There was something in his eyes—in the way he was

looking at Belle—that suggested he wasn't talking about food.

Amusement twitched my lips, but before I could say anything, Belle said, *Go there, and this dish of lasagna will end up in your lap.*

Whatever happened to the motto of doing no harm to your witch?

Doesn't apply when said witch is about to be evil.

I grinned but managed to restrain my evilness and, once Belle had placed the tray on the table, began serving everyone. The conversation moved on to other matters, but once the lasagna was eaten and dessert served, Monty leaned back in his chair and said, "Tell me about every encounter with the wild magic."

I did so, only omitting any mention of the second wellspring. He'd no doubt find it once he'd been here long enough but we—Katie, Gabe, and I —could deal with the consequences of that when it happened.

"I'll do a search through the archives and see what they have on wild magic—and don't worry, no one is going to think twice about such a request given I was ordered to investigate the stuff." His sudden grin was wide and filled with anticipation. "I have to admit, I'm rather looking forward to being the witch for this reservation now."

"Meaning you weren't before?" Belle asked, eyebrows rising.

"Well, no. I took it because I was bored to death with spell logging."

"I'm sure there would have been a multitude of options open for Frederick Ashworth's oldest—"

"But not, as you well know, for one whose power was deemed less than desirable." He half shrugged. "I just needed to go somewhere different than Canberra. Something with a little more life and a little less restriction."

I snorted softly. "It's always wise to be careful about what you wish for—especially when it comes to an area in which a major wellspring has been left unprotected for a year."

"Ashworth and Eli were filling me in on all that on the way up here. I hate to say it, but it's probably going to get worse before it gets better."

"That much we figured—"

I stopped as energy surged into the room. Its feel was bright and sharp, and filled with an odd sort of cognizance.

Not just wild magic, but the portion controlled by Katie.

And with it came an odd sort of urgency.

She wanted me to follow her. *Now.*

Monty drew in a sharp breath. "What the fuck is going on? That's wild magic, and yet not."

"You were told some parts had gained awareness. This is one of those parts." I thrust to my feet. "It wants us to follow it."

"What? Why?"

"I don't know, but I've learned not to ignore it." I ran behind the cake counter, pulled my purse out of the hiding spot, and tossed my keys to Belle. "You'd better drive."

Monty thrust upright and swung his coat off the back of the chair. "Don't think you're going to leave me behind."

"Not a chance—you're the official witch here now, so you can goddamn deal with whatever horror we're about to be shown."

"Sounds like you're expecting the worst."

"That's because when the wild magic turns up, it

usually is." I grabbed the backpack—which we hadn't yet unpacked—and ushered him out the door.

"Where are we heading?" Belle asked, as she carefully reversed out of the parking spot.

I hesitated, and silently called the force that was Katie to me. Her energy rushed through me, but the intensity of it was not as fierce as previous times. Either she was learning control, or I was getting used to being inhabited—however briefly—by wild magic. But even so, everything around me suddenly seemed brighter—sharper. I could clearly smell Monty's aftershave—it was musk based, with hints of orange, lavender, and geranium. Could hear the distant thunder of an oncoming storm, and feel the electricity of it in the air—a sharp force that had the hairs on my arms standing on end. Heard her words in my mind, faint compared to the other sensations, and yet nevertheless clear. And then she left.

But I had my directions.

"Left at Hargraves, and then continue straight down."

"And how the fuck do you know that?" Monty said from the back seat. "The wild magic went through you—I saw that much—but please don't tell me it's aware enough to give *directions*."

"It's not."

"Then what the fuck just happened? If that wasn't the wild magic, then what the hell was it?"

I glanced briefly at Belle. *What do you think?*

You have to tell him at least part of the truth, she said. *Otherwise he's going to go searching—and that could be bad news, as I'm not sure how Gabe will react to the intrusion. He seemed pretty intent on keeping the second wellspring a secret.*

Good point, I said, and then added out loud, "From

what we can ascertain, it appears that parts of the wild magic have been infused with the soul of a werewolf."

Monty laughed. "That's not possible."

"You keep saying that," Belle said, amused, "despite evidence to the contrary."

"But a soul can't—" He cut it off. "Do you know how?"

"No." Which wasn't a lie because I had no idea just what spell Gabe had used—although I *did* suspect it hadn't come from any known spell book. "But I do know the soul is that of Katie O'Connor—the youngest sister of Aiden O'Connor, the head ranger here. She's appointed herself the reservation's guardian, and I appear to be the only one she can communicate with."

"Because of your connection to the wild magic?"

"I suspect so."

"Which only deepens the mystery of your connection."

I didn't bother replying because there was nothing I could really say. I concentrated on the darkening countryside, looking for the next turning point. After a couple of minutes, I said, "The road curves to the right up ahead, but there's a dirt track on the left that goes into the old dry diggings area. We need to head into that area."

Belle immediately slowed and then pulled off the road. The headlights swept across the scrubby-looking forest of eucalypts and then pinned a less than pristine track.

"We're not going to get this car through that," she said. "That's four-wheel drive territory."

"Then we'll walk. I don't think we're far away."

She stopped just short of a ditch that had at some point been created by water runoff and then switched the engine and lights off. The night closed in but held no threat.

I grabbed the backpack, then climbed out of the car and studied the nearby trees. The gentle breeze stirred through the leaves, making them rustle gently, but there was little other sound to be heard.

"I don't suppose either of you has a flashlight," Monty said, as he stopped beside me.

"That's what flashlight apps on phones are for." I moved forward without bothering to retrieve mine. Right now, with the stars so bright and clear, there was little need for it.

We'd barely entered the forest when Katie's energy spun around me again, leading me away from the main track. As shadows grew deeper, I finally used my phone. Its bright light ran across the nearby trees and briefly highlighted a large mound of rocks—tailings from a disused gold mine.

"Is it safe to be walking around an area like this?" Monty asked.

"If we stick to the trail, most likely," I said.

"A statement that doesn't comfort me much."

It didn't comfort me much, either, given I'd almost fallen to my death down a disused mine shaft only a few months ago.

The path gradually grew steeper and rockier, forcing us to slow down even further. Frustration ran through the energy guiding us, but there was little urgency. It was a point that had trepidation stirring, if only because it meant what we were being led toward was death rather than life.

Something that was all too quickly confirmed as the scent of rotting meat began to taint the air.

"I'm not liking the smell of that," Monty muttered. "And I'm seriously hoping its source is a dead animal rather than a human."

"Katie wouldn't be leading us to an animal," Belle commented. "So you'd better prepare yourself for the worst."

Energy tugged me left, off the smaller track and into the trees. I paused briefly, running my light across the ground, and then followed her in.

The smell of death was sharper. We were getting close.

Up ahead, light began to glimmer. It wasn't starlight or even the pulse of wild magic. It was, I suspected, a will-o'-the-wisp—or ghost candles, as they were more commonly known around these parts. Wisps weren't actually ghosts, despite their nickname; they were spirits, and very fragile by nature. Wind could tear them away, rain could wash them out, and they couldn't stand the touch of sunshine. Sometimes they were helpful, and other times they weren't. The myths of them leading travelers astray were very much based on truth. I'd encountered them a couple of times over the last few months, and each time they'd chosen to help me. I very much suspected the one up ahead might be doing just that—that it was standing guard over whatever it was Katie had led us here to find.

"Is that a wisp up ahead?" Monty asked, a hint of surprise in his voice.

"Yes." I glanced over my shoulder at him. "You've never seen one?"

"I've lived in Canberra all my life," he said, expression amused. "Opportunities have been few and far between."

"You'd better get used to seeing all manner of weird, wonderful, and often very deadly things in this place," Belle commented. "In fact, you may find yourself longing to be back at the capital."

"No matter how bad it gets here, Canberra will never be a better option."

"At least we agree on that," I muttered.

I flicked off the phone's flashlight app and, after a moment, Belle and Monty did the same. The wisp's light immediately grew brighter, its blue-white light washing through the small clearing and highlighting the figure it hovered above.

That figure wasn't moving.

It also wasn't clothed.

And, like Mrs. Dale, it had very obviously been skinned.

"Oh fuck," Monty said softly. "Is that what I think it is?"

"Yeah, it is." I paused on the outskirts of the clearing, my stomach churning as I scanned the area. The wisp's light was bright enough to view the immediate area; there were no clothes or personal items to be seen. Once again, it appeared as if this woman had been killed elsewhere and simply dumped here.

My gaze returned to the body and, after a slight hesitation, I forced my feet on. The wisp pulsed in response but it didn't flee. Part of me wondered if it was the same wisp that had helped me previously—it was certainly the same size—and whether Katie's presence within the wild magic was enabling her to influence or at least call on those beings who existed alongside it. Either way, the wisp's presence needed formal acknowledgment.

"I appreciate you staying to highlighting the area for us," I said, as I stopped short of the body.

One thing was very obvious—this death wasn't new. The remains had the look of meat left too long out in the sun, and smelled like it too. I pinched my nostrils together with a hand and started breathing through my mouth, but it didn't seem to help any. The smell clawed at the back of my throat and had my stomach churning even faster.

The wisp spun lightly, as if in acknowledgment, and then moved back several feet as Monty stopped beside me. It was uncertain about his presence, but not enough to flee.

"It's a female," Monty said, shoving his hands in his pockets. "Married, too."

My gaze leapt to her left hand. A silver wedding ring gleamed brightly on the raw remnants of her finger.

"Why would anyone bother skinning a body and then go to the trouble of putting a ring back on?" Belle asked. "That makes no sense at all."

"I guess until we understand who or what we're dealing with, making no sense will continue to be a problem," Monty said.

Katie's energy stirred around me again, lightly tugging at my fingers. "There's something else here—something else we need to find."

"What?" Monty said.

"That I don't know." I glanced at Belle. "Could you ring the rangers while I go find whatever else there is?"

She nodded, and as she made the call, Monty and I followed Katie's lead. We took a wide detour around the body and walked across to the clearing's other edge. The wisp followed us into the trees, highlighting the faint trail.

Twenty feet in, we discovered another death.

But it wasn't a body. Or, at least, it wasn't a full body.

It was instead the skin of one.

FOUR

I briefly closed my eyes and took a deep breath. *Big mistake.* While the smell of decay had been bad enough in the clearing, it seemed ten times worse here. My stomach lurched and rose, and it took every ounce of control I had not to lose the dinner I'd only recently eaten.

"Is that what I think it is?" Monty whispered, horror filling his voice.

"Yes."

"Why the fuck would anyone go through the arduous task of skinning a human, and then simply dump the skin a few yards away?" He shook his head. "It makes no goddamn sense."

"As you noted only a minute ago, until we know what is doing this, it probably won't." I swallowed heavily. It didn't ease the bitterness of bile in my throat or the churning in my gut. "One of us will need to guard the area until the rangers get here, just to be sure a stray dog or cat doesn't wander in and start eating the evidence."

The thought of that happening only helped to increase the intensity of the churning.

"If it hasn't happened yet, I doubt it will, but I'll stay. It'll give me a chance to look around and see if whatever did this left behind some sort of energy spore or tell." He glanced at the wisp still hovering nearby. "You might want to return with Lizzie, my friend, as I'll be raising a light sphere."

The wisp immediately retreated, and Monty smiled. "Who knew they could understand us so easily?"

"Spirits have been in this world as long as we have," I replied, amused. "So it's not really that surprising."

"It is for someone like me, who has only ever read about such things."

Which I guessed could be said about a lot of those in Canberra. My parents might be the capital's power couple and very sought-after mentors and advisors to both political parties and private business, but even *they* had never stepped outside Canberra's confines—not since before I was born, anyway. And I couldn't help wondering just how different their worldview would be if they'd done so.

Probably not a great deal, Belle commented, mental tones dry. *I think your dad was born a set-in-his-ways, over-bearing stick in the mud.*

They wouldn't have remained at the top of the witch tree if they were unwilling to bend with new ideas and ways.

True, Belle said. *I do think, however, that the more power and influence they gained, the more determined they became to ensure they and their family kept it.*

And the latter they ensured by arranging marriages for their children that forged strong magical alliances. Whether or not said children had actually wanted them.

At least Cat did love the man chosen for her, Belle said.

That she had—and in that, she'd at least been lucky. But Charlie had been yet another who'd held me accountable for her death, and that had perhaps hurt me more than anything my parents had said or done, if only because he and I had actually gotten on well until that point.

Grief does strange things to a person, Belle said softly. *I think there was a chance he would have seen sense if we'd hung around.*

Maybe. And maybe not. It wasn't like I could afford to actually hang around and find out.

Belle squatted several feet away from the body, a slight haze of energy surrounding her. Not wild magic, but rather the energy runoff from her spirit guides. "Do you think the skin you found belongs to this poor soul? Or does it perhaps belong to Mrs. Dale?"

"I really have no idea." I stopped beside her and did my best to breathe shallowly. The wind was at our backs and blew the worst of the smell away, but that didn't stop it from lodging in my nostrils or churning my stomach. "Why?"

She pushed upright. "The spirits think we might be dealing with some kind of skin walker."

"The spirits actually offered helpful information? Color me shocked."

She lightly whacked my arm—twice. "That's one from me, and one from the spirits."

I grinned. "Even they have to admit helpfulness is a rarity."

"They wish to remind you that they are not here to provide information we are more than capable of uncovering for ourselves." Her tone was haughty—an echo of whatever spirit she was listening to.

While most witches only had one spirit guide, Belle usually had at least two, but sometimes as many as four. Neither of us really knew why that was the case, although it might have something to do with the fact she was an extremely strong spirit talker.

I frowned down at the body. "Why do they think it's a skin walker? Aren't they extremely rare here in Australia?"

"Yes, which is why they mention the possibility—it's likely we'll have to search the US witch archives to find anything about them."

"*We* won't be doing anything of the sort. As you keep reminding me, that's Monty's job, not ours." I hesitated. "I don't suppose they can tell us why they think it's a skin walker? From the little I know about them, they're a form of evil witch who can turn into, possess, or disguise themselves as animals. That's not what's happening here."

Her gaze became slightly distracted as she listened to the other side. "No, but there are legends of skin walkers through many cultures, even if they are not known by that name. It is just a matter of finding the variation we might be dealing with."

"Which means another search through your gran's books, I'm thinking."

"Possibly, although if skin walkers *are* as rare as the spirits are saying, then it's unlikely she'll have anything of note."

The distant sound of sirens began to cut through the stillness of the night. The rangers weren't far away. "Do you —or the spirits—think the two skinning deaths are in any way linked to the quasi vampire attack from last night?"

Belle hesitated, and then wrinkled her nose. "If the skinnings are being done by a walker, it's unlikely, as they don't feed on blood. Why?"

I shrugged. "It just seems weird that we're now dealing with three supernatural murders so close together."

"Not really," she said. "Not given the amount of time

the wellspring was left unguarded. In fact, this sort of thing is likely to start happening more often."

Which was *exactly* what I feared, and also something we could do absolutely nothing about.

The sirens abruptly cut out and the ensuing silence somehow felt heavier. "Who answered when you called the rangers?"

"Aiden. He wasn't happy."

"He never is when it comes to supernatural crimes."

Belle snorted softly. "Well, he's only got the damn council to blame."

"He knows that." I paused. "Did he say who he was sending out here?"

"No."

The wisp's light abruptly went out, throwing us into darkness. A few seconds later, Aiden stepped through the scrub and strode across the clearing.

"How did you get here?" I said. "I've got your truck's keys."

"Mac picked me up." He stopped beside me, his shoulder lightly brushing mine, sending a wave of warmth rolling through the rest of me. "This looks like a repeat of what you found at the cold store."

"Except this time we also found the skin." I motioned toward the trees. "Monty's keeping an eye on it while looking for energy spores."

Aiden glanced at me, eyebrows raised. "The thing that did this has spores? Meaning it's some sort of plant?"

I couldn't help smiling. "No, but there are some supernatural beings who give off detectable energy patterns, and each one is unique to that particular demon or spirit."

"So if he finds a spore, we know what we're dealing with?"

"In theory, yes."

"Good." He glanced toward the trees, his nostrils flaring. "The skin in those trees smells older than this body."

"Yes, although it doesn't look as if it's in the process of decomposing."

"I'm presuming, then, that there's some sort of magic involved?"

"If there's magic preserving the skin, I didn't feel it." I shrugged. "But that doesn't mean Monty hasn't."

He grunted. "Do you and Belle want to head home? I'll grab your statements when I drop by in the morning for my keys and breakfast."

I nodded. Truth be told, now that the adrenaline of the hunt was drifting away, weariness was well and truly settling in. "Have you met Monty yet? Do you want me to do the introductions?"

"I'm a big lad—

"So I believe," Belle murmured.

"And I can introduce myself just fine," he continued, obviously ignoring her comment. "Mac and Ciara are almost here—do you want an escort back to your car?"

"No, we'll be able to find our way back." I rose onto tippy toes to kiss his cheek, but he turned and my lips caught his instead. It was a heated but all too brief moment.

"Go to sleep," he said, voice gruff. "We'll talk tomorrow."

I licked the taste of him on my lips—a taste that was a lovely mix of coffee, heat, and desire—then turned and walked away. It didn't take us long to get back to the car, but by the time we got home, I was yawning loudly and could barely keep my eyes open. I had a quick, hot shower to wash the stink of death and decay from my skin, then all but fell into bed. If I dreamed, I certainly didn't remember it.

The smell of bacon woke me the next morning. A quick look at my phone told me it was just after five, which was way earlier than our usual wake-up time on a working day. I stretched the kinks out of my muscles and then flung off the blankets and quickly pulled on jeans and a dark green tank top—my current wardrobe of choice when working in the café.

As I clattered down the stairs, I said, "You're up early this morning."

"Heard Aiden's truck starting up, and had a mild panic attack thinking someone was stealing it." She came out of the kitchen carrying two plates filled with bacon, eggs, and toast. "Thankfully, it was Aiden rather than a thief, but it was pointless going back to sleep so I started the prep instead."

I headed across to the coffee machine to make her a coffee and me a hot chocolate. "Did he say why he was here so early?"

"Another dead body, apparently."

"Fate has obviously decided to greet Monty with a baptism of fire." Or death, as the case was. "I don't suppose he gave any details?"

"No. He did say he'd exchange the breakfast date for a dinner one, if that was okay with you."

It was, and not just because dinner would inevitably lead to bed but also the fact I'd avoided having to explain my past to him for another few hours.

"Five supernatural murders in almost as many days is a little extreme, even for this reservation."

Belle's gaze shot to mine. "Where did you get five from? If we include the one he's investigating now, it's four by my reckoning."

I hesitated, but the certainty that if this *was* another

murder, then that made five rather than four wouldn't go away. I shrugged, picked up the two filled mugs, and walked over to the table. "It's not like the prophetic part of my soul is renowned for giving details. It's even more obstinate than your spirit guides."

"Ain't *that* the truth." She wrinkled her nose. "You know, I think I'm going to miss not being in the thick of the action."

I snorted. "May I remind you of how close to death we've come on a number of occasions?"

She grinned. "The whole death thing aside, it did liven up our days—even you have to admit that."

"I can live without *that* sort of excitement, thank you very much." I tucked into my breakfast. "But I really don't believe we're off the hook when it comes to crime investigations. Katie's the reservation's self-appointed guardian, and I'm currently the only one able to communicate with her. We'll be dragged into events, willing or not."

As if to emphasize my point, my phone rang, the sound sharp in the brief silence. The tone told me it wasn't someone I contacted regularly and, with my pulse skipping into overdrive, I thrust to my feet and walked around the counter to grab it. The number that popped up on the screen was Alice Dale's.

"I hope she's not ringing to accuse us of holding back information," Belle said. "Because it wasn't like we had much choice."

"No." I took a deep breath then swished the screen across to answer the call. "This is an early call, Alice—are you okay?"

"Oh God, yes." The joy voice was so fierce it practically vibrated down the line. "I just thought I'd ring and let you know that my mom is home—I was worrying over nothing, obviously."

Dread curled through me. Alice's mom *couldn't* be home—her body lay in the morgue sans its skin. The rangers might not have formally identified her as yet, but I had absolutely no doubt that the body we found in the dumpster was that of Mrs. Dale.

So if she'd suddenly turned up at her house, either she'd risen from the dead or something else was going on.

"Have you talked to her yet?" I said, trying to keep the urgency from my voice. "Or gone to see her?"

"No—I was just driving past, just on the off chance that she'd come back, and saw her peeking out of the blinds."

It was far too early to be out for a drive, but I guessed if it'd been my mom who was missing, I might have done the same thing. My relationship with my mother might have deteriorated once I'd hit my teens, but she was still my mom and, despite everything, I did still love her.

The same could *not* be said about my father.

"Are you sure it was her?"

"Of course. Why?"

"No real reason." I hesitated, that sense of dread getting stronger. "I've still got her necklace, Alice—would it be okay if I drop by in a few minutes and return it?"

"I can come by the café this afternoon—"

"I've got to go to the wholesaler's to pick up some supplies for the café before it opens, so it's really not a problem," I cut in. "Saves you the hassle."

"Sure." She seemed surprised rather than suspicious. "I'll go in and put the kettle on, if you'd like."

Don't, I wanted to scream. *That's not your mom; it's someone—something—else.* But I had no proof, and Alice wasn't likely to believe me anyway. All I could do was get there as soon as I could.

"That would be lovely, thanks."

My voice was edged and a little too sharp, but she didn't seem to notice. She gave me the address, said a quick "see you soon," and then hung up. I spun and raced to the reading room. Thankfully, I'd simply dumped the backpack again rather than unpacking it—a fact that gave me a few precious extra seconds.

"You might want to ring Monty," Belle said, as I came back out. "His place is on the way, and that's what he's here for after all."

"Could you make the call? Tell him I'll be there in three minutes."

Her answering grin held a little too much delight. But then, Monty had been a well-known night owl with a long history of arriving late for the first session of school. I couldn't imagine that would have changed greatly over the last twelve years as, for the most part, government and witch departments up in Canberra worked on flexible hours.

I grabbed my purse and car keys, then headed out. By the time I got across to Monty's, he was—rather surprisingly —already waiting out the front. But as he climbed into the front passenger seat, it became very obvious his brain hadn't yet kicked into gear.

"Your shirt is inside out." I pulled back out onto the road. "And you've different colored sneakers on."

"Is it any wonder?" He scrubbed a hand across his bristly face. "It's almost indecent to be up at this hour."

"Next time, I'll bring one of Belle's wake-up tonics for you."

He grunted. "I'm not sure it would help, but I suppose it couldn't hurt, either."

I grinned. He hadn't yet tasted her tonics, and I wasn't about to spoil the surprise—or Belle's delight—by mentioning just how foul they could smell and taste.

"What are we racing toward again?" he added. "I think I remember Belle mentioning something about a dead person coming back to life but nothing else really sunk in."

I explained the situation and then added, "It may be nothing but—"

"Your gut says otherwise," he finished for me. "Aiden's already mentioned just how helpful your psi abilities have been when it comes to tracking down perps, so I'm not about to discount them."

"Perps?" I glanced at him. "Seriously?"

He smiled. "I do love me some crime dramas. Right now, it's starting to feel like I'm in my very own."

"And *I* suspect you might not feel so happy about it after the first few fights for your life."

"Probably not, but no matter what happens, it's still far better than sitting behind a desk cataloging other witches' shitty spells." He paused. "Of course, it would be preferable if said perps chose better hours to do their thing."

"Up until now, most of them have." I flicked on the blinker, braked to allow several cars to go past in the opposite direction, and then swung right. "Isn't it rather unusual for a spirit to be active this close to dawn? I thought most of them preferred the comfort of darkness?"

"They do, but that doesn't mean they can't move around in daylight if necessary."

Which was *not* something I really wanted confirmed. "Were you able to find any clue as to what we might be dealing with?"

He shook his head. "Tells like spores tend to fade fairly

rapidly, so unless you're on the scene very quickly, there's not much hope."

I grunted and slowed enough to check house numbers; we were at the wrong end of the street. I accelerated again. "So you have no clue what killed the woman last night?"

"Aside from her being skinned, you mean?"

I glanced at him in annoyance and his amusement grew.

"There did appear to be what looked like burn marks on the heels of the victim's feet," he added, "but I couldn't say for sure they're supernatural in origin."

"But you think they are?" I slowed down again as we neared number fifty-one. There were two cars in the driveway—a gray Hyundai SUV and a white Ford Focus.

"I've absolutely no credible reason for believing so, but yes, I do." He leaned forward. "I can't see or feel anything wrong in that house."

"No."

I found a parking spot several houses further up the road. The wind whispered around me as we climbed out, its touch filled with nothing more than the promise of warmth. The street was silent and there was little noise coming from the nearby houses, although I could see TV screens flickering through several windows. No sound came from Mrs. Dale's house and all the curtains were drawn.

Trepidation stirred anew. I slung my pack over my shoulder and joined Monty at the front of the car. "What do you think?"

"I don't know." He frowned at the house for several seconds. "I still can't feel anything out of place, yet there's something about that house that is making me very uneasy."

"That makes two of us."

"Then we'd better get over there and see what's going on."

He hitched his pack higher onto his shoulder then strode quickly down the footpath, forcing me to run to catch up. I touched the hood of the SUV as I passed it; it was still warm. Mrs. Dale—or rather, the thing that was now impersonating her—couldn't have gotten here much before her daughter.

Monty took the steps two at a time, then strode across to the front door and knocked loudly. The sound echoed inside the house, but there was no immediate response.

The sense that something was very wrong grew stronger. I silently gathered a repelling spell around my fingers as Monty knocked again.

Still no response.

He looked at me. "What do you think?"

"I think we need to go inside and see why neither Alice nor her mom are answering."

"Wouldn't it be better to call the rangers? There're laws about breaking and entering, remember."

"We're in a werewolf reservation that has in recent months been overrun with supernatural events." My voice was dry. "I think it's fair to say they're not going to be bothered with us entering unlawfully if our suspicions pan out."

"And if they don't?"

I grinned. "I also happen to be sleeping with the head ranger."

Which wouldn't actually help me if I *did* commit a serious crime—Aiden was by nature a law-abiding man and very unlikely to ever take a bribe, be it sexual or monetary in nature—but Monty was new here and wouldn't yet know that.

Monty snorted softly and energy stirred—a force that was bright, sharp, and so strong it burned across my skin like fire. He wove his spell around his fingers in much the same manner as I had the repelling spell, and then launched it. The spell's energy caressed the door with a finesse that only came with training, briefly splaying out across the wood before merging into it. There was a soft click, and the door slowly opened.

The hallway beyond was dark and silent.

Monty took one step inside and then stopped. "While there's no feel of magic, there's definitely *something* here—some kind of foul energy."

I squeezed in beside him and unleashed my "other" senses—the ones that seemed more attuned to the evil forces of the world. Malevolence stirred through the house, a wash of foulness that already seemed to be fading.

"I think whatever was here has already gone."

He glanced down at me sharply. "What makes you say that?"

"My psychic senses were always stronger than my magic, remember?" I paused. "What I'd really like to know is what has happened to Alice, given her car is still here."

"I guess there's only one way we're ever going to find that out."

"Indeed." I motioned him forward. "You're the official witch, so lead the way, cousin."

He snorted, but nevertheless cautiously moved further into the house. I followed, every sense alert, the repelling spell swirling lazily around my fingers in readiness.

There were three doorways that led off the small hall and an arch down the far end. We moved forward, switching on lights as we did. The door to our right revealed a living room, the one on our left was a bedroom, and next to that was the bathroom. Each room was empty of both life *and* death. Which wasn't really a surprise, as the fading sense of evil was coming from whatever rooms lay beyond the arch.

Monty glanced at me, his face pinched with tension. I didn't say anything; I simply nodded. After a moment, he moved toward the arch. The repelling spell tingled around my fingers, its soft buzz seeming extraordinarily loud against the thick pall of silence.

Monty stepped through the arch, turned on the light, and again stopped. I did the same. The room ran the width of the house and comprised a kitchen—which was to our left —and a dining area to our right.

In between the two lay a body.

And beside it, the almost inevitable pile of skin.

"Oh fuck," Monty said. "Another one."

"But is it Mrs. Dale, or is it Alice?"

"That I can't tell you." He moved around the skinless body and squatted at the end of it. "There're burn marks on the soles of her feet, though, and I doubt that's a coincidence."

"Meaning it could have something to do with how this spirit is stealing—" I broke off the rest of the sentence at the sound of a car's engine roaring to life.

That sound was close—at the front of the house close.

I glanced at Monty, then swore and ran for the front door, getting there in time to see a woman in the seat of the Focus.

That woman was Alice.

Or was it?

Something within me suddenly wasn't so sure.

I leapt off the front porch, yelling her name as I ran for the car. She didn't look at me; either she couldn't hear me, or she simply wasn't acknowledging me. Maybe it was shock. Maybe she'd walked into that house expecting to see her mother, and instead had found a raw body and a pile of skin beside it. It was a sight that would certainly send even the strongest of minds into turmoil—and I doubted Alice would ever have been described as strong.

I lunged for the door handle, but at that very point, she hit the accelerator and reversed out of the driveway. Tires squealed and rubber burned as the car lurched back. The mirror clipped my hand and pain surged; I swore loudly and flung the repelling spell. It was designed for flesh rather than metal, but it nevertheless hit the front of the car and sent it spinning sideways.

Alice didn't brake, didn't ease her speed, and the smoke coming from the tires grew thicker as she fought to control the spinning car. I leaped the small brick fence, gathering magic across my fingertips as I ran again for the car. But somehow, Alice had regained control and was now reversing down the street.

"Duck," Monty yelled, and I immediately did so.

Magic sizzled over my head and hit the front of Alice's car. It didn't stop.

"What the fuck?" I spun around, only to see Monty leap the fence and then sprint down the street.

"It's a tracker," he said. "So get in the fucking car, Liz, and let's stop this bitch."

I ran after him, grabbing my keys and opening the car just as he reached for the passenger door. I jumped in, reversed out as quickly as possible, and accelerated after the Focus. The wagon's headlights were barely reaching the other car.

"I take it you think it's not Alice in the Focus?"

"I do." His voice was grim. "After all, if it *was* Alice, would she have reacted so violently?"

"If she thought we were the ones who killed her mother, it's possible."

"Except that she must have seen you—"

"She didn't look at me, Monty. She just got the hell out of there."

The taillights of the car ahead flashed briefly, then it spun around and disappeared into another street. I reached for the seat belt and pulled it on.

"It's okay," Monty said. "The tracker spell has a very good range, so it's unlikely we'll lose her."

"That may be so, but given the fact things keep happening in this reservation that shouldn't, I'd still rather keep her in sight."

I swung around the corner, the tires squealing in protest. The street ahead was all but empty.

"She took the next right," Monty said.

I grunted and swung into it. Something flashed toward us —something that was round and sunlight bright. I swore and automatically wrenched at the steering wheel in an effort to avoid it. As the car slewed sideways, the bright ball hit the back of the wagon, and we were sent spinning in the opposite direction. Around and around we went, the speed of our turns gut-wrenching. I swore again and fought for control, trying to stop—or at least slow—our spinning. Then smoke began to curl through the cabin—thick black smoke—and panic surged.

It wasn't smoke from the tires. It was much worse than that.

The car was on fire.

"Get out," Monty said. "*Now.*"

"We're still moving—"

"Yes, but the fire is supernatural in origin, and it'll take too long to craft a spell to stop it. We'll die if we don't jump." He unclipped his belt, did the same for me, then reached across and thrust my door open. "Go."

I hesitated and, in that moment, the choice was taken from me. Magic hit me, thrusting me into the air and away from the car. I hit the ground hard, scraping my arms and hands as I rolled along the verge for several meters before coming to a sudden stop against the thick trunk of a tree. My breath left in a gigantic whoosh, and for several seconds I saw nothing but stars.

What the fuck is happening out there? Belle's mental tones were filled with urgency. *Do you need help? Are you okay?*

I am, but I have no idea if Monty is as yet. You'd better call in Aiden and an ambulance, just in case. Give him Alice's address and then tell him to follow the smoke trail.

Why the hell is there smoke?

We were supernaturally firebombed. I pushed onto hands and knees and looked around. Saw our car still spinning down the road. Saw one door flapping open, the other still closed. Saw the smoke and fire burning inside as well as out. *It's not looking good for the old wagon, let me tell you.*

I couldn't give two hoots about the damn wagon. It can be replaced—you can't. Are you sure you don't want me out—

Yes. And yes, I'll also be careful.

Heard that before, and I'm still not believing it.

There were faces peering out of windows in the houses opposite but no familiar figure anywhere nearby.

"Monty?" I croaked. "Where are you?"

He didn't answer. I twisted around and called louder. Still nothing. I returned my gaze to the car.

At that precise moment, it exploded.

FIVE

"Monty!" I screamed, as a huge cloud of thick black smoke, metal, and unnaturally bright fire that plumed toward the brightening skies.

He *couldn't* have been trapped in the car; he was too damn strong magically to have let something as simple as a jammed door stop him from escaping.

He *had* to be here. Had to be alive.

I pushed upright, ignored the dozen different hurts that instantly assaulted me, and staggered toward the blazing car. I didn't get far. The heat was too damn intense.

I flung one hand up to protect my face, hastily created a grasping spell around the other, and then flung it at the remains of the car. Once it had locked onto the front passenger door, I took a deep breath then wrenched the spell back to me. Such was the power of my desperation that the remains of the door were ripped from its hinges.

Monty wasn't inside.

Relief surged. I released the spell and, as the door crashed to the road with a loud clang, spun around and desperately scanned the area. After a moment, I caught sight of a red sneaker poking out from the deep drain that ran along the other side of the road, and sprinted over.

Monty.

His clothes were singed and there were bloody scrapes on his face and his arms, but he was breathing, his fingers were twitching, and his magic stirred through the air.

I jumped into the ditch and knelt beside him. One of the strands of magic ran around me and then quickly faded. He might not be fully conscious, but he was nevertheless aware enough to create a protective spell and *that* was pretty damn impressive.

The other strand of magic slid past me, growing ever thinner—the tracking spell. Still attached, still working.

I touched his shoulder and his eyes sprang open. For a moment, there was nothing but confusion, then awareness surged and his gaze sharpened on mine.

"Are you okay?"

"Battered and bruised, but alive. The same can't be said of my car, however."

He tried to move but I pressed him back down. "It's probably best you don't move until the ambulance—"

"Fuck not moving." Though his voice was little more than a hoarse whisper, his silver eyes were afire with anger and determination. "That bitch tried to kill us and I'm *not* about to let her get away with it."

"The tracking spell is still on her car—"

"Yes, and while it *does* have a good range, it's not infinite. We can still lose her." He knocked my hand away and pushed into a sitting position. His breath hissed between clenched teeth and beads of sweat dotted his forehead. "Help me up."

I rose, took his offered hand, and helped him up—an effort that left my head briefly spinning. I took another of those breaths that really didn't do a whole lot, and then glanced around at the sound of sirens. Headlights swept around the corner down the far end of the street, and then a SUV raced toward us, red and blue lights flashing.

I scrambled up the ditch, ran to the edge of the road, and waved my hands.

The SUV slid to a halt beside me, Jaz at the wheel. We didn't give her a chance to get out, instead flinging open the doors and climbing inside, me in the back, Monty in the front.

"Go," he said urgently. "She's getting away."

"Who the hell is 'she,'" Jaz said, even as she obeyed. "And who the hell are you?"

"Jaz, meet the new reservation witch, Monty Ashworth—no relation to Ira," I said. "And the 'who' is April Dale. Or, at least, something that's currently impersonating her."

"And your car? How did that end up ablaze?"

"The thing impersonating April set it alight."

"Meaning it's possible she can do it again, to us?"

"No, because she won't catch me unawares a second time." Monty motioned to the left. "Head down the next street then turn right three blocks down."

As she obeyed, the onboard computer came to life. "Jaz, report in. What's happening?"

Aiden's voice was flat and very, *very* controlled. I knew him well enough now to understand it meant he was very worried.

Jaz touched the screen and then said, "I have Monty and Liz onboard. Both okay, though Liz's car is a burning wreck. We're currently chasing a supernatural entity."

I leaned forward. "And there's a body and more skin in Mrs. Dale's place."

"I'll head there, then. Keep me posted." He paused. "And be careful, all of you."

"Right at the next street," Monty said. "And go faster if you can—the spell is almost at breaking point."

"What spell?" Jaz asked.

"A tracking spell—but if we don't damn well move faster, we just might lose her."

Jaz swore, but the SUV didn't noticeably increase its speed. We were obviously already at its top.

"How long will the remnants of the spell last on the car once the connection breaks?" I asked. "And will you be able to sense it if we get close to it?"

He motioned to another street then glanced over his shoulder. "I created the spell on the fly, so it could fade within minutes or it could last a couple of days."

"If it *did* last, then it at least still gives us one means of finding the vehicle even if the tracking thread snaps."

"Yes, but finding the car won't help us find the entity. She'll be long gone."

"But maybe *not* her spore."

"*That* depends entirely on how quickly we can find the car."

"So we drive around until you find the damn thing," Jaz said. "Because the sooner you two know what you're dealing with, the better off everyone else is going to be."

Monty grunted and continued giving directions. The chase soon led us out of Castle Rock, off the main roads, and deep into a heavily forested area.

As the trail moved from paved roads to gravel and then onto what was little more than a rough track, the silken thread that was the connection between Monty and his spell broke.

"She's driving a damn Focus," I said immediately. "She

can't have gotten too much further up this track—the car isn't equipped to deal with this sort of road."

"Unless she's using some sort of magic to force it through," he said.

"Why would an entity capable of creating fireballs and stealing human flesh bother? Even dark spirits have energy limits—she's more likely to abandon the car and run than make a futile attempt to force it through the damn trees."

"It would seem the latter is the case." Jaz slowed the SUV down and pointed. "There's a car in the trees up ahead."

"Stop," Monty said.

The SUV slid to a halt and dust plumed, briefly cutting the Focus from sight despite the brightness of the headlights.

"Stay here," he added. "I'll make sure it's safe."

"Jaz can stay here but I'm sure as hell not. It may take two of us to pin this bitch down."

Monty didn't say the obvious—that my magic probably wasn't going to be strong enough to handle this entity if his failed. He simply got out and moved to the front of the SUV. I scrambled out and joined him.

"What do you think?" I asked.

"Hard to tell whether she's still there or not, as the whole car is practically vibrating with the force of her nature."

And that force was *very* dark. It definitely *wasn't* Alice who'd run from her mother's house—and that meant the body was probably hers. But I doubted the skin beside it was. This thing was obviously—for whatever reason—shedding one skin and then stealing another.

I glanced at Monty. "What do you want to do?"

Power stirred around him; the spell was one I recognized but had never actually tried simply because we'd run just as they'd begun teaching us the more complex stuff. He was creating a demon snare.

"I'll take the direct approach," he said. "If she's still there, she'll sense my magic and react to that. You move around the side and hit her only if you sense my magic failing."

Tension wound through me but I didn't say anything. I simply nodded, moved into the trees, and carefully made my way through the shadows, making sure I kept the same pace as Monty. If I got there before him, the dark spirit might well attack, even if it was also aware of Monty's magic.

So much for you being sensible and it being Monty's job not ours, came Belle's thought.

He's battered and beaten. If this thing is here and attacks, he might need magical help. Not that my magic alone would have much hope if his *did* fail, but there were glittering, silvery threads of wild magic drifting through the trees here and—

How long have you been able to see the wild magic as threads? Belle's mental tones were sharp.

I don't know. I studied the threads through narrowed eyes. They were as fragile as moonbeams and yet pulsed with a power I could both see *and* feel. I reached out as one drifted by. It curled around my finger and warmth tingled across my skin. With it came a sense of acknowledgment. Of kinship.

It should have frightened the hell out of me.

It didn't.

This stuff was a part of me now, even if that should have been impossible.

There has to be a reason for it, Belle said. *I know Monty said he'd check the archives, but maybe we should also ask Ashworth to do some discreet research.*

To what end? I crept past a few more trees, watching the ground more than the car ahead, trying to keep my steps as silent as possible. *If the wild magic was going to cause me harm, it would have done so by now.*

It's already changed both your eyes and your power output. We need to know if that's it, or if there's more to come.

I grunted. She was right—it would be better to know than not. *I'll ask him next time we see him.*

Depending, of course, on how busy he was. He and Eli might have decided to move into the reservation, but Ashworth still worked for the Regional Witch Association— or would once his arm healed.

There was no movement inside the car ahead and, despite the pulse of wrongness coming from the vehicle, little indication that the spirit remained.

I glanced at Monty. His expression was a mix of determination and trepidation, and the barely leashed spell that spun around his fingertips was an interweaving connection of furled strands that glowed with power.

I blinked. Not only could I now see the wild magic rather than just feel it, but I also saw ordinary magic. Not just the creation threads of the actual spell—which was something most witches saw if they took the time and concentrated—but the actual *force* of it.

I could see—and understand exactly what it was—with just a look.

What the hell was happening to me?

I had no idea and, right now, no time to wonder or worry. I needed to concentrate. I took a deep breath to quell the stirring fear and studied the car. The closer I got, the more evident it became that the spirit had already fled. But that didn't mean she hadn't left a clue behind. Didn't mean we couldn't still track her via her power output or spore.

Monty motioned me to stop; I immediately did so. He continued on cautiously, a thread of magic spinning out from his free hand—the hand not enmeshed by the leashed spell. It gently probed the car, then slipped in through the open window. After a moment, the thread dissipated and some of the tension left Monty's body.

"She's gone." He turned and motioned for Jaz to come up.

I rubbed my arms against the chill gathering inside, though I wasn't sure whether its source was the sudden uncertainty of what was happening to me, or the growing certainty that the thing that had tried to kill us was far from finished yet. "And her spore?"

"Is fading fast, even though we can't have missed her by more than ten minutes." He moved around the car and studied the trees beyond it. "She ran through the trees, going up the hill rather than down, from the look of it. Do we risk trying to track her?"

"Well, we certainly can't risk *not* tracking her. The sooner we catch this bitch, the sooner we can concentrate on finding the other one."

"Other one? Oh, the thing that drained the guy of blood." He paused. "You know, it's possible they're one and the same being, given what you said about the heat and the fact this thing flung fire at us."

He walked into the forest. I hurried around the car and caught up to him. "But how many fire spirits can actually take on human form and then drain their victims of blood?"

He raised a hand, grabbed a tree branch and pushed it

aside. I grabbed it from him as I passed by then let it swish back.

"I don't know offhand, as I didn't actually study demonology in uni. But there'd have to be a few."

"It says a lot about the high council's view on reservations," Jaz said, as she caught up to us, "that they'd send a witch with so little arcane knowledge."

"Which under normal circumstances wouldn't have been a problem," Monty fired back. "It only is in *this* reservation thanks to the fact your elders left the wellspring unguarded for so long."

"A fact your council was made aware of before your appointment," Jaz said. "I would have thought it'd be a point mentioned when applications were called for."

"Why would it be when any witch appointed here has a major arcane library up in Canberra to access at will? No witch these days really needs in-depth knowledge of demons and spirits unless they intended to make the study —or the hunting—of them a career choice." Monty glanced over his shoulder, his expression somewhat bemused. "And anyway, why would you presume this sort of position is a much sought-after one by those in Canberra? Because I'm here to tell you it's not. In fact, there were only five applicants—the man who was initially chosen, but who literally missed the plane, three older witches looking to get out of Canberra and semi retire, and me."

Annoyance flared through Jaz, something I felt rather than saw. "What's wrong with reservation life?"

"Nothing, I'm guessing, but it's a far cry from the bright lights of Canberra."

Jaz snorted. "I've been to Canberra. The place is all but dead after six."

"Only if you don't know where all the action is."

I cleared my throat and said, "Can we concentrate a little more on the hunt? Because it seems to me that the trail of this thing is starting to fade."

"Maybe her magical scent is," Jaz said. "But her physical scent lies heavily in both the air *and* on the ground. It's actually quite putrid."

"Demonic scents tend to be," Monty commented.

I frowned. "I thought we were dealing with a spirit rather than a demon?"

"We probably are—I'm just using the term interchangeably."

"So there's a difference?" Jaz asked.

"Demons are *always* malevolent," Monty said, "and while some can have physical form, most simply possess the body of another. Spirits can either be good or bad—many witches do in fact have spirit guides—and can either be human related, such as a ghost, or be an entity in their own right."

"This thing isn't possessing bodies, though," I said. "It appears to be stripping off their skins and fleshing them out."

"Which is why I'll need to go through the library's databanks and see what I can find," he said. "Because if we *are* dealing with one entity rather than two, then it could be something that hasn't been seen for a while."

He brushed past a couple of scrubby-looking trees and then stopped and swore. "The trail's gone dead."

"To you, maybe," Jaz said.

Monty stepped to one side and motioned her forward. She strode past us both and continued on up the rocky slope, her steps light and sure—unlike me and Monty.

As the path grew steeper, I started to struggle, and my

breath became little more than a harsh wheeze. It was yet another reminder of just how unfit I was.

After another few minutes, the path flattened out as we neared the summit. Jaz stopped, tension emanating from her body and her aura filled with uncertainty and perhaps a little horror.

"What's wrong?" I stopped beside her, my breath a harsh rasp that echoed through the surrounding silence.

The path widened out to a narrow, stony plateau, beyond which there was nothing but air. Obviously, there was a sharp dip downward. I couldn't see or smell anything untoward in the immediate area, but then, I didn't have wolf senses.

"There's something dead up ahead." Her nostrils flared as she drew in a deeper breath. "It's not large, and not fresh."

"Which really doesn't tell us anything," Monty commented. His breathing was even worse than mine, which at least made me feel a little better.

"Can you feel any sort of magic or evil presence nearby?" she asked. "Because I'm not going anywhere near that clearing until I know for sure this spirit or whatever the hell it is isn't just waiting to attack."

A smile tugged at Monty's lips. "I have no idea what you're smelling, but there's no sense of magic coming from the clearing."

"And no sense of evil." I glanced at Monty. "And that suggests this thing has escaped."

His amusement faded. "Which means the smell is another abandoned skin."

"Either way," Jaz said, "I'm thinking the reservation witch should lead the way from this point on."

He snorted but nevertheless strode past Jaz and into the

clearing. We followed. The wind picked up as we left the trees, blowing my hair around my face and briefly blinding me. I tucked it back behind my ears and looked around. The only thing I could see was rocks and hard earth.

"The scent is coming from the left," Jaz said.

Monty spun on his heel and headed that way, but he'd barely taken half a dozen steps when he stopped. "It's skin."

I halted beside him. The rather sad remnant of humanity lay near the edge of the plateau, wobbling unsteadily in the strong breeze. I walked over to the edge. The ground dropped down vertically for forty or fifty feet then ended in a huge pile of rubble, suggesting the cliff had given away at some point in the past. I carefully leaned over a little further, trying to find some way down. There was none.

I stepped back. "It's obviously resumed its real form to escape.

Jaz knelt next to the pile of skin and hair. "There's one thing I want to know."

"And that is?" I crossed my arms and tried to ignore the vague sparkle of energy that was hovering nearby. I rather suspected it was Alice's ghost.

"What happens to the clothes?"

My gaze jumped back to the skin. While there were visible remnants of hair left, there was nothing that suggested material of *any* kind. "I don't know."

"If we're dealing with a fire spirit," Monty said, "then they're probably being destroyed when the spirit leaves the flesh and resumes its normal form."

"Except you'd expect there'd be at least *some* material or at the least ashes to remain," I said. "And if the material *is* being cindered so completely, why isn't the skin? Why is it instead being left in a misshapen pile?"

Monty shrugged. "That's one of the many questions I can't answer—not until we uncover what we're dealing with."

I rubbed my arms. Though the wind was in no way cold, a chill gathered deep inside of me. One that was, I suspected, due in part to the nearby ghost and the anger emanating from her. Whether it was caused by the situation or my presence, I couldn't say. Belle was the one who could talk to spirits, not me.

Do you want me up there? It's usually fairly slow on Tuesdays—I'm sure Penny will be able to cope for an hour or so.

Not if the brigade come in. And they would, given Mrs. Potts would need to update them all on the murder of her neighbor. *If it is Alice's ghost I'm seeing, do you know why she's here rather than with her body?*

Couldn't say, but it is rather unusual. She paused. *It's possible that she was rising when the spirit claimed her flesh, and somehow got entangled in the process.*

Meaning she's bound to her skin, wherever it may be?

Unless she was set free when the dark spirit fled, possibly. She paused. *We could always do a deep-level connection, and I can tell you what I see.*

Could you communicate with her remotely? Through me, I mean?

I honestly don't know, but we can give it a try.

Give me a second to word up Monty and get comfortable.

Penny's just arrived so she can open up. I'll head into the reading room, just to be safe. Give me a shout when you're ready.

Will do.

Jaz's phone rang, the sharp sound making me jump. As

she unclipped it from her belt and stepped away to answer it, I said, "Monty, I've just been talking to Belle—"

His expression held a hint of confusion. "I thought there were distance limits to telepathy?"

"There are, but we're witch and familiar, remember?"

"Oh. Yeah. Handy."

"Especially in a case like this, when she's the spirit expert and there's a rather cross soul hovering nearby."

His gaze turned to the sparkling wisp that now hovered above the mound of skin. "Is she coming out to talk to it?"

The soul has a name, came Belle's comment. *Tell him to use it if he doesn't want to rile her up some more.*

I did so, and then glanced around as Jaz returned. "Everything okay?"

She nodded. "It was just Aiden wanting a check-in. I've got to go back to the car to get the crime kit and record events here. Do you two mind staying here to keep an eye on things?"

"No," I said. "In fact, I'm going to try and talk to Alice's ghost—"

Jaz's gaze darted around. "There's a ghost here?"

"Yes. I'm going to attempt to talk to her and see if she can tell us anything."

She frowned. "I didn't think you were the one who could talk to spirits?"

"I'm not."

"Then how—"

"It's complicated," I said. "But it basically involves a telepathic connection between Belle and me, and her using my eyes to see what might be going on."

"Oh." Her expression suggested the explanation had left her none the wiser. "I daresay Aiden will want me to record—"

"There won't be anything to see beyond me asking questions. You won't hear the replies, and because Belle is working through me—basically taking me over—I won't be able to repeat them." I returned my gaze to Monty. "I'll need you to keep an eye on things magically—"

"I'll go one better." He pulled a small silk bag from his pocket. "I can create a protection circle for you."

"That would be great." Especially given the anger still emanating from Alice.

"So you don't need me here?" Jaz said.

I shook my head. "If she's able to give us anything, I'll tell you."

She nodded, then spun and quickly disappeared down the hill. I watched Monty set up his protection circle, sensed the caress of his magic as he raised the spell, and felt wholly inadequate in the face of such power. Although I had to wonder if it was nothing more than a rogue emotion from the past—from a time when I was constantly reminded of my lack, not just by my father, but also by the never-ending energy haze that came with being in the presence of witches who hadn't yet learned to contain their output. Truth be told, in this place—thanks to the wild magic—I wasn't powerless. It might yet prove to come with undesirable consequences, but for the moment, at least, I was the equal of any other witch here.

And if I told myself that often enough, I just might start believing it. One day. Far in the future, possibly.

The threads of Monty's magic wove in and out of each other in the air above his spell stones, the golden strands glittering brightly in the morning light, until a dome-like structure hovered in the air.

He lowered his arms and stepped back. Wisps of gold circled lazily around his fingertips, an indication that while the protection circle had been created, the spell had yet to be activated.

"Ready?" he said, glancing at me.

I nodded and stepped inside the protection circle. The force of his spell flared around me briefly then dropped away. I sat crossed-legged in the middle and then said, "Right, ready."

As he closed the circle, I reached out for Belle. Her thoughts flowed through mine, then her being, until we were fused as one—not so deeply that her soul left her body and became a part of me, but deeply enough that she could use her talents while seeing through my eyes.

A shudder went through her—through me.

That's one pissed-off ghost, let me tell you.

Can you talk to her? Or is she one of those ghosts who are all emotion and no real sense of being?

I can connect. You ready?

Yes. Go for it.

Belle took a deep, mental breath, then her energy centered inside of me and took over. Alice's form abruptly sharpened—she was still ghostly, but her form was complete rather than a mere sparkle. Her fury was evident in the glitter of her eyes, in the flexing of her fingers.

What have you done? she all but spat. *Why didn't you tell me—*

"Alice," Belle cut in, her voice—my voice—holding the whip of command. "You need to calm down."

Would you be fucking calm if you were me? If you'd walked into your mom's house and found not your mom, but a thing that was in her body?

The meek, mild Alice who had come into the café had obviously died with her flesh. Or maybe losing her life had finally unleashed some long-repressed but deeply fierce part of her nature.

"Of course not," Belle replied evenly. "But fate has a plan for us all, and sometimes it's not always pleasant and fair."

You can say that again. She paused and appeared to notice her surroundings for the first time. *Where am I? And where is Mom?*

"Your mom has moved on," Belle said gently. "It was her time and she has other lives to live."

So why am I still here? Alice asked. *Why haven't I moved on?*

"Because your murder wasn't part of fate's plan and, as a result, your soul remains here in this lifetime."

Belle's soothing tone was working—Alice's anger was leaching from her expression. *Meaning what?*

"Meaning you may or may not be able to move on."

So I'm a ghost? That hardly seems fair.

Life isn't fair, I wanted to say, but kept the comment down. It would only inflame her again and that wasn't what we needed right now.

"It's possible that I could help you move on, if you wish," Belle said. "But I need you to answer a couple of questions first."

What happens if I do move on?

"Your soul is reborn and you get to live a new—and hopefully longer—life."

And if I don't?

"Then you remain here, in this form, unable to experience all that life has to offer ever again. You won't even be able to communicate with anyone other than the occasional psychic."

Well, fuck, there's not really a choice then, is there? She paused, a slight frown marring her ghostly features. *Will Mom and I be together again in the next life?*

"There are always souls who are destined to travel with us through eternity. Your mother could well be one of yours."

Which wasn't exactly the confirmation Alice was seeking, but it seemed to satisfy her. *What do you wish to know?*

"What was your mother doing when you went inside the house?"

She was just sitting in the darkened living room. She looked asleep except she couldn't have been, given she'd looked out the window at me only a couple of minutes before.

Which suggested the spirit in control had probably shut things down to conserve its strength. I might not know much about skin walkers—if indeed that was what we were dealing with rather than some sort of fire spirit—but I did know that most spirits were somewhat weakened by daylight.

"Did you notice anything unusual? Either about your mom or the house itself."

No, not really. Alice hesitated. *Well, other than the fact she was sitting there naked.*

It was a comment that had me thinking—had Alice been wearing clothes when she'd left her mother's house? Everything had happened so fast that I couldn't actually remember if she had been or not. It would certainly explain why there hadn't been much in the way of clothing—or remnants of such—near any of the flesh piles, but still left the question of why none had been discovered near any of the bodies.

"Can you tell me what happened after that?" Belle asked.

I woke her up, of course. She hesitated again. *She was*

kinda out of it, though. Speech was slurred, eyes unfocused. I thought she might have had a stroke or something, so I went into the kitchen to call an ambulance.

"Why the kitchen?" Belle asked. "You had your phone with you, because you rang us."

Because mine died just as I started calling, so I went into the kitchen to grab Mom's.

"What happened then?"

Just for a heartbeat, Alice's form shimmered. Fighting the memories that rose, perhaps?

She hesitated. *I remember my mom grabbing me, holding me. I remember dancing—*

"Dancing?" Belle cut it curiously. "As in, arm-in-arm type dancing?"

Yes. Mom was never much of a dancer, either, so it was rather weird.

To say the least.

"What happened then?" Belle said.

I'm not entirely sure. Again her form shimmered. She was definitely battling the memories. *I remember feeling so dizzy it was only Mom's arms keeping me upright. I remember it getting so hot it felt like I was burning. I remember Mom burning, but that couldn't be right, could it? And then I was somehow standing outside my body, watching me standing over a body that was red and raw and really didn't look right....* Her voice faded and tears that she could never shed glimmered briefly in her ghostly eyes. *That wasn't Mom, was it?*

"No," Belle said gently. "That wasn't your mom on the floor, and it wasn't your mom who danced with you."

It wasn't surprising she hadn't realized the body on the living room floor was hers, but it was rare for a ghost to so quickly realize the truth about her murder in this sort of situation. Most of them were either too confused or too angry to connect the dots.

Then who was it? And why did she look so much like Mom?

"We haven't got much time if you want to move on, Alice, so you need to stop worrying about the body and tell me anything else you remember."

Alice frowned, her form fragmenting slightly as the strengthening wind swirled around her. *I don't remember all that much more. Just the heat and... the hunger.*

"Whose hunger?"

Mom's.

"Did she kiss you?" This time the question was mine rather than Belle's. "Or even bite you?"

Confusion ran through her expression. *Why would Mom bite me? That makes no sense.*

It would if the fire spirit was the same spirit was also responsible for the murder of Kyle Jacobson.

"You can't remember anything else?" Belle asked.

Not really. Alice hesitated. *What happens now?*

"That depends on whether you're ready to move on or not," Belle said.

I am. Alice shivered and crossed her arms. *I don't want to stay here. It feels strange. Cold.*

"Then I can help you," Belle said. "May fate bless you with happiness and old age in your next life, Alice."

Even as Alice's thank-you rolled around us, Belle silently whispered the words that would set Alice on the path to rebirth.

As Alice's form faded away, a shudder ran through my body and tiredness beat through my soul. While this wasn't the first time Belle and I had merged to share senses, it was the first time we'd done anything this deep. The toll was far greater than I'd been expecting.

I'd better go, Belle said, her mental tones weary. *I'll see you when you get home.*

As the connection between us broke, I took a deep breath and then glanced around. Monty was watching me closely; Jaz had returned with her kit and was in the process of taking photos.

"Did you get anything useful?" Monty asked.

"Not really." I scrubbed a hand across my eyes and repeated everything Alice had said.

"A dancing demon?" Monty frowned. "That definitely seems rather odd."

"Unless what she was actually describing was being caught up in some sort of vortex of fire, and in her confusion, she's described it as a dance."

"Possibly." His lips pursed. "The bit about the dizziness was interesting—I wonder if it means the fire spirit was feeding off her energy or whether Alice was feeling the spirit's state of being as it invaded her body and killed her?"

"A question neither Alice nor I can answer."

"Indeed." He drew in a breath, his expression somewhat frustrated. "But at least it gives me a starting point. You ready to come out?"

I nodded and watched as he deactivated the protection circle; the golden threads of his spell quickly and silently faded into the sunshine. Once he'd picked up his spell stones and tucked them carefully back into the silk bag, he stepped closer and offered me a hand. I clasped it gratefully and let him pull me upright. Just for an instant, the world spun around me, and it was only his grip that kept me standing.

"You're looking rather pale," he commented. "I wasn't

aware that psi powers took such a great toll."

"Any power, psi or magic, has a cost, Monty. They taught us that in school, remember?"

"Must have been in one of the many lessons I missed." Amusement glimmered in his bright eyes. "Does this ability to share psi abilities come from the fact you're witch and familiar? Can you two also draw on each other's magical strength?"

"Yes, and yes," I said. "But the latter isn't unusual— you've a familiar, so you must know that."

"Mine's a cat, and a goddamn grouchy one at that. Not quite the same as having another witch as a familiar."

"No one ever saw it as an advantage, Monty. Not even you."

"I guess not." He hesitated. "But now I can't help wondering why."

I shrugged. The only reasons I could ever come up with was the fact it went against all tradition. Of course, if my sister had been gifted with a human familiar rather than me, it might have been a different story.

"Right," Jaz said, as she slapped the lid down on her kit. "You two finished here? If so, we'll head back."

My gaze automatically went to the spot where the skin had been dumped. Jaz must have seen it, because she added, "I was ordered to record positioning and collect all relevant evidence. There's really little point in doing anything else, because the actual crime didn't happen here."

"You're not going to collect the skin?"

"Ciara's second—"

"Wait—when did Ciara get an assistant?"

"He arrived about a week ago," Jaz replied. "He hails from the Raine pack up in the Northern Territory. His name is Luke."

I grunted. "You were saying before I sidetracked?"

"There aren't any scavengers around this immediate area, so the skin should be safe enough until he can get up here."

I hoped she was right. Even though Alice had moved on, she deserved a proper burial—one where her body and her skin were present.

We followed Jaz down the hill. By the time we got back to her car, my head was thumping, weariness had settled into my limbs, and all the scrapes and bruises I'd gotten when I was pushed out of the car were hurting like a bitch. What I needed was several large buckets of coffee, a good dozen chocolate bars, and maybe even a painkiller or two. And while I didn't have the first or third of those, I did at least have three of the middle option stashed in the side pocket of my backpack. I offered one to Monty and Jaz, and was totally relieved when both said no.

Ciara's second—who was a tall and rangy man with carrot-red hair, pale skin, and lovely dark brown eyes—appeared as I was finishing my second chocolate. Jaz gave him directions and then jumped into her car and drove us out of there. By the time we got back to Castle Rock, the headache had at least eased slightly even if the weariness remained. Jaz dropped Monty home first and then ran me around to the café.

I opened the door once she'd stopped and then said, "Do you want to come in for a coffee?"

She shook her head. "I've got to go write up a report, but thanks."

I nodded and headed inside. Though it was close to lunchtime, there were only half a dozen people inside. Penny—a middle-aged woman with long gray hair tied back in a ponytail and a lined, interesting face—stood behind the counter making coffees and either Frank or Mike—our kitchen hand and chef—was whistling softly in the kitchen. I couldn't hear the rattle of pots and the dishwasher wasn't going, so obviously there wasn't much to do as yet.

Penny glanced up as I neared the counter and gave me a wide smile. "Everything's under control here. Belle's upstairs doing some research if you want her."

I nodded. "Has the brigade come in?"

"Not as yet, but Mrs. Potts rang twenty minutes ago, asking if we could shove some tables together, as there was twenty of them."

"What time?"

"Around two."

"That shouldn't be a problem." I pushed away from the counter. "Give me a shout if things start getting busy."

She nodded. I headed upstairs to find Belle sitting in the middle of our two-seater, her feet up on the coffee table and an old, rather large leather-bound book resting on her lap.

"There's an energy drink in the fridge," she said, without looking up.

"Thanks. I'll grab it after a shower."

Once I'd cleaned up and slathered the various scrapes with a potion that would not only numb them, but also help accelerate healing, I dragged on jeans and a top then went back out to grab the drink.

"What are you reading?"

"I went through the index to see if Gran had anything on skin walkers, and found a book on different types of fire demons instead."

"Is ours in there?"

"There's a couple of possibilities, but it'd be handy to know if we were dealing with one entity or two."

"Even Monty isn't sure of that as yet."

"Monty hasn't been here long, and didn't see the first victim," she commented. "What are your instincts telling you?"

I half smiled. "They flip-flop between one being and two."

"Which is absolutely no help."

"I know." I walked over to the sofa and plonked down beside her. "Why? What have you found?"

She turned the book so that I could see it more clearly and then pointed to a picture. It was a hand drawn but beautifully detailed depiction of a bite wound—one that looked almost identical to the wounds that had decorated Kyle Jacobson's body.

"And the demon responsible?"

"A soucouyant, apparently." She turned the book around to read the text. "According to this, it's a demon who takes on the form of an old woman by day but who sheds her skin at night and takes on a fire form to hunt and kill her victims."

"By draining their blood, I take it?"

She nodded. "It can apparently enter victims' homes through any hole, including cracks and keyholes."

"Which is what happened at Kyle Jacobson's place but not any of the others." I studied the picture for a little bit longer. "Is that all it does? It's not a shape shifter of any kind?"

"There's a side note that says she found some references in a couple of medieval manuscripts that stated a soucouyant can also transform herself into to a gorgeous-looking young woman at night. She then seduces her victims with her looks and her dance, and once fully enthralled, she drains them of blood."

"I'm gathering 'dance' is a metaphor for sex in this case."

"I suspect so. Scholars of old were pretty cagey when it came to that sort of stuff."

"Does it say how to kill it?" I warily took a sip of the energy drink, but it was surprisingly free of its usual muddy taste.

Belle grinned. "That's because I wasn't about to drink something that tasted like boiled socks."

"So the secret to getting decent-tasting potions is to ensure you also need a dose?"

"It depends on how drained we are but generally, yes. But you're well aware of why most of them taste like shit."

"Because sugar interferes with the efficiency of the brew," I intoned, imitating her voice. "I know, but a little bit of honey—"

"Is still a sugar. Stop whining and just drink the muck."

I grinned, gulped it down, then pushed up and walked over to the kitchen counter. "Would you like a coffee?"

"Yeah, thanks." She flipped the page of the old book. "According to this, the best way to kill a soucouyant is to find its skin and salt it. That prevents it from returning to its own form."

"But still leaves it in fire form, which—if today's events were any demonstration—is decidedly more dangerous."

"That's if it's the same demon responsible for both the attack on you and all the other deaths. There are some inconsistencies."

I made the coffees and walked back, handing her one before sitting down again. "Like why, if it had its own skin, was it stealing others?"

"Precisely."

"I don't suppose any of the other fire spirits mentioned strip their victims of their skin and then steal their identities?"

"No—or, at least, they're not mentioned in this book."

Of course not. When were things ever that easy? "Hopefully Monty will be able to find something in the witch archives."

"You'd think so," she said. "After all, it *is* the major collection center for any and all information on the supernatural in Australia."

"And yet it was still your gran—and her books—that bluebloods came to when they wanted information on all things magic and the occult."

"That's because she was awesome, Sarr witch or not."

She wasn't going to get an argument about that from me. Nell might have died before either Belle and I had been born, but Belle's mom had told us so many stories about her that she felt very real to the both of us. And now her legacy —the vast majority of her books—was Belle's. Not all of the books were here, though—we simply didn't have the room. Most were carefully stored in a humidity controlled off-site storage unit that was surrounded by multiple layers of both protection and repellent spells. Nothing was getting into that unit without our consent—not even smallest of bugs.

"So if we *are* dealing with two separate demons," I said, "how do we kill a fire spirit?"

She wrinkled her nose. "There's a couple of options, and no guarantee any of them will work. I think Gran was just compiling information rather than speaking from experience when it came to these sorts of entities."

"Anything would be better than what we've currently got."

"Which is nothing." Her grin flashed. "A containment spell, holy water, and silver are all suggested. No guarantees, as I said."

"Maybe not, but it at least gives us a starting point."

And yet another reason for me to keep carrying the small bottle of holy water around with me.

A babble of noise drifted up from below and, a second later, Penny's face appeared at the top of the stairs. "The brigade just arrived."

"On my way." I pushed upright, gulped down my coffee, and headed downstairs. Belle followed me a few minutes later.

The twenty ladies kept us busy for the next couple of hours, but none of us minded because it certainly balanced the books for the day. We closed just after four, but by the time we'd done the till and cleaned up, it was well after five. I made us both a coffee, then walked across to the table.

Belle accepted her mug with a nod of thanks and then said, "Don't sit. Aiden's about to knock on the door."

Happiness shot through me. I placed my coffee down then walked over, opening it just as he raised his hand to knock.

"About damn time, Ranger," I grumbled, and then threw my arms around his neck, and kissed him very, *very* thoroughly.

"I missed you too," he said eventually, his breath warm against my lips and his eyes bright with desire. He brushed a stray strand of hair away from my eyes, his fingers so warm and tender against my skin. "And I am totally glad to see you are indeed unhurt."

"I wouldn't say unhurt. There are a few new scrapes and bruises, but all in all, we were lucky."

"I've seen your car," he said. "Trust me, I'm well aware of just how lucky you both were."

"I'm gathering the car's a write-off then?" Belle said.

Aiden looked past me. "I'm afraid so. It's insured though, isn't it?"

"Yes, but I'm doubting being firebombed by a supernatural entity would be covered in the policy."

Belle's voice was dry and Aiden grinned. "Given the current situation, you might want to look into that when it comes to insuring the next one."

I stepped back to allow him inside the café. His fingers lightly squeezed mine and then he walked across to the table where Belle was sitting.

I relocked the door then headed over to make him a cup of coffee. Once I'd placed the steaming drink in front of him, I pulled out the chair beside him and sat down.

"What's been happening since we last saw each other?"

He snorted softly. "Too fucking much. We're going to need more rangers if this pace keeps up. We're stretching both ourselves and our capabilities to the limits. Especially Ciara. She's got an assistant now, but I really think the council will have to employ a third coroner—and urgently."

"It would make sense," I commented. "And given we're in this situation because of the committee's actions, it's also only fair."

A smiled tugged his lips. "That's something they're now more than aware of, thanks to both Ashworth and Monty."

I raised an eyebrow. "Monty has said something?"

Aiden's smile grew. "Let's just say he more than amplified what Ashworth had already said."

That surprised me, as Monty had never been one to rock the boat. But I guessed it *had* been a long time since we'd been at school together—things could change in a few minutes let alone over twelve years. I certainly had.

"Was the murder you and Tala were called to this morning another skinning?"

"No, thankfully. It was a fencing dispute that escalated rather abruptly, and wasn't actually a murder. One neighbor hit the other over the head with a star picket, split his head open, and knocked him out. The victim is currently in hospital under observation, but he's certainly not dead."

"At least that's one bit of good news," Belle commented.

"This time," Aiden said. "But the pair of them have been at each other for years, and one day it will end badly."

"Have you identified either of the first two skinning victims?" I asked.

"The body in the dumpster was Mrs. Dale, but the skin we found in there wasn't a match for her DNA."

"Have you got a time of death as yet?"

"Sunday night. The accelerated rate of decomposition thanks to the heat has made it hard to pin down an exact time, but Ciara thinks it happened around eight."

So just after dusk, then. "And the body in the forest clearing?"

"Belonged to a Marilyn Jones, who went missing a few days before Mrs. Dale. We haven't yet got the DNA of the skin that was with her, but if it's not a match for either woman, it means we have another body somewhere within the reservation."

I grunted and glanced at Belle. "All of which are just more pointers to the fact that we're dealing with two entities rather than one."

Aiden frowned. "What makes you think there's two?"

Belle quickly filled him in on what we'd discovered about soucouyants and then added, "Nothing I've found suggests the soucouyant is, in any way, a skin walker, which means it could be behind the death of Kyle Jacobson but not the skinning victims."

Aiden scrubbed a hand across his eyes. "Do I need to ask what a skin walker is?"

Belle once again filled him in. "But if that's what we're

dealing with here, then we're obviously dealing with a very obscure branch of walker—one that *actually* steals the skin of their victims."

Aiden picked up his coffee and leaned back in his seat. "Monty didn't mention that possibility when we were discussing the situation last night."

"Monty hasn't the advantage of spirit guides." I took a sip of coffee. "And it's not like skin walkers are a common variety of witch here in Australia."

"For which I'm extremely grateful," he muttered. "I take it your books haven't much on them?"

"No, but that's not really surprising."

"Monty has access to the witch archives in Canberra," I said. "If there's any place in Australia that will have information on them, then it should be there."

"He did mention going online to search through some archive last night." He drank some coffee and then added, "How likely is it that this soucouyant will strike again?"

"That's an unknown, simply because we just don't know enough about it."

He grunted, then shifted in his chair so that he was looking straight at me. My heart instantly skipped into overdrive.

This was it.

This was the moment of truth. The time when I either came clean about my history or walked away from a relationship that had barely even begun.

Because there was no other option now—that was very evident from the determination in his eyes.

I took a deep breath and released it slowly.

I knew what I had to do.

I just didn't know if I had the courage to do it.

SIX

"So that chat we were supposed to have yesterday morning," he said softly. "You want to do it here, or over dinner?"

"And *that's* my cue to get out of here." Belle rose. "You two can nut this one out on your lonesomes."

Coward, I grumbled, as she grabbed her coffee and made a hasty retreat.

No, just being sensible. Three is always a crowd when it comes to this kind of heart-to-heart.

I'm not ready for a heart-to-heart with the man. I just wanted to enjoy being with him for a little while longer.

Now who's the coward?

I think the fact that it's taken me so long to get into another relationship has well and truly proven it's one of my character traits—at least when it comes to the emotional stuff.

"Liz, will you stop talking to Belle and look at me?"

I sighed and did so. For the first time in ages, his expression was guarded.

"Aiden—"

"No more lies, Lizzie. No more half-truths. I don't want to be a part of *any* sort of relationship based on either."

Even though I'd been expecting such a statement, a chill nevertheless went through me. "That sounded an awful lot like an ultimatum."

"I suppose it is." He hesitated. "The problem, you see, is that I've been through all this once before, and I'll not do it again."

"With the wolf you mentioned once before—the one who loved and left you?"

"It's debatable whether she ever really loved me, but yes."

"That's still different to this situation though, because you and I can never—"

"This isn't about us being wolf and witch," he cut in. "This is about *trust*, and whether you're actually willing to let someone other than Belle into your life."

"Except if I *do* let you in, I'm setting myself up for heartache further down the line, and for the simple reason that I *am* a witch rather than a werewolf."

Something flared in his eyes—something that spoke of understanding and yet held an odd hint of... not desire, not even yearning, but something close to both. He grabbed my hands, held them gently but securely, his skin oh-so warm compared to mine. But then, my lack of heat had nothing to do with being cold, but rather the fact I didn't want to be doing this—not here, not now, and certainly not with a man who would probably end up breaking my heart.

But Belle was right. If this reservation was *our* end destination, then we'd certainly need Aiden, his rangers, and even the council in our corner.

Whether it would, in the end, make any difference was an unknown point at this stage of the game.

"Do you really think you're alone in taking that risk?" he asked softly.

The smile that tugged my lips held little in the way of amusement. "Why would I think otherwise? You've certainly sent out enough warnings over the last few months that you'll never get *deeply* involved with someone who wasn't a werewolf."

"And for the most part, that's true. But that doesn't mean the risk isn't there. Doesn't mean I won't be hurt if you decide you've fooled around long enough with a were-wolf and walk away." He released one hand and lightly brushed the back of his fingers down my cheek. "None of us know what the future holds, Liz. None of us know which relationship will develop into a meeting of heart and soul. I can't ever promise that I won't find someone else, but neither can you. All I know is, at this point in time, I want to be with you. I want to explore the full breadth and width of this attraction between us. But *only* if honesty is a part of that relationship."

His words had tears stinging my eyes. I blinked the ridiculous things away and took a deep, somewhat shuddery breath.

"Fine," I said eventually. "But you can't share this with anyone, Aiden. The gossip brigade has enough to talk about already."

"You have my word that I will *never* willingly share anything with the brigade." His brief smile died as quickly as it had appeared. "And no one else has the need to know."

"Good." I paused to drink some coffee and wished it were something stronger. "While my real name *is* now Elizabeth Grace, it's not the name I was born with—that's Elizabeth Marlowe. My father is a leading member of the high witch council."

He didn't say anything. He just waited for me to continue. Perhaps he knew that if he spoke, my courage might falter.

"I was an utter disappointment to my parents. They're two of the strongest witches of their generation, and both my sister and brother were similarly gifted. I was not, and they never let me forget it."

"Is that why you ran?" he asked softly.

"No." I paused again. "When I was sixteen years old, my sister was murdered; to say it had a devastating effect on my parents—but particularly my dad—is something of an understatement."

He squeezed the hand he still held, but didn't offer any of the usual platitudes. But then, having lost his own sister, he knew well enough how little they helped.

"She was the final victim of a serial killer," I continued after a moment, "and my father took his grief out on me—"

"Why?" Aiden cut in. "What did you have to do with her death?"

I smiled, but only because it was better than releasing the pain and the tears that were gathering. "Nothing. My crime was finding her when they, for all their abilities and power, could not."

"That hardly seems reasonable—"

"Grief and reason don't often go together, Aiden. You know that."

"True." He hesitated. "So you ran to get away from your dad's anger?"

"Not so much his anger, but his punishment."

"What did he do?"

I briefly closed my eyes and took another of those deep breaths that did little to ease the turmoil inside. "He decided that the only possible use I could have was as a breeder—that in my children, the power that I was missing might be found."

Or rather, the power that had been lost with Cat's death would be reborn in one of my offspring.

Aiden didn't say anything. He didn't even move. And yet a wave of disbelief and fury hit me, a force so strong it damn near blistered my senses.

"As I've said before," I continued, "arranged marriages remain very common amongst witch families—"

"But you were *sixteen*—"

"Which only meant I couldn't marry without his consent." My mouth twisted. "*My* consent apparently didn't matter."

"Fuck, Liz, no wonder you ran." He tugged me closer and rested his forehead against mine. "Did you even know the man?"

I closed my eyes, drawing strength from his closeness. "Yes. He was one of my father's friends—a man who divorced his first wife because he discovered she couldn't have children, and who'd lost both his second wife *and* child after she'd suffered a major hemorrhage when she was five months pregnant. He was thirty-eight years old, Aiden. More than double my age."

And, like my father, a disciplinarian. My father knew Clayton would keep me in line no matter what it took—be it by word, hand, or even magic. My mother *had* objected, but those objections had fallen strangely quiet on the eve of the marriage. It would have made no difference anyway. By that time, the agreement certificate—and my fate—had been signed, sealed, and delivered.

At the time, I'd felt stranded and horribly betrayed, but I couldn't help but wonder now if I'd been the only one. I hadn't sensed any sort of spell on my mother—and she was certainly a strong enough witch to have sensed and retaliated against any sort of effort to magically change her mind or mute her objections—but there were other ways to silence. Telepathy, for instance.

"Fuck, Liz, that's—" Aiden stopped and shook his head. "That a father could do that to his own daughter—wow."

"Oh, that wasn't the worst of it." I paused and swallowed heavily against the bitter taste of bile rising up my throat. "One of the conditions of the marriage contract was ensuring I was fertile and fully capable of carrying a child to term. I was sixteen years old. I'd only just started my period and hadn't even had sex yet. You can imagine what that did to me."

"I'm surprised it didn't scare you off both men and sex for life." His voice was grim and there was anger in his eyes. Deep anger. For me. For the child I'd been and what I'd been forced to endure.

And suddenly, all the doubts, all the fears, and the so very deep-seated reluctance to trust disappeared.

Because if the future I feared *did* come to pass—if my father and Clayton did come to this reservation to claim what they considered theirs—then Aiden would stand by my side, ready to go into battle for me.

Whether or not we were still together.

It felt like a huge weight had been lifted from my shoulders. No matter what happened now, Belle and I were no longer alone.

And that made me want to cry all over again—but this

time in utter happiness and relief rather than in fear and pain.

"Was there nothing you could do to stop this insanity?" he asked. "No one you could turn to?"

"No. My father is a man of power and influence—there are few who'd dare gainsay him." My grandfather might have, but by that stage he was long dead.

Aiden hesitated, and then asked softly, "Was the marriage consummated?"

I closed my eyes for a moment, battling the wave of fear, horror, and pain that rose with those words. "Almost."

Aiden didn't say anything. He didn't even move. Not for several seconds. But his fury was so fierce that it flowed over me, *through* me, filling every breath with its heat.

"Belle?" he said eventually.

I swallowed heavily and nodded. "I was underpowered and *she* was a Sarr witch. No one understood our connection and they certainly had no respect for Belle, despite the fact she's one of the strongest telepaths out there. And let me tell you, that night she was *fierce*."

"I can imagine," he murmured. "I've never seen her truly angry, but she still scares the fuck out of me."

I laughed, but it came out a hiccup and ended as a half sob. Aiden quickly moved out of the chair, onto his knees in front of me, and pulled me close. I closed my eyes against the sting of tears and relaxed into his body, letting his warmth and strength batter away the worst of the memories.

"So how did you escape Canberra?" he asked eventually.

"I might be underpowered, but I'm not stupid." My lips twisted, but there was little amusement in it. "And, thanks to my grandfather, I also had access to a rather large inheritance. Money really does talk, especially when you're dealing with people who aren't exactly law-abiding."

But—now that I was actually thinking about it—the fact that I *had* been able to access the money at sixteen was rather unusual, as most trusts didn't mature until the recipient was either eighteen or even twenty-one. But perhaps my grandfather had had some inkling of the trouble headed my way and done his best to counter it. Without his money, I would never have escaped.

"Even so, I wouldn't have thought the sixteen-year-old daughter of a high-flying witch would have any idea where to even look for such people."

"I didn't."

I pulled back a little and met his gaze. The blue depths were filled with so much caring and understanding that my stomach twisted. It would be so very easy to fall in love with this man....

I swallowed the thought and added, "But Belle's a Sarr, and it was through her family's 'questionable connections' we were able to change our names and disappear so completely."

"Thank God for questionable connections, then." He leaned his forehead against mine, his breath warm on my lips and oddly comforting. "And thank God you were able to get away."

"Yes." A memory of cold hands on warm flesh stirred, and a shudder went through me.

My father might have stolen so much from my childhood—simple things, like the love and the caring of a father —but it had been Clayton who'd stolen my innocence.

Even if, in the end, the innocence he'd coveted most had escaped him.

I shuddered again and thrust the memories back into

the box where they'd long been locked. I wasn't ready to confront the full extent of them yet.

And probably never would be.

"At least I now understand why you hate your parents," he said, "and why you've been so afraid to confide in anyone."

"My parents are *the* power couple in Canberra, Aiden. They have allegiances and allies scattered throughout Australia and Europe. I couldn't ever trust that someone wouldn't give us away if they thought they could gain either an advantage or favor by doing so."

"Which is why you never settled anywhere permanently, and why you confide in so few."

"We've never fully confided to *anyone*. Not until now— not until you."

"Thank you." His gaze briefly searched mine. "There is one thing you've forgotten in all this, though."

I raised my eyebrows. "And what might that be?"

"The fact that forced marriages are illegal in Australia." He brushed some hair away from my eyes, his touch tender. "It may be common practice amongst witch kind to arrange a marriage—but forcing someone into one *is* illegal. You have the weight of the law on your side."

"And *they* have the weight of influence and position on theirs. I know which side I'd put my money on if it ever came down to a court of law."

"If your father values his power and influence as much as you imply, there's no way known he'd go to court over such a matter. He'd have too much to lose."

Which was true enough. But it would never get to court. He'd simply wrap his magic around me and force me to return to Clayton, just as he'd forced me to sign the documents of agreement and the marriage certificate.

"And Monty?" Aiden asked. "Will he out you?"

"No. We made an agreement—we tell him all about the wild magic, and he keeps our presence here a secret."

"So Belle hasn't—in any way—stepped in to ensure that?"

A smile twitched my lips. "Maybe. Just a little."

"I'd be almost disappointed if she hadn't." He slipped his hand around to the back of my neck, holding me still as he kissed me. Softly—gently—but with so much underlying emotion that those damn tears threatened again.

"I'd really like you to spend the night with me. I know we both have to work tomorrow, but I can get you back here in plenty of time."

"I'd really like that." I kissed him again then pushed to my feet. "Give me five minutes to gather a few things."

It took me three. Forty-five minutes later we were back at his place, where he cooked for me, pampered me, and then escorted me up to bed. But we didn't make love. Not then. Not until the morning.

He simply held me in his arms and made me feel safer than I'd ever felt in my entire life.

———

The café was back to its usual busy self the next day even if I was a little slower. Despite the numbing salve I'd rather liberally applied when I'd gotten home, the various aches and pains felt the need to protest every time I either moved too suddenly or twisted the wrong way.

And obviously, the slowness of body had extended to my brain, because it took me entirely too long to realize Monty was sitting at one of the corner tables, sipping coffee and munching on a piece of carrot cake as he scrolled through a screen on his phone.

"When did he get here?" I asked as I finished plating up cake for a couple of customers.

"Monty?" Belle brushed past to get the cream. "I felt a vague surge of energy about twenty minutes ago, but I didn't really pay much attention to it as there was no sense of threat."

"Odd that I didn't feel it."

She shrugged and swirled cream onto the top of the hot chocolate she was making. "We've been flat-out, so not really."

"I guess." It still niggled though, so once I'd delivered the cakes to the table I was looking after, I walked over and sat down opposite him. This close, the tiny threads of red and gold energy that swirled around his body were very evident. Though I had no idea what the spell was, I very much suspected it had been designed to mute his energy output.

"Morning," he said, all too cheerfully. "Lovely day for it, isn't it?"

"That depends entirely on what you mean by 'it.'" My voice was dry.

He absently waved a hand. "You know, witch stuff."

I snorted. "By witch stuff, do you mean you're sitting here enjoying cake while you scroll through Canberra's libraries, or are you simply spying on Belle and me?"

He raised his eyebrows. "What, I can't just drop in to see my long-lost cousin without said cousin becoming suspicious?"

"No. Give, Monty—what are you up to?"

His lips twitched. "Thought you'd like an update."

"I would indeed, but on what, exactly?"

"I had a look at the body of the first victim—the one with bite marks everywhere. I believe this skin walker could actually be a soucouyant—"

"Except for the fact that while they leave their skins in a safe spot to go hunting at night, they always return for them. They're not skin walkers as such, and they certainly don't steal the skin off their victim's backs."

"I know, but—" He stopped and blinked. "How the hell do you know what a soucouyant is? Do you know how deep I had to go down the information rabbit hole to find anything concrete about them?"

I smiled. "Belle and I aren't just pretty faces, you know."

"Yes, but I spent hours talking to the head of the Occult Studies department at the uni last night, and even *he* struggled to find anything more concrete than the usual myth disinformation."

Which was just more confirmation that the library Belle had been gifted was very precious indeed.

"Did he find out how to kill them? Because the only suggestion we uncovered was salting their skin to prevent them reclaiming it. The problem with *that*, of course, is finding the skin in the first place."

"Indeed." He frowned. "We didn't get anything else, but I suspect the usual methods of dealing with a fire spirit would work for a soucouyant."

I had no idea whether the "usual methods" were the ones Belle had found or totally different but I wasn't about to admit that. I leaned forward and crossed my arms on the table. "What about skin walkers? Did you find any information about them?"

"Not really." He scooped up a big chunk of cake smothered in cream cheese frosting and munched on it contemplatively. "But we've put an urgent request in with the US Witch Archive, and we'll see what they come up with."

"Which doesn't help *us* if this thing attacks again in the meantime."

"I know, but baby steps and all that." He paused as his phone rang and pulled it out of his pocket. After a quick look at the screen, he hit the answer button and said, "What can I do for you, Aiden?"

I clenched my fingers against the need to grab the phone out of Monty's hand and find out what was going on —or rather, who or what had been murdered. I doubted Aiden would be ringing him for any other reason.

I listened to the very one-sided conversation for several minutes, but didn't really learn anything more than another body had been uncovered in Greenhill, a small town on the reservation's border.

"Skin walker or soucouyant?" I asked, the minute he hung up.

Monty shrugged. "Unknown at this stage. Apparently the woman who called it in was pretty hysterical, and they barely even got the address." He scooped up the last bits of cake then downed his coffee in several gulps and rose. "I'd better go and grab my gear. Aiden said he'd pick me up in five."

With a sharp nod, he strode out the door. I couldn't help the wisp of envy that followed him. I should have been glad that the weight of looking after this reservation was no longer mine to bear, and yet... it just didn't feel right sitting here doing nothing. Not after everything we'd been through since our arrival here.

Which was a seriously *stupid* way to be thinking given everything we'd been through had resulted in several hospital stays and near death. I rose, gathered Monty's plate and the cup, and dropped them off in the kitchen before returning to help Penny clearing and serving.

But as the evening drew closer and no word came from either Aiden or Monty, worry stirred. And with it came an odd sense of restlessness.

"If anything had happened to Aiden, Katie would have come running for you," Belle said. "So whatever you're feeling, I doubt it stems from any danger to him."

"I know." I leaned a shoulder against the sliding door that led out onto our small balcony area—the only bit of private outside space we had—and watched the gathering twinkle of lights as another sunset faded into night. "But something is happening out there, Belle. I can feel it."

"Is that a 'my internal radar is twitching and evil is on the move' something? Or is it an 'I hate not knowing what is going on' something?"

My lips twitched. "The former, I'm afraid."

"And you're sure it's not your psychic self being totally pissed about being left out of the action and wanting something to do?"

"Totally—though it is indeed a fact that I really *don't* like being kept out of the loop like this."

"Well, that makes two of us." She pushed to her feet. "Given we have no other plans tonight, why don't we just jump in the car—oh. Fuck."

"Yeah. And it's far too late to hire one."

"There are times when living in a small country town is a right royal pain." She slumped back onto the sofa. "It leaves us with two choices—we contact the rangers, or we ring up Ashworth."

My eyebrows rose. "Why Ashworth?"

"Because the man has a truck he can't drive, and

because he came into the café last week and stated he was bored out of his mind."

"I thought he and Eli would be enjoying the time together?" Especially given Ashworth's job at the RWA generally had him working at all hours and away from home for days—or even weeks—at a time.

"According to Eli, a bored and restless Ashworth is not a pleasant one to be around." She smiled. "He all but begged me to give them a call the next time your radar went off."

"Why me? Why not Monty?"

"I asked the exact same thing. Ashworth promptly told me that if we thought this reservation was going to let us off the hook so easily, we had rocks in our heads."

I snorted. Ashworth had never been backward when it came to stating an opinion, and it was one of the reasons why I liked him. That and the fact he very much reminded me of my grandfather.

As I continued to stare into the gathering darkness, the nebulous feeling that evil stirred strengthened, and my gaze went to the green and purple glow coming from Émigré.

Whatever I was sensing, it was at the club, hunting.

"Which suggests that whatever this evil is, it's not very bright." Belle pushed upright again. "I'll get the backpack ready—do you want to call a cab?"

"Yes, and I'll also call Maelle, just to give her a heads-up." She might have said she had no capacity to feel the presence of spirits or even demons, but she was still a very old vampire and one capable of magic. Even if she had no overt awareness when it came to the supernatural, there were certainly spells that could temporarily provide that ability.

I unplugged the phone from the charger, quickly called for a cab, and then dialed Roger. I didn't have Maelle's direct number, but given the intimate connection between vampire and thrall, calling him was basically the same thing.

"Lizzie Grace," he said, cool tones edged with surprise. "To what do we owe this pleasure?"

"An undefined but growing certainty that evil currently lurks in Émigré, waiting to pounce."

"If you're referring to my mistress, I can assure you she is well fed and of no danger to anyone."

Although there was no change in the tone or timbre of his voice, it was rather obvious he was making a joke. If he'd believed, in any way, that his mistress was the evil I'd referred to, then Maelle would have taken him over and refuted the statement directly. And it would have also ended any future hopes I had of remaining unbitten.

"News I'm ecstatic to hear," I replied, voice dry, "but not the point I was trying to make."

"Indeed." He suddenly sounded more serious, even if his tone remained the same. "And what evil do you think visits our establishment?"

His use of "our" suggested Maelle was now listening in on the conversation.

"At this stage, I'm not really sure. I'm just ringing to give you a heads-up, and to inform you that Belle and I will be over there in ten minutes."

"We'll be waiting," he said. Or she. His voice was a strange mix of both. "In the meantime, we'll do a sweep of the venue and see if anything can be sensed. Thank you for the warning, young Elizabeth."

That last bit had been pure Maelle.

I hung up, ran into my room to grab a jacket and my purse, and then clattered down the stairs. Belle was just coming out of the reading room, the backpack slung over her shoulder.

"I packed everything I could think of, and every bottle of holy water we have in stock," she said. "I figure if we are dealing with a fire spirit, it couldn't hurt."

The cab pulled up just as I slammed the café's front door closed. Thankfully, Émigré wasn't that far away and it didn't take long to get there. Security hustled us straight in without asking any questions.

Maelle was waiting in the main room, but Roger was nowhere to be seen. She was wearing a deep blue aviator outfit this evening, and her hair had been swept up into a tightly bound topknot. Her appearance was as immaculate as ever, and yet there was something less than controlled emanating from her. Something that could, at any moment, unravel and create chaos.

That something was the vampire.

Someone—some*thing*—was hunting in her territory, and she was *not* pleased.

"We've done a circuit of this entire area, but I cannot feel anything untoward."

"We may not find anything either," I admitted. "But it's always better to be safe than sorry."

"Indeed," she agreed evenly. "What do you wish to do?"

I hesitated, and briefly scanned the room. The club only opened at sunset, but it was already half-full. There were plenty of clubs in Melbourne that didn't get this type of turnout on a Friday or Saturday night let alone a Wednesday. The colorful lights that swept the lower dance floor didn't stay long on any particular face but, even so, my psychic radar remained mute. Whatever I was sensing wasn't currently amongst those on the dance floor.

"I think Belle and I need to do a circuit. If I sense anything, I'll let you know."

"I'll be accompanying you," Maelle said. "I can react against an attack far faster than you can throw a spell."

The thought of having Maelle at my back sent a chill down my spine. But I wasn't about to admit that, even if—as a vampire—she would have noticed the sudden jump in my pulse rate.

"That's probably *not* the best idea," I said carefully. "Please don't take this the wrong way, but your closeness will dilute my ability to sense the evil stalking this venue."

A small smile touched her lips but didn't do much to lift the coolness from her eyes. "Then I will allow Roger to shadow you. His presence has not affected your skills in the past."

Because he *wasn't* a scary old vampire—just the servant of one.

I nodded and glanced at Belle. "Ready?"

"I'll go right, you go left." She opened the bag and handed me a small bottle of holy water. "Just in case we *are* dealing with a fire spirit and the damn thing attacks."

I tucked the bottle into my pocket and, as I resolutely went left, reached out to Belle's thoughts and lightly linked our minds. This time, it was at a deeper level than our usual telepathic connection. All witches and familiars could mesh thoughts and share energy—in fact, one of the reasons familiars existed was to provide a last-ditch well of energy their witch could draw on in a worst-case scenario. Few witches ever went that far, as it was absolutely possible to drain a familiar to death—and while a witch could survive the loss of their familiar, they were always left far less than they had been.

But the fact that Belle was also a witch meant that we

could, under certain circumstances, share abilities as well as energy. While I couldn't use her telepathic skills, we could share others—as we had yesterday, when she'd remotely talked to Alice through me. So while she had no radar for evil, our current connection allowed her to borrow mine.

I walked into the deeper shadows haunting this portion of the main room. The upper tier was divided into two distinct sections—the alien-themed bar lay to the right of the main door, and a series of seating "pods" on the left. Each pod seated between four and twelve guests around a metallic table, and offered some degree of privacy for those who wished it. The only lighting in each one came in the form of tea candles housed in grotesquely shaped lanterns, and while they didn't throw off a huge amount of light, they did at least provide enough to see the faces of those within.

Not that I actually needed to *see* anyone. Not when my "radar" was scanning each and every person and almost instantly rejecting them. The thing that had set it off wasn't in any of these booths—it was somewhere up ahead.

And on the move.

Roger appeared out of the gloom, but this time there was no welcoming smile. His expression was as blank as his eyes. He might be physically here, but Maelle was in charge.

"Anything?" Though it was softly said, it carried easily across the pounding beat of the music and the underlying babble of multiple nearby conversations. I rather suspected it was a subtle form of magic, just as his ability to have the crowd part before him was.

"Not yet."

I stepped around him and continued on. He silently followed, but the weight of his stare had my shoulder blades twitching. Even though there was no threat in that weight, the stirring uneasiness got stronger.

One day, there would be.

I shivered and forced myself to concentrate. The pods became more crowded—and far noisier—the farther around the room and the closer to the bar we got. A strobe of bright light briefly gave me a glimpse of Belle, but someone else almost immediately caught my attention.

She was blonde, statuesque, and absolutely, mind-blowingly stunning. And a man who looked rather star-struck accompanied her.

Our hunter, and her next meal.

Belle, are you close enough to get any sense of her?

Not really. There're too many damn people in the way. She paused. *But I caught a brief glimpse of her aura, and it had a really strange glow.*

Auras were one of those things Belle normally couldn't see, and it spoke of just how well this connection of ours was now working. I couldn't help wondering if the wild magic—or rather, the changes it had made to both me *and* my magic—had something to do with that.

Define strange.

She hesitated. *It's a weird dark purple-red, and didn't surround her as such—it looked more like streams of heat trailing after her. It sort of reminded me of a comet and its tail.*

Suggesting it isn't so much her aura but rather something to do with her energy output.

Possibly. Belle hesitated. *They just disappeared into the crowd on the dance floor.*

I swore and started pushing toward it, but very quickly realized there was a better way. I swung around. "Roger, I need a path cleared."

He glided past me, a small smile touching his lips. The throng of people standing between the dance floor and us parted as easily as Moses had parted the sea and, in very little time, we were standing at the top of the steps that led down to the lower level.

My gaze swept the ever-moving mass of dancers, but I couldn't immediately see the blonde or her victim.

"Who are we looking for?" he asked.

"A tall, absolutely gorgeous blonde." *Belle, can you see her?*

No. She paused. *Oh wait, there she is—in the middle, right underneath Maelle's glass lair.*

My gaze briefly jumped up to Maelle's office in the roof to get the right position and, after a moment, I found her. "I think she's heading for the exit."

"Point her out," Roger said. "So that my mistress can stop her."

"Middle of the dance floor—tall blonde in a red dress."

He studied the area and his frown deepened. "I cannot see her."

Confusion swept me. Aside from the fact she was a good six inches taller than everyone currently around her, her hair shone like a beacon in the multicolored lights sweeping the floor. "Seriously? She's right there." I pointed. "Just passing that guy in the gold lurex shirt."

"I see the shirt, but I cannot see the woman."

"Fuck," Belle said, as she came to a halt beside me. "She must be using some form of concealment spell."

"I can't feel any magic, though, so maybe it's an innate part of her nature." I glanced at Roger. "Is it possible to lock down the main doors temporarily?"

He was shaking his head before I'd finished. "The health and safety people are here this evening—shutting the doors will not be viewed favorably unless there's a very good reason."

"What about stationing a couple of security guys near the door, and getting them to pull aside any tall blonde that attempts to leave. Tell them they've won free drinks next visit or something."

"A good idea except for one flaw—if I cannot see her, it's possible that no one else can."

"Her victim certainly can," Belle commented. "He wouldn't have the boner he has if he couldn't."

Roger raised an eyebrow, amusement lurking briefly in his eyes. "I find the things you ladies notice very interesting indeed."

The woman and her star-struck companion were now moving toward the stairs leading up to the main exit. "We need to get over there, and fast."

"Then follow me."

Roger spun and strode around the top tier, moving quickly and easily through the mass of people. As we followed in his wake, my gaze went to the stairs and the two people unhurriedly climbing them. Halfway up she paused briefly and looked over her shoulder.

Straight at me.

A small smile touched her perfect lips and then she lifted the hem of her long dress and continued climbing. She didn't increase her pace, but the comet-like tail that trailed behind her shifted and flickered with renewed fierceness.

Whether that spoke of vexation at being spotted or something else, I couldn't say.

Either way, she was going to reach the door before us.

"Is your mistress near the exit?" I asked.

"Yes. Whether she will see or sense this woman if there is magic involved is another matter entirely."

"But she'll see the guy with her—whatever magic she's using isn't hiding him," I said. "Besides, Maelle is capable of magic, so she should at least be sensitive to its presence."

"I am, in some circumstances," he replied, his voice once again taking on Maelle's tone, "but the cleaner the magic, the less I'm aware. It is the nature of the beast, I'm afraid."

The beast being the vampire, I presumed. "I wouldn't classify the soucouyant's magic as clean, Maelle."

The bigger news here is the fact she just admitted she's attuned—and capable—of darker magic, Belle said. *We seriously need to step lightly around this bitch.*

Like we haven't been?

I know, but we've now got confirmation that she's a dark witch as well as a vamp. And it means that while she may not be radiating power, it's totally possible she's stronger than either of us magically.

I still think the vampire is the bigger danger. I scanned the area near the door, but there were far too many taller people standing between it and me. Despite the fact she should have towered over them all, I couldn't see her.

I can. They've just reached the top step and have tucked in behind another couple. Belle gave Roger the second couple's description and then added, *The bitch just looked over her shoulder again. She knows we're here.*

Yes. And, from all appearances, remained totally unworried by the fact.

We came around the final curve and strode toward the door. Up ahead, Maelle had stopped the couple Belle had described, but the woman and her victim weren't with them. I swore, pushed past Roger, and bolted toward the door.

Maelle glanced over her shoulder and raised an eyebrow.

"She's not with them," I said, and ran around the three of them.

To see the woman gliding out the airlock doors.

She must have sensed my nearness, because she paused and turned. Our gazes met—her eyes were full of fire and glittered in amusement.

In that moment, I realized two things.

One, she was a very old spirit and had no fear of a witch such as myself.

And two, she was about to unleash hell.

SEVEN

Fire sprang across her fingertips, a fierce and violent storm of circular energy that reminded me of the orb that had taken out our car.

I swore and hastily constructed an ensnaring spell. As the bitch unleashed her fire, I released my magic. The two intersected at the doorway and, for an instant, nothing happened. Fire and magic boiled around each other, neither getting the upper hand.

Then, with a rush of power, the two exploded.

I swore, spun around, and knocked Belle down. Heat sizzled over our heads as we hit the ground hard, and the smell of burning material and screams of fear filled the air.

You okay? I asked, even as I disentangled myself from Belle.

I think I'll have one hell of a bruised shoulder tomorrow, but that's better than being crisped. She hesitated. *The bitch has left the building.*

I know.

I scrambled to my feet. Saw Roger helping Maelle up— saw the scorch across his shirt and the bubbling skin underneath. He'd taken the brunt of the heat to protect his mistress *and* the two patrons standing with them.

I grabbed Belle's hand, helped her up, then spun and raced through the door. There were spots of fire burning in the foyer and smoke drifted, a black cloud that stung my throat with its foulness. As we ran past the cloakroom, the fire alarm sounded and the sprinklers activated, soaking the two of us in an instant.

The street door was already open. I ran out and looked right and left. Saw a glimmer of red disappearing around a corner to our right. Spun and ran that way, my shoes squelching water with every step.

We reached the corner and turned into the street. A couple with a kid in a pram strolled toward us, but there was no sign of the blonde or her next victim. I swore softly and ran out onto the road, my gaze sweeping the other side of the street.

She was here somewhere—I could feel it.

After a moment, I spotted her. Or rather, spotted the flash of red as she climbed into the passenger side of a silver car halfway up the road.

"Belle, can you call the rangers?" I said, as I sprinted toward the car. The pair would be gone long before I got anywhere near them, but I still had to try.

The car's engine roared to life and the headlights came on, a bright flare that had me blinking. As the car pulled out of the parking spot, the blonde turned and raised her hand, idly waving at me. Anger surged and energy flowed across my fingertips in response. As the car pulled away, I flung the twisting threads of magic at the fast-disappearing vehicle. It didn't stop it and it certainly wasn't designed to track it. I wasn't Monty, and I didn't have the power or the knowledge to create something like that on the run.

Instead, my magic hit the back of the vehicle and briefly enlarged the number plate. I memorized it then spun around and stalked back.

Belle was still on the phone. I gave her the number to pass on and then added, "If Monty's still helping Aiden with that other murder, we'll need to be present when they go after that bitch."

"Aiden and Monty are still returning from Greenhill, and are still a good forty-five minutes away."

"We can't afford to wait for them. Not if we want to save the man accompanying the soucouyant."

She hesitated, listening to whoever was on the end. "Tala will be here in five."

"Good." I reached up and squeezed the water from my ponytail, and wished I could do the same to my clothes. "I don't suppose you asked about the Greenhill murder?"

Belle shoved her phone into the back pocket of her jeans, her expression grim. "Apparently, it's another skinning victim."

I wrinkled my nose. No death was a good one, but Greenhill was a very small, close-knit border town community that consisted of little more than a pub and a hundred or so people, and this would hit them hard.

"Which to me suggests we *are* dealing with two different entities."

"Bit of a coincidence that both of them can throw fire, though."

"Yes." I hesitated. "If they're capable of taking on alternate forms when required, why are they stealing skins?"

"We don't know that they both are."

"True." I started walking back down the road. While we had absolutely no hope of catching the pair on foot, the restlessness inside refused to let me be still.

Belle fell in step beside me. "I wonder if she's capable of attaining multiple forms, or whether the one she used tonight is her only one?"

"I have absolutely no idea." I glanced at her, eyebrow raised. "Why?"

"Because that woman is stunning. If she's staying in a motel or rental, it should be a fairly easy task to find her."

"Except for two things," I said. "The first being the sheer number of motels and rentals within the reservation."

"I didn't say we'd be doing the ringing," she replied, amused. "That's a ranger type job, not witch. And the second?"

"The fact that your gran's book said that by day, a soucouyant is an old woman."

"Well, damn, forgot about that." She thrust a hand through her wet hair, dragging it out of her face. "How the hell are we going to find someone who possibly has three different forms?"

"I don't know." I hesitated. "We might be able to create a spell that could track down her energy output, but to do that we'd first have to get some sense of said output."

"I could run back to the club," Belle said. "She had to have been in there for a while before she found her target. Even if her energy isn't lingering, the damage caused by the fireball might just hold enough of her essence to design a spell around."

"And if we can't, surely Monty will be able to."

"Exactly." She swung the pack off her shoulder and handed it to me. It was waterproof, so even though water dripped from the straps, everything inside the pack should be dry. "Be careful if you do track the bitch down."

"I've been fireballed twice now. I do not intend to suffer through a third."

"Then we'd better start figuring out a proper fire dousing spell." She glanced around at the sound of a siren. "That'll be Tala. I'll head off."

"Tread lightly around Maelle. She's going to be mighty pissed."

"I think *that* may win the award for understatement of the year."

She jogged away. Several seconds later, a green-and-white SUV slid around the corner and roared toward me. I could see two figures inside—one was Tala, the other had reddish hair, which meant it was probably Duke, a ranger I'd seen on a couple of occasions but never been officially introduced to.

The SUV slid to a halt beside me and Tala motioned me to hurry and get in. I ran across the road and jumped into the back of their vehicle.

I'd barely pulled on the seat belt when Tala took off again. "I take it you managed to get an address from the rego number?"

"Yes." Duke's voice had a decidedly Irish lilt to his voice, which suggested he was yet another wolf who'd come into the reservation under the exchange program. "It belongs to one Jason Harding, who lives in Louton."

Louton was one of a handful of small gold mining towns that ringed Castle Rock, and only ten minutes away. But that still gave the soucouyant too much of a head start, and more than enough time to hastily seduce and then kill.

"So what, exactly, happened at the club?" Tala turned onto the highway that led down to Louton. "We got a report that the fire brigade had been called to the scene."

I gave them a brief rundown on what we were chasing and then said, "The bitch wasn't trying to burn the club down—she was just trying to delay me."

"Successfully, it seems," Duke commented.

I glanced at him. "Yeah. But she's aware her attack wasn't fully successful and would expect us to track her victim down fairly quickly."

"Meaning she may not be there when we arrive."

"*If* they're going to his place, yes. But she can seduce and feed anywhere between here and there."

"Meaning we'd better keep an eye out for an abandoned silver Kia."

Given this whole area was a rabbit warren of scrubby trees and intersecting tracks, it would be fairly easy for a Land Rover to disappear let alone a smallish sedan. But there was little point in stating the obvious.

We roared down the highway—though calling it *that* was something of a misnomer given the road consisted of a single lane each way—and were soon out of Castle Rock and heading into Louton. Tala slowed enough to do a right into the street just past the local pub and then switched the siren off. The sudden silence was decidedly eerie.

"The registered owner of the Kia lives in the last house at the other end of the street," she said. "How do you want to play this?"

I undid the seat belt and leaned forward. The glow of the SUV's headlights revealed a street that was single lane and roughly asphalted. Light peeked out from the covered windows of the three nearest houses, but the far end of the street remained wrapped in shadows.

I had no sense of the soucouyant; in fact, my senses were tugging me back down the road and out of Louton. And yet we couldn't leave—not until we'd checked the house out. My instincts hadn't been wrong often of late—and the star-struck stranger certainly couldn't afford them to be wrong now—but the truth was, we knew very little about soucouyants and just what they were truly capable of. Given her ability to disappear to the senses of others, it was totally possible she was using a similar magic here.

"Well?" Tala said, a touch impatiently.

"I'm not feeling anything on the psychic radar, but I don't think we can leave without checking that house out."

"And if they're not there?"

"We can discuss *that* after we uncover whether they're there or not."

Annoyance ran through her expression, but she didn't say anything and shoved the SUV back into gear. The house at the top of the hill was a single-story, tin-roofed old weatherboard cottage that was painted in an ugly brown. Rather weirdly, though the front door pointed toward the main street, there was no street access or even a pathway, and between the picket fence that surrounded the entire place and us was a rather large embankment.

Tala continued past it and then swung left. A small carport and a number of old tin sheds lined the back fence, but there was a gateway at the far end.

Tala stopped and the two rangers climbed out. I grabbed the pack and followed them. The night was still and quiet, and there was absolutely no sense of evil riding the darkness.

The soucouyant wasn't here.

Duke's nostrils flared briefly. "I can't hear any sound coming from inside that house and there's no olfactory evidence that anyone has recently passed by."

"Would there be after twenty minutes?" I asked curiously.

"To normal senses, no. To a wolf or a dog, or indeed anything else that hunts by scent, yes." He glanced at Tala. "What do you want to do?"

Tala grimaced. "We'll have to check it out, just in case this creature has done the deed and fled."

She'd certainly fled, but the deed hadn't been done here. I rubbed my arms lightly and followed the two rangers through the gate. The path was broken and weed filled, but there was enough moonlight to prevent any slips or tripping over on my part.

Tala motioned Duke to the back door and then moved around to the front. I stopped and crossed my arms. There was nothing here—nothing but cobwebs and silence. Duke tested the back door, peered in through the laundry window, and then moved around to the other side of the house.

After a moment, they both returned. "The doors are all locked and there's no sign or scent of life within the house," Tala said. "What do you want to do?"

"Go back onto the highway and head out of town."

She raised her eyebrows. "It's still on the move?"

I hesitated, prodding the tenuous psychic thread for answers. "No. But it's somewhere outside of Louton."

Tala grunted. Though she looked dubious, she led the way back to the SUV. In very little time, we were on the move again.

As we drove out of Louton and the road began a series of sweeping curves that climbed up the mountain, the tenuous thread of evil grew stronger.

I leaned forward. "Slow down. We're getting close."

As Tala immediately did so, Duke said, "This isn't a brilliant area to be killing someone. There's no room to park on the verge, and the entire area is a mix of large allotments and small holdings."

"There're no street lights here, though, so if she goes off

road, it'd be hard to see her," Tala said. "And there are plenty of places along this road to do that, too."

We swept around another corner. The road ahead dipped down a slight incline and then ran straight. The headlights gleamed off the trees lining the hillside to our right, but to our left, beyond the metal guardrail, the land fell sharply away. In the distance, a house light shone, but between them and us was a wide, dark surface on which moonlight glimmered. It was a large dam or a small lake.

The tenuous thread sharpened abruptly.

"There," I said, pointing to the water. "They're near that lake."

"I can't see anything," Duke said.

"You may not," Tala said. "I know that dam—it's part of Old Benson's property. There's a dirt road that goes around the back of it, and if they're on that, then they won't be seen from here."

The protective guardrail ended as we hit the straight section of the road and, in the headlights, the land to our left began to look rather park-like. Tala swung onto a gravel entrance and killed the siren. Up ahead, the driveway split into two.

"Take the left fork," I said.

She did so. As the headlights picked out the rusting metal structure of an old windmill, the tenuous thread of evil that had lead me here surged—and both trepidation and urgency spiked with it.

I clenched my fingers and peered out through the windscreen, but there was nothing beyond trees, darkness, and that windmill to be seen.

It was what I *couldn't* see that was worrying me.

"There," Duke said. "Up ahead to our left, just off the road in the trees."

I shifted and, in the gleam of the headlights, saw what appeared to be a rear bumper bar. The rest of the car was little more than a shadowed outline; if there was anyone inside the vehicle, it wasn't obvious from here.

"I'm not liking the feel of this." Tala halted the SUV but didn't turn off the engine or get out. "At the very least, there should have been some reaction to us pinning them with our headlights. Is the soucouyant still here?"

"Yes."

But why couldn't we see her? Or, for that matter, her victim? The Kia wasn't a large car and there wasn't a whole lot of room in the back seat to stretch out in *any* way—something I knew from rather disastrous and totally unsatisfied experience. The soucouyant's human form was well over six feet tall, and her victim had been at least several inches taller than me. Seduction room would have been sparse.

"How do you want to play this?" Tala asked.

I swung the pack onto the seat and quickly unzipped it. "I think I'd better go on alone to investigate—"

"And I think that's a *bad* idea," Tala cut in. "If all three of us spread out, then it divides her attention and gives one of us a chance to take her down."

"Except you're dealing with a fire spirit—the only way bullets could take it down is if they're blessed." And I didn't know of many priests who actually did *that*. We'd had a hard enough time finding ones who would bless our knives. "She can also use fire as a weapon, as she did in the club. I managed to contain it then, but I may not be as lucky a second time."

"So why put yourself in the line of fire? Why not call in Monty and let him deal with this thing?"

"Because if we do wait, we void any chance of rescuing Harding."

"I think we all know the chances of him coming out of this alive is practically zero," Duke commented.

"Practically zero still gives us a chance, however minute," I said. "And if it were you up there, wouldn't you want someone to at least try?"

He grunted and didn't bother replying. I tucked two more bottles of holy water into my pockets and then clipped my silver knife onto my belt.

The presence of unguarded silver had both Tala and Duke pulling back from me, though I rather suspected it was an instinctive reaction.

"Right." I took a deep breath and then opened the door. "If the shit hits the fan, don't come running."

Another of those tight smiles touched Tala's lips. "Just don't get yourself injured or dead. The boss will be mightily pissed if you do."

"I think it's safe to say I wouldn't be overly pleased if that happens, either."

I climbed out of the SUV. The bright glare of the headlights cast the car up ahead into deeper shadows, but I didn't need to see the car to know the soucouyant was still there.

And waiting.

Fear shivered through me, and it took every ounce of control not to climb back into the SUV and beg Tala to just get us out of here.

I swallowed heavily and then said, "Can you turn the headlights off?"

She immediately did so. The night closed in, still and thick with menace. I shivered again then silently began weaving a demon snare around my free hand. I might have only read the theory of the spell, but I'd seen the threads of its creation when Monty had called it into being, and that helped. Whether my spell would have anywhere near the necessary strength to contain the soucouyant was anyone's guess. But I had nothing else in my arsenal right now.

I forced my feet forward, but the closer I got to the vehicle, the greater my uneasiness became. There was no sign of anyone inside—no silhouettes and no movement. If not for the fact I could feel the presence of the soucouyant, it would have been easy to believe they'd abandoned the car and gone elsewhere.

My grip on my knife was now so fierce that my knuckles glowed white. The encasement spell flowed around my left hand, a mix of gold, silver, and red threads. The power of it pulsed across the night, and yet it was little more than a breeze against the storm of heat and energy now rising from the car.

I crept around the edge of the trunk and moved to the back door. While there was still no movement, there was now light—flickering, orange-red light.

Fire.

Fire that rather eerily bore human form, but in miniature.

The soucouyant.

Sitting on the center console, watching me.

I tore my gaze from it to the back seat. Saw the pale gleam of unmoving flesh. Saw the bruises decorating his flesh and the look of utter horror frozen onto his face.

Her first victim might have died in bliss, but Jason Harding had not.

I wrenched open the door and raised my hand. But before I could unleash the encasement spell, the soucouyant charged.

I reacted instinctively, throwing myself backward and raising the knife. As my butt hit the ground, the soucouyant's fiery form flowed around the blade and then fled. I cursed and flung my spell after it; the soucouyant spun around, as if daring the spell to catch it, and then continued on into the trees. I flicked my hand and sent a bright thread spooling after her. It was a last, desperate lash of power. Just for a moment, I thought it had succeeded, as fire flared briefly through the trees. Then the darkness returned and the fiery thread was left trailing behind the main portion of the spell as it sped on into the darkness. It would stop as soon as it hit something. Unfortunately, that something wouldn't be the soucouyant, as the spell hadn't included a tracker.

I swore in frustration at my own lack of knowledge then turned to look at the car—and only then realized the damn thing was on fire. She might have fled, but she'd left a parting gift.

As thick smoke billowed from the interior of the vehicle, I scrambled upright, grabbed Harding's arms, and heaved him out of the car. Or tried to. His body was quite literally a dead weight.

"Here, let me." Duke pushed me out of the way and grabbed Harding from me. As he pulled Harding from the car, Tala stepped past him, a fire extinguisher in one hand. There was a fierce hiss of air, then foam erupted into the car. But this fire was *not* natural, and there was no extinguishing it. Not until it had done the task it had been set.

"Tala, Duke, *run*," I said, and immediately did just that.

We were perhaps a dozen steps away from the car when it exploded. A blast of heat and air hit all three of us and sent us tumbling. I skidded through the dirt for several yards and stopped just short of the SUV's front tires. As bits of metal, plastic, and flaming fabric rained all around me, I swore again and scrambled under the truck for protection.

Between the fiery deluge and the thick smoke billowing from the remains of the Kia, visibility was down to practically zero. I couldn't see either Tala or Duke, but Harding lay on the ground ten feet away.

He was on fire.

And the smell....

I gagged and pinched my nose. Breathing through my mouth helped, but only a little.

So why him? Belle asked. *Why not you or the rangers?*

I have no idea.

She'd certainly had both the time and the opportunity to attack us—and could have done so even before I'd opened the back door. So why wait until the last moment?

Why sit on the console waiting for me to see her? She certainly didn't appear to fear either me, my magic, or the knife.

Perhaps she's taunting you.

Why on earth would a fire spirit do that?

Maybe she's a very old spirit. Maybe simple seduction is no longer enough for her. Belle mentally shrugged. *Until we know more about soucouyants, we won't know if this is normal behavior or not.*

Hopefully, Monty's searches will have more success than ours.

Given he's got both the national and international libraries at his disposal, I suspect he will. She paused. *Aiden's just sent me home, so I'll go through Gran's books again and see if I can find anything else on them.*

Is everything okay at the club?

Yeah. As expected, Maelle's not a happy camper—especially now that Aiden's confiscated the security tapes for the last week.

I'm betting she has a backup system somewhere.

The fiery rain of car bits had eased, so I carefully climbed out from under the SUV. My shoulder vehemently protested the movement, and there was moisture running down my right thigh, but all in all, I'd once again escaped relatively unharmed.

But between these new scrapes and the previous ones, I was going to be a sore mess in the coming days.

Oh, she definitely has. I think it's more a case of her not wanting him to see who, exactly, visits her establishment.

That made sense, especially given she apparently had a series of "special rooms" that weren't open to the general public. *Did she say anything else?*

Just that Roger was in the process of going through the secondary tapes, and would contact us if he spots her first victim with the soucouyant or anyone else the night he was murdered—though I'm not sure how knowing that will help the situation any.

It'll tell us if she's using the club as her hunting ground. It'd also tell us whether she was capable of taking on more than one form.

True. Belle hesitated. *Other than the scrapes, you okay?*

Yeah, though I have to wonder how much longer I can keep pushing my luck.

Hopefully for many years yet to come, she said. *And given the shitty nature of our teenage years and the twelve years we've spent constantly on the move, I think we deserve all the goddamn "good" luck in the world.*

Here's hoping fate agrees with you.

A twig cracked behind me. I twisted around, my pulse rate leaping into overdrive again. Thankfully, it was Duke rather than the soucouyant arriving to charcoal the three of us. He gave me a nod, limped past Harding's still burning remains, and continued on to the remnants of the car.

Let me know when you're on the way back, Belle said. *I'll run you a bath to help ease the aches.*

Thanks.

A good familiar always looks after her witch, she stated, her voice philosophical, *especially when the brigade has booked half the café out tomorrow, and said witch will probably have to work her ass off.*

I snorted softly but didn't comment as Tala came out of the trees. Her left shirtsleeve had been torn and there was a bloody scrape down the right side of her face, but like the rest of us, she'd escaped the explosion relatively intact.

"Why would she blow up the car and then burn Harding rather than us?" She stopped several feet away from his remains and thrust her hands on her hips—a movement full of frustration and anger. How she was standing the smell, I had no idea. "It doesn't make any sense."

"No, it doesn't."

"Do you think it was an attempt to cover up evidence?"

"Nope. Nor do I think it was a serious attempt on our lives—if it had been, we'd be dead."

"And the thing that did this? Is it still around?"

I shook my head. "No. But I wouldn't send me home unless you call in Monty first."

She glanced around at that, a smile on her lips. "I wasn't going to, but I *will* point out that your magic doesn't appear to counter that of this fire creature."

"Hey, we're all still alive, are we not?"

"That we are." She motioned toward the truck. "Do you want to wait inside while we examine what's left of the car?"

I shook my head. "I'll head into the trees where she disappeared and see if she left anything behind."

Tala raised her eyebrows. "How likely is that?"

"Not very." I shrugged. "But I still have to try."

"Just give both the body and the car a wide berth, then."

I did so then climbed the slight incline into the trees. The moonlight disappeared and the darkness closed in, but this time it held no sense of threat. The encasement spell had snared itself between two trees several meters in. I quickly disengaged it, but as the threads of power faded away, a second glimmer caught my attention. I studied it, my heart beating somewhere in my throat even though there remained no threat in either the night or that glimmer.

After several moments, I realized it was a will-o'-the-wisp—the same one who'd been in the clearing when we'd found the second body and the skin. I walked toward it. "It is good to see you again, my friend."

The wisp spun, as if in acknowledgment. While they undoubtedly had their own language, it was one most witches didn't understand.

"Are you simply passing by, or is there another reason you wait for me?"

The wisp's light pulsed briefly, but before I could decide what that meant, it spun and darted through the trees. When I didn't immediately follow, it returned, spun around, and raced away again. Obviously, it wanted to show me something.

It was casting just enough light for me to pick my way through the trees, which meant I could move through the small forest relatively quickly. In very little time we came out into the wide, almost park-like area. Before me lay a long, smooth slope that led down to the bank of a large dam —the same dam I'd seen from the road.

The moon remained behind the clouds and the lake's surface was little more than a black mirror that barely reflected the light of the distant stars. I half wondered what the wisp would do when it got to the water—and whether it'd actually expect me to go into it. The question was quickly answered when the wisp jagged left and then stopped. In the pale glow of its light, there was a small but bloody glow of red.

Excitement surged, even though I had no real idea as to why. The wisp didn't back away as I approached, but it did rise, keeping itself slightly above my head.

I knelt on one knee—wincing as my newly scraped thigh protested the movement—and then reached out, but didn't quite touch, the spark.

I didn't have to, not to understand exactly what it was.

The energy that rolled off it might be dying, but it nevertheless told me what it was and where it had come from.

This ember was a piece of the soucouyant.

While my spell hadn't ensnared her, that last, desperate flick of energy I'd sent spiraling after her *had* caught her. Maybe not enough to capture, but certainly enough to tear a small piece of essence from her body.

But if I didn't immediately do something to protect it— to somehow keep it alive—then we might just lose our one and only means of tracking the soucouyant down.

I'd never been taught the sort of spell needed to contain something like this, but I *had* witnessed it being done—and very recently. Eli had done exactly that when he'd drawn together the filaments of a dark sorcerer's essence, and then contained them in a small, spellbound container. I'd memorized the spell, but whether I'd actually be capable of reproducing it, I had no idea.

I took a deep breath and then created a protection circle around the ember, using both the holy water and a spell.

Once inside the circle, I activated the spell and sat cross-legged on the ground.

I glanced up at the wisp. "I'm about to weave a spell to contain this remnant of a dark one. It shouldn't affect you, but, just in case, it might be wise if you put some distance between us."

The wisp immediately retreated to the trees but didn't totally disappear. I somehow felt safer, even though a wisp wasn't in any way capable of defending me if someone or something decided to attack.

I grabbed the end of my T-shirt and quickly dried out the inside of one the small bottles that had contained the holy water, and then did the same with the cork. After another deep breath to center my energy, I closed my eyes and mentally crossed fingers, toes, and all things in-between that I remembered the spell correctly. Then I began. Energy immediately stirred around me, thin threads that gleamed in the darkness as they gathered pace and power—something I could see despite the fact my eyes remained closed. As the filaments and the spell gained momentum, the tiny ember began to twist and turn, as if fighting the pull of my magic. The glowing threads continued to gather, until a fist-sized sphere was formed. I spelled on, not entirely sure I was doing it right but not really caring if the end result was the same.

The ember was lifted from the ground. I carefully wrapped the sphere around it, then picked up the bottle and gently guided the sphere inside. Once the ember was contained, I corked the bottle and then wound the remaining threads of my magic around it to seal and protect it.

It was done.

I closed off the spell and took a deep, shuddering breath

that did little to ease the weariness that washed through me or the growing ache in my head. But that was to be expected; new spells always drained far more from you than ones in regular use. And I couldn't help but seriously hope *this* sort of containment spell was not one I needed to repeat too often.

I opened my eyes. Inside the small bottle, sitting in the middle of the constantly revolving filaments of my magic, was the small piece of the soucouyant. I'd successfully contained it; now all I had to do was hope the spell could keep the ember alive long enough to use it as a tracker.

I quickly dissolved the protection spell, but even that small task had the ache in my head intensifying. And, unfortunately, every other part of my body now seemed intent on going along for the ride.

I slowly pushed to my feet, biting my lip against the groan that surged up my throat. The wisp pulsed and spun its light forward, lighting my way as I slowly—wearily— made my way back up the slope. When we neared the spot where it had met me, I stopped and said, "Thank you for the assistance tonight, my friend. I wouldn't have found this ember if not for you."

The wisp spun again, and then, with little fanfare, fled into the trees. Leaving me alone but not without light—the tangled threads of the spell around the glass bottle were emitting just enough to see by.

Tala glanced up as I emerged out of the trees. "What the hell happened? You look like shit."

"That's probably because I feel like it."

Amusement flared briefly in her eyes. "Who were you talking to in the trees?"

"A wisp."

Duke glanced around sharply. "A what?"

"She means ghost candle," Tala said. "I had no idea there were any in this area, let alone them being able to understand conversation."

"Wisps are spirits," I said. "We may not know their language, but they can certainly understand ours. Which is why I always recommend you be polite if you ever come across one."

"Suggesting those led astray weren't?" Duke said, disbelief evident.

"More than likely." I raised the small bottle. "It led me to this—a means of hopefully tracking down the soucouyant. But we'll need to get Monty here, and pronto, because I'm not sure my magic is strong enough to keep this ember alive long."

Tala grunted. "He's actually on his way here—and rather pissed that he missed out on the action, from what I can gather."

"He's already been flamed once. I would have thought *that'd* be enough."

"Apparently not." She motioned toward the SUV. "There's a first aid kit in the back of the truck—you might want to head down and look after that wound on your thigh."

"I will. Thanks."

I hobbled on down to the truck. Once I'd found the first aid kit, I carefully washed away the worst of the muck and grime from both the scrapes on my arms and the one on my thigh. It was the worse by far—a long, deep wound that probably needed stitches. But I found some antiseptic and some butterfly Band-Aids inside the kit, so applied all that instead and then wrapped a crepe bandage around the thigh wound for additional support.

With all that done, I climbed into the truck and leaned

back against the headrest, drawing in deep breaths in a vague attempt to ease the weariness and lingering wisps of pain. It didn't really help. Nothing but a mountain of food and a solid ten hours of sleep would do that.

After a few more minutes, I opened my eyes and reached down for the backpack. Belle had said she'd packed everything, so hopefully that also meant some snack bars. It did.

I spent the next fifteen minutes munching on a variety of nuts, chocolate, and protein bars, and washed it all down with some painkillers and water. While it didn't in any way mute either the stiff soreness or the overall tide of weariness, it did at least boost the energy reserves.

Tala's SUV was briefly spotlighted as another truck pulled up beside it. I glanced across and saw it was Aiden and Monty.

I climbed out but kept my grip on the door handle. Despite the painkillers and all the food, my head remained a little spacy.

Monty jumped out of the truck. "How come you get all the fun?"

"Born unlucky, I guess." My voice was dry. "Believe me, I'd much rather have stayed at the café and avoided this bitch, but that really wasn't an option once my psychic radar went off."

"And did you manage to avoid getting hurt this time?" Aiden came around the back of the truck, his gaze sweeping me. "No, you did not."

I grimaced. "It's only a few more cuts and—"

"It's more than *that*." His voice was edged with anger and concern. "You're holding on to that door for grim death."

"Yeah, but that's because I've been spelling. It's not

from the scrapes." I tossed Monty the small bottle. "Found this for you."

He caught it easily, and his expression went from curious to fascinated. "It feels like a piece of the soucouyant—how did you get this? And where the hell did you learn this spell? It's something they teach in uni, and one you shouldn't have known."

Let alone have the power to construct. He didn't add that last bit, but he didn't need to. It was very evident in the look he gave me.

"I tried caging the soucouyant in the demon snare, but missed, so I flicked one of the spell threads out after her. It obviously got close enough to slice an ember off."

His gaze narrowed. "You skipped out of school before they taught that particular spell—which, by the way, normally doesn't have a tendril variation."

"Yes, but I *did* read the basics of that spell at school, and I saw you perform it." I shrugged. "The variation came out of desperation."

"Didn't anyone ever tell you it's dangerous to create new spells on the fly?"

"Obviously not."

He shook his head and raised the thread-wrapped bottle. "And the spell around this? Where did that come from?"

"It's one Eli did not so long ago. Thankfully, I remembered it."

"Your witch powers might not be up to scratch, but your memory sure as hell is." He glanced down at the bottle again. "I'm not sure I'll be able to work a spell through this to track her, though."

I frowned. "Why not? The essence is still active—"

"Yes, but to weave a tracking spell into it, I'll first have to dismantle your spell, and that might just extinguish the ember."

I swore softly and shoved a hand through my hair, catching tangles and bits of leaf matter. "So it's all been a wasted effort?"

"No, because I can certainly walk you through the tracking spell. It just depends entirely on whether you've got the energy to do it all again."

"Does it have to be done tonight?" Aiden asked. "I'm all for catching this bitch ASAP, but not at the cost of putting Liz in hospital."

A smile touched my lips. "I'm fine—really, I am."

"You'd say that if you had a leg cut off and were spurting blood everywhere," he grumbled.

His concern was so very evident in both his eyes and his expression, and my heart did a dangerous sort of flip-flop. The sort that said I was getting in far deeper than was wise with this man. No matter how much he cared for me, no matter how much he wanted to explore where this relationship of ours might go, the fact was, it would only ever have one outcome. Heartbreak.

He'd already said he would never marry someone like me, and there would never be enough magic in the world to change me from a witch to a wolf. Of course, that hadn't stopped people from trying in the past, and *that* was generally where the myths of wolfmen—beings who were neither human nor wolf, but a deranged and thankfully short-lived version of both—came from.

If I were the sensible type, I'd stop this thing in its tracks. Maybe not right here and now, because this was neither the right time nor place. But certainly in the next day or so. It would hurt, of that I had no doubt, but not as much as it might six months, or a year, or even more down the track.

Unfortunately, I'd never really been the sensible type. Not when it came to matters of the heart.

"The sooner we catch the soucouyant," I said, somewhat surprised my voice came out so even given the errant direction of my thoughts, "the better everyone is going to be."

His gaze had narrowed, and I had a vague suspicion he knew exactly what I'd been thinking. Which was stupid. Werewolves might have heightened senses, but they *weren't* telepathic. I returned my gaze to Monty. "What do I need to do?"

"Right now? Relax. I'll set up a protection circle and then guide you through the process." He grabbed his pack from Aiden's truck and then walked down the track for a few meters.

Aiden caught my hand and tugged me into his arms. I rested my head against his chest, listening to the steady beat of his heart and feeling far safer than I ever had in my entire life.

Which was a rather sad statement about my life.

He didn't say anything, not for several minutes. Then he kissed the top of my head and said, "You need to stop worrying about the future and just enjoy the present."

He may not be telepathic, but he *had* guessed my thoughts. I obviously needed to work some more on containing my emotions. "Easier said than done, Aiden."

"I know. But the future you fear may never happen."

Part of me wondered which future he was referring to, but in the end, it didn't really matter. Both were equally troubling. Both would lead to heartbreak of one kind or another.

"As much as I'm enjoying *this* moment," I said, "haven't you got a job to do? I'd hate for you to be accused of dereliction of duty because of me."

He laughed, the sound vibrating delightfully through his chest. "I don't think anyone would *dare* accuse us of that after the last few days."

"Tonight especially—it's been rather eventful."

He snorted. "For you, maybe. Not so much for us."

"Being called to another skinning is hardly *un*eventful."

"The victim had been dead for several hours and we didn't come under attack. So yeah, compared to this, it was."

I frowned and pulled back from his embrace. "Several hours? So he'd been killed during the day rather than at night, like the other victims?"

"Technically, Alice *wasn't* killed at night." He frowned. "Why?"

I hesitated. "It just seems out of character."

"Give how little we know about either skin walkers or soucouyants, isn't it a little early to be saying what is and isn't out of character?"

"Well, yes, but that doesn't mean I'm wrong."

"I'm not saying you are, but Monty didn't appear to think there was a problem—"

"Monty's a witch, not a psychic, and neither of us actually know what we're dealing with—especially when it comes to the skinning victims." I hesitated. "If I'm being honest, I'm still not convinced we're dealing with a skin walker. But until we can get confirmation from Canberra, we're both just guessing."

A smile tugged at his lips but didn't fully bloom. "If there's one thing I've learned over the last few months, it's to trust your guesses. What do you want to do?"

I hesitated again. "Right now? Nothing. But I wouldn't

mind going back to Greenhill and having a look over the murder scene."

"Monty's going to think we don't trust him."

"Monty doesn't have to know about it."

"I feel the need to point out that, whether I like it or not, Monty *is* the reservation witch, and should be included in any investigation involving magic and the supernatural."

"Words I bet you never thought you'd utter."

"*That* is a fact." He brushed a few stray strands of hair out of my eyes, his fingertips warm against my skin. "But I'd rather be safe than sorry—you're bone weary, Liz. I can see and smell it. You *will* end up in hospital again if you're not careful."

I rose on my toes and said, my lips so close to his that I could almost taste them, "Then you'd better ensure I'm kept warm and well fed, hadn't you?"

Someone cleared their throat. Loudly. "Folks, there's a time and a place for that sort of muck."

I laughed, dropped a quick kiss on Aiden's lips, and then glanced at Monty. "I take it the protection circle is constructed?"

"Yes, and given the ad hoc nature of the spell around the ember and the fact neither of us know how long it'll last, I think we'd better get a move on."

Aiden released me. "You'll let us know if this works or not?"

"Ranger, if this works, I'll be as surprised as hell, but yes."

"The lack of belief." I clapped a hand to my chest. "It hurts."

Monty didn't reply. He just rolled his eyes, then spun on his heel and walked away.

I followed. He'd constructed his circle at the base of the

slope, on a flat bit of ground. His spell stones gleamed in the cold light of the moon, and the threads of his magic swirled lazily above them, ready to be activated. I stepped over them, then carefully sat down.

Monty sat opposite then shuffled closer. Energy stirred and meshed where our knees met, and it was oddly comforting—but also rather alarming—that the pulse of mine was in no way inferior to his.

He raised the protection circle around us and then gave me the small glass bottle containing the ember.

"I think it's better if we keep your spell completely active, and just attempt to weave the tracking rider through it," he said. "That way, the core remains intact and will hopefully continue to keep the ember viable."

I nodded and tried to quell the rising tide of tension. Though what I was so nervous about, I couldn't say.

"Ready?" he added.

I nodded again.

"Right. Unpick the outer layers of your spell, and then I'll guide you through the rest of it."

"And if, for any reason, my magic *isn't* up to the task?"

"I'll risk stepping in. But you'll be fine, Liz."

I gave him a quick, tense smile, and then centered my energy and glanced down at the small bottle. After a moment's hesitation, I carefully picked up the first thread of magic and disengaged it, then repeated the process until the bottle was uncorked and the tangled mass of filaments that surrounded and protected the ember once again floated free.

"Good," Monty said, his voice so soft it could have been coming from a great distance. "Now we get into the real work."

He carefully guided me through the process, teaching

me how to weave the threads of the tracking spell through the sphere's filaments and then how to connect it to the core protection spell and the ember itself without in any way disturbing either. It required utter precision, and it left me physically and mentally drained. By the time I guided the sphere back into the bottle and spelled it closed, sweat was dribbling down my face. But the ember remained active, and was also now connected to a tiny filament of silver.

Monty carefully plucked the bottle from my hands. "It worked. It goddamn *worked.*"

I scrubbed a hand across my eyes, smearing sweat. "You sound awfully surprised."

His gaze jumped to mine. "That's because I didn't actually think it *would.*"

I would have laughed if I'd had more energy. "Not the impression I received at all."

His grin flashed. "It's always better to fake it until you make it, trust me on that."

"I'll remember that when you start rabbiting on about spells in the future." I nodded toward the bottle. "How long do we have to use it?"

"That I don't know, as everything depends on the stability of your original spell." He quickly dismantled the protection circle and then thrust upward. "To be completely safe, I think we'd better go after it tonight."

I nodded and watched as he collected his spell stones and then strode off. He must have realized I wasn't following, because he stopped several yards away and spun around. "Are you coming?"

"Nope. Not unless you help me up."

"Ah. Sorry."

He shoved the bottle into his pocket and then walked

back and offered me his hands. I gripped them tightly and was pulled up so quickly my head spun.

"Are you okay?" He didn't immediately release me, and his expression was concerned. "I have to say, you look like shit."

"Theme of the night, it seems." I took a deep breath and gathered determination. "I'm fine. You go get Aiden—I'll wait in his truck."

"Are you sure you can make it that far?"

"Yes. Go."

He hesitated, and then walked off. I slowly made my way up the hill, grabbed my pack out of Tala's truck, and then climbed into the front of Aiden's. And discovered he'd added energy drinks to the stash of chocolate he now kept in the glove compartment for me. I downed both in quick succession and then started in on the chocolate. Tonight was *not* my waistline's friend—not that I'd ever really given a damn about that sort of thing.

The two men came back. Monty handed me the spell-wrapped bottle and almost instantly I felt the directional tug. It was faint, suggesting the soucouyant was some distance away, but at least it was working.

Aiden turned the truck around and drove back to the main road.

"Turn right," I said, as he slowed down.

He immediately did so and then accelerated up the hill. We sped through the sweeping curves and then on into Louton. The locational pull got stronger as we neared the outskirts of Castle Rock, and the tiny filaments started untwining, until what was formed was a tiny map.

"Go left at the next street," I said, and then turned around in the seat and showed Monty the bottle. "Is it supposed to do that?"

"In theory, yes."

"In theory? I thought you'd performed the location spell before?"

His grin flashed. "I have, but this particular one had to be layered in and that's not something done too often."

"Surely the uni would have ensured everyone practiced spell alterations."

"They did, but you're forgetting I've been a cataloger of spells for nigh on five years now, so while plenty of new and unusual spells crossed my desk, I haven't actually done much spell work since I left uni."

"I suspect that is *not* something you mentioned to the council when you were interviewed for the position," Aiden said, voice dry.

Monty chuckled softly. "Actually, I said I'd probably forgotten more spells than the other applicants had ever performed, which is nothing other than the utter truth."

I glanced down as the filaments stirred. One pulsed brighter than the others, giving me a direction. "Swing left. I think we're getting close."

Aiden obeyed, then slowed down and studied the street ahead. "This entire area is filled with families and kids— why would a soucouyant hide here?"

"If its daytime skin is that of an old woman," Monty said, "what better area is there? Families these days are generally too busy to be worrying about what their elderly neighbors might or might not be doing."

"Not sure what type of neighborhood you grew up in," Aiden said, "but we tend to look after our old folks here."

"Werewolves might, but I'm betting the human residents don't."

Aiden didn't bother disputing that statement, though

his expression suggested he didn't exactly agree with it, either.

As the filaments in the bottle drew tightly around each other again, and the tracking pulse grew stronger, I leaned forward and studied the houses up ahead. My gaze swept past a house with a large old gum out the front of it and then snapped back.

That was it.

That was the soucouyant's hiding place.

"It's the brown brick place." I tucked the bottle into my pocket and then dragged my backpack onto my lap.

Aiden stopped two houses down. As the headlights went out and darkness closed in once again, he said, "How do we play this?"

"We need to know if the soucouyant is there before we can actually do anything," Monty said. "I know the spell led us here, but this thing is obviously smart, and it's possible it left that ember behind deliberately."

I twisted around again. "And why didn't you mention this possibility before?"

"Because it only just occurred to me." His grin appeared, but just as quickly faded. "What are your psychic senses telling you?"

"Right now, absolutely jack squat. I think our best option is to just suss the situation out."

I opened the door and climbed out. Various bits of my body had stiffened up over the short journey, but I studiously ignored the aches and kept my gaze on the house ahead. There was no light coming from inside the house, no sound, and absolutely no indication from my psychic self that there was anything to fear, either inside that house or out.

And yet....

And yet, uneasiness was once again stirring.

But maybe it was based on nothing more than the notion that if something *could* go wrong, it most certainly would.

Aiden came around the truck and stopped beside me. "Anything?"

"Maybe." I wrinkled my nose. "And maybe not."

"I'm not sensing a spirit in that house," Monty said. "Although there's an odd pall of evil shrouding it that certainly suggests occupation by some form of entity, even if not our one."

I narrowed my gaze and, after a moment, saw the dark shroud he was talking about. It was almost as if the air around the immediate vicinity of the house had been stained by its presence.

"I've never seen anything like that before." I rubbed my arms against the chill that was gathering. "And the fact that it's falling so heavily around the house suggests the soucouyant might have been here for a while."

"Or that it's an extremely old and powerful spirit," he said.

"Well, she certainly appeared to be daring me to go after her."

"Why would a dark spirit do that?" Aiden asked.

"Humans aren't the only ones addicted to the thrill of the chase," Monty said. "And for the very old spirits, the prospect of danger or of being caught and killed is the only thing that makes them feel alive. Or as alive as the spirit would ever actually get."

"Which suggests the spirit world can be just as fucked up as the real."

"It can indeed." Monty's gaze returned to the house. "I'm not sensing anything untoward in that house, but that doesn't really mean anything. As a fire spirit, she can pretty much blow that house apart from some distance away."

"Now isn't that a cheery thought," Aiden muttered.

"It's always better to consider the worst outcome when undertaking these sorts of investigations," Monty said cheerfully. "That way, they're less likely to catch you unawares."

"Says the man who's done *so* many investigations," I said, voice dry. "Do you want to go around to the back door? Aiden and I will hit the front."

"And if the door is locked?"

"I dare say you've a spell that'll fix that." Aiden touched my back, his hand warm against my damp shirt. "You ready?"

I nodded and moved forward. Aiden matched my pace, his fingers lingering on my spine. Perhaps he sensed just how close to the edge I was.

That niggling feeling that something wasn't quite right within that house grew stronger the closer we got, but Monty was right—other than the shroud, which in itself appeared to be little more than some kind of anomalous stain few would ever see or notice, there was absolutely no indication of any kind of supernatural entity nearby.

But there certainly *had* been, and very recently. The shroud would have dissipated otherwise.

I crossed the neatly mowed lawn, then skirted the rose bed that lined the front patio, my pace only slowing when I approached the shroud. Stepping into it was not unlike stepping into a kind of supernatural fog—it clung unpleasantly to my skin, but there was no threat or harm in it. I continued up the steps and along the patio to the door. It was locked, but that was easily enough remedied.

"Just as well you witches are generally a law-abiding

lot," Aiden said as I pushed the door open. "Because you'd sure as hell make brilliant burglars."

"It's that whole 'what you do to others comes back threefold' rule thing that keeps us on the straight and narrow more than anything else." My gaze swept the dark hall beyond. Shapes loomed, and the warm air was musky and stale.

"Anything?" Aiden asked.

"The soucouyant isn't here." I pulled the small bottle out of my pocket. Though the directional pull was fading, it still seemed to be suggesting there was something here to be found.

I stepped warily into the house. The light coming from the twin spells wrapped around the dying ember provided just enough light to pick out the coat stand to our left and the three doors farther down the hall. The light flickered and briefly pinned the first doorway.

I edged forward, every sense on high alert. Neither my psychic senses nor my witch ones were picking up anything untoward, and yet the certainty that something was here grew.

I stopped in the doorway. The room was darker than the hall thanks to the closed curtains, and the dying embers of the spell weren't doing much to lift the gloom.

"Can I turn on the light?" I asked.

"Not without a glove. I'll do it." He pulled on a glove from the seemingly endless supply of them he had in his pockets, and then flicked on the light.

The abrupt brightness not only had me blinking but also revealed the room's horrifying secret.

Lying on the top of the queen-sized bed that dominated the small room was a body.

Or rather, the complete skin of one.

EIGHT

Aiden stepped passed me and walked across to the bed. "Does this mean our two separate cases just collided? That we have, in fact, only the one soucouyant rather than two?"

I stopped beside him. The skin on the bed looked remarkably intact. In fact, it rather reminded me of a life-sized doll that had simply been deflated. There was nothing hasty or messy about the way this skin had been left lying here. Even her hair—which was cut short and gray—looked immaculate.

"I don't think so," I said. "The other skins we've found were left in untidy piles—this was a deliberate choice. The others weren't."

Aiden frowned. "What makes you think the other skins were abandoned involuntarily?"

I hesitated and waved a hand in frustration. "Gut instinct, nothing more."

Out in the hall, footsteps echoed. "Aiden? Liz? You found anything?"

"You might say that," Aiden replied. "We're in the bedroom to the right of the front door."

I glanced around as Monty stepped into the room. "We might not have found the soucouyant, but I think we've just found her skin."

"Well, I'll be...." Monty stopped beside me. "I know the legends all said that they left their skin to go hunting, but I hadn't believed it actually happened."

"If this *is* the soucouyant's real skin," Aiden asked, "then where did she get the one she was wearing in the club?"

"There is one legend that says soucouyants are capable of taking on the form of a beautiful woman," I said. "But maybe they have to shed their actual skin before they can take a different form."

"So what do we do with this one?" Aiden asked.

"We salt it, and stop her from claiming it again," Monty said. "And then we set a trap for the bitch."

I glanced at Monty. "I'm not entirely sure either of us has the power to restrict let alone kill this particular fire spirit."

"Maybe not, but we have to try."

A smile tugged at my lips. Nothing like having my own words used against me. "What about we call in Ashworth and Eli? They've been chafing at the bit to get in on some action."

Aiden snorted. "I'm beginning to believe the lot of you are crazy."

"That's more than possibly true," Monty said. "Especially when you consider I gave up a very secure, very well-paid—if boring—position to take up this one."

"And I'm betting you don't regret it," I said.

"Hell no." His grin flashed. "Never felt more alive, in fact."

"Certifiable, for sure." Aiden shook his head, his eyes gleaming sapphire bright in the light. "What do we need to do?"

"Liz, can you make the call to Ashworth and Eli? I'll salt her skin, then throw a protection spell around the entire bed, just to be doubly sure."

"And if she returns before you've set everything up?" Aiden said.

"Then we'll probably end up crisped," Monty said cheerfully. "But I doubt it'll happen."

I glanced at him curiously. "Why would you think that when she's already fed tonight? She has no reason to remain away."

"Except that after draining that poor sod from the club, she then proceeded to make him crispy meat while completely destroying his car. That takes a lot of energy, and not even the most powerful spirit has an endless supply of it. I'd bet every cent I have in the bank that she's out there feeding right now."

Aiden scrubbed a hand across his face, the sound like sandpaper in the hush of the house. "I hope to hell you're wrong, because the last thing we need this evening is another goddamn body. There's enough unease stirring through the reservation as it is—we don't need it developing into full-blown panic."

Monty frowned. "Can't the council just put a clamp on the media? They've got the power to do that, from what I understand."

"It's not the media that's the problem," Aiden replied. "It's the gossip brigade. They never miss a morsel—and certainly not when it's as juicy as this."

"Especially when one of them was the neighbor of our first victim," I said.

Monty's gaze went from Aiden to me and back again. "The gossip brigade?"

"A force of nature that generally works for good but has been known to occasionally flirt with the dark side," Aiden said.

Monty's expression was somewhat bemused. "And that totally clarifies everything."

"The brigade is a group of retired ladies who meet a couple of times a week to discuss all matters great and small," I explained. "And if you know what's good for you, you'll never get on their bad side."

"Huh." He swung his bag off his shoulder. "On the off chance the soucouyant does return early, Ranger, it might be best if you and Liz—"

"And let you face this thing alone?" Aiden cut in. "No."

"Aiden, you're about as useless as I am in *this* particular situation." I touched his arm lightly; his muscles jumped in response. "If we remain, we'll not only be targets if the soucouyant appears, but also a distraction, as Monty and co will be forced to protect us rather than hit the soucouyant."

"Well, the co might," Monty commented. "I wouldn't be too sure about me."

I whacked him lightly. He yelped and rubbed his arm, but the pretense of hurt was somewhat diminished by the laughter creasing the corners of his eyes. "How about the two of you just get out of the house so that I can get down to business?"

"Done," Aiden said, and led the way out of the house.

As I followed him, I tugged my phone out of the backpack and called Ashworth.

It rang a couple of times, then a somewhat gruff voice

said, "If you're just ringing for a chat at this hour of the night, I will be extremely pissed off."

I grinned. "According to Eli, that's a standard state of being for you recently."

"That's because he keeps trying to mollycoddle me," Ashworth bit back. "Do I look like the type who enjoys being mollycoddled to you?"

"Not really, but it wouldn't be the first time I've been deceived by appearances."

"A somewhat common problem—at least when it comes to certain witches. What can I do for you, lass?"

"We have a situation—"

"Oh thank God for that," Eli said in the background.

I grinned. "We've tracked down the skin of the soucouyant—"

"Hang on, hang on, back up," Ashworth said. There was now movement in the background, suggesting Eli was getting things ready. "When exactly did the reservation gain one of them? Because they're nasty pieces of shit, let me tell you."

I quickly gave him an update on the situation, and then added, "Monty's in the process of salting its skin and running a full circle around the bed to ensure she can't access said skin, but he's going to need help if we're to have any hope of containing this spirit. It's old, and it's nasty."

Doors slammed and then the sound of a truck rumbling to life came down the phone line. "Well, they're not called evil spirits for nothing. Where are you?"

I gave him the address. He repeated it to Eli, then said, "And why aren't you helping out? With your ability to call on the wild magic, you're probably stronger than the three of us combined."

"Except she's dead on her feet and actually doing something sensible for a change," Aiden said, loudly enough for Ashworth to hear.

I might not have had the phone on speaker, but I didn't need to given the acuteness of his hearing.

The older man chuckled softly. "Ah, the sensibilities of a man in lust will *always* outweigh those of common sense."

"There's nothing sensible in Liz running herself into exhaustion and ending up in hospital," Aiden growled. "We've potentially two entities running amok in the reservation, and no idea if even the combined magic of the three of you will suffice to contain this one let alone the other. Given the toll the wild magic takes, it's far better it's left as a last option, and used only when Liz is back to full strength."

He opened the truck door, helped me into the cabin, then slammed the door shut and stalked around to the driver side.

"Well, that's me told," Ashworth said, clearly amused.

"Yes, but he's right. I copied the spell Eli used to contain the essence of that dark witch on a piece of the soucouyant, but it's really drained me."

"If you want me out of your life, lass, you'd best stop doing things that you damn well shouldn't."

"I never said I wanted you out of my life, just out of my personal business." A smile twitched my lips. "As I've also said, you remind me of my grandfather, and I really miss the grumpy old bastard."

"This would be the dead grandfather?"

"Yes, and if you could avoid the same fate, I'd appreciate it."

He grunted, and it was an oddly pleased sound. "I'll do my best. We should be there in ten minutes."

He hung up. I shoved my phone into my pocket, then leaned back in the seat as Aiden climbed into the truck. But

I didn't close my eyes, as much as I was desperate to sleep. It was very possible the soucouyant might decide to come back before the cavalry arrived and if that did happen, then I needed to be ready to attack.

Though how exactly I'd do that when I felt like crap was another matter entirely.

Thankfully, the soucouyant didn't return, but the flip side of that meant Monty was right—it was out there somewhere, regaining its strength in the arms of another man.

Headlights swept into the street up ahead and raced toward us. "That will undoubtedly be Ashworth and Eli."

"Yes." Aiden glanced at me. "Are you staying here or getting out?"

"Monty can update them. One of us needs to keep a watch for the soucouyant." And the less I had to move, the better right now. It wasn't just the weariness thumping through me, but also the ache from the various scrapes and bruises.

He nodded and got out as the other truck pulled to halt. Aiden spoke to the two men briefly and then led them inside. The nosier section of my soul that didn't want to be left out of any part of action regretted not following them, but the more sensible side was quite content to simply sit there and do nothing.

That side should come out to play more often, Belle commented. *It might result in fewer aches, scrapes, and bruises.*

That's highly unlikely.

Also true. Her amusement echoed down the mental line. *I found an interesting side note in the book on fire spirits.*

And?

It states that those bound by skin will sometimes claim the skins of others if for any reason they lose their own.

I blinked. *Which is what appears to be happening here with the skinning murders.*

Yes. It also states that a soucouyant can often feel its skin being salted, and this will often result in a vengeful counterattack.

Which means Monty and co had better be damn sure they contain and then destroy the soucouyant tonight.

If she did feel her skin being salted, she may not even come near the place. She doesn't actually need to—she can fling fire from some distance, remember.

Unease stirred at the comment. I leaned forward and scanned the surrounding area, but there was no sign of fire in any form, be it spirit or not.

Which didn't mean anything. Not in this situation.

Maybe luck will be with you for a change, Belle said. *Maybe she's simply too far away to have felt her skin being salted.*

I wouldn't like to take a chance on that being the case—especially when she's already shown a propensity to blow things up.

I think that's something that goes with the territory when it comes to fire spirits.

And I think we need to start digging deeper into your gran's books, and see if any of her old spell collections deal with deflection or containment—and not just for fire. I've got a bad feeling we're going to be batting away all sorts of foul energy in the near future.

Aside from the fact Monty must still have access to the catalogue section, isn't it his job to be worrying about counter spells?

I hesitated. *Of course it is, but I've just got this feeling that we'd better have our own spells handy—and that we're going to need them.*

My, your psychic self is chock-full of cheerful news of late, isn't it?

I smiled. *Aren't you glad your bedroom is shielded against the worst of my prophetic tendencies?*

I opened the door and climbed out of the truck. The night air swirled around me; while it held no heat, it *did* hold power. The wild magic was near, but it came from the main wellspring rather than Katie. And there was a *lot* of it.

I walked to the front of the truck. The glittering threads of wild magic fell around me like a scant but powerful cloak. It was almost as if it was trying to protect me.

But from what?

And why, Belle commented. *I can understand it protecting you if it was from the wellspring Katie's soul has infused, but this is the real thing. It has no awareness and it certainly shouldn't interfere or interact with either you or anyone else. Not without any kind of direction.*

I know that, Belle, but there's a whole truckload of things involving the wild magic that shouldn't be happening right now. And *this* was just another thing to add to the ever-growing list.

I rubbed my arms, my fingertips tingling every time I brushed a thread. The night remained dark and, other than the wild magic, there was little indication of anything supernatural.

And yet the uneasiness was sharpening.

It might be wise to warn the men, Belle commented. *If something's coming, they may not have enough time to get out.*

I immediately grabbed my phone and dialed Aiden. I could have called out easily enough, but I didn't want to wake or alarm the neighbors. And I dared not go inside; if the soucouyant or her fire *was* headed this way then I needed to be out here to spot it.

What I'd be able to do if I *did* was another question entirely.

"What's wrong?" Aiden said, without preamble.

"Maybe nothing, but I think the four of you had better get out of the house."

"Is the soucouyant coming?"

"Something is." My gaze was drawn skyward. Other than the extraordinarily bright glimmer of the evening star, there was absolutely nothing untoward to be seen.

"Liz," Monty said in the background, "we've got a network of spells surrounding the place, but they all depend on the bait—us—being inside."

The glimmer of that star was getting stronger. Growing warmer. The cloak of wild magic stirred in agitation and my heart began beating a whole lot faster.

"The bait will be of no use to anyone if it's crisped. Get out," I said. "Get out *now*."

Monty swore, but I could hear Ashworth telling him to shut up and just move.

"Hurry, Aiden," I said, and hung up.

That star was brighter. Closer.

But it wasn't a star. It was a fireball.

It looked big enough to cause an explosion that would take out not only this house but also those on either side. Worse still, it was moving so damn fast that even if we made it to the trucks, we'd very likely get caught in the backwash.

I swore and briefly closed my eyes in desperate anger— at the situation and the fact that no matter what I did or how fast I learned new spells or new ways of interacting with the magic of this place, it wasn't ever enough. But as the anger surged at my own inadequacies, so too did the wild magic. The silvery threads shifted and flowed across my body, winding their way down my arm and forming a ball of thick, pulsing energy.

One power to contain another, I realized.

But it meant me standing in front of the house, holding steady against the heat of that fireball until it was close enough for me to throw the wild magic. I swore again, moved into position, and then looked around as Aiden came out of the house.

He studied me for a heartbeat and then looked up. "What the hell is that?"

"Retribution for salting her skin."

"If that thing hits the house, she'll destroy not only her skin, but everything in the near vicinity."

"Given her skin is now inaccessible to her, I don't think she really cares," I said. "I need you and the others to get beyond the trucks, at least."

"I'm not abandoning—"

Anger surged—anger that was based as much in fear for his safety as it was at his stubbornness. "Damn it, Aiden, stop arguing and just do what I ask for a change. You can't help but you *can* get in the way, and that might be dangerous to us all."

Anger flashed across his expression, and it was every bit as fierce as mine. But all he said was, "What about the neighbors? Should we at least try to evacuate them?"

I hesitated, my gaze darting back to the fireball. It was now close enough to see it was the size of a Swiss ball; close enough to feel as if we were standing under a heating vent.

And yet it was nowhere near close enough to throw the wild magic at.

"You can try, but we've only a few minutes, if that."

He nodded and looked around as Ashworth and Eli came out of the house. "Can you two go right, and get the neighbors out? I'll go left."

Ashworth nodded. As the three of them departed, Monty finally appeared.

"Okay, now I understand the urgency in your voice." He stopped beside me and squinted up at the fast-approaching fireball. "It's kinda large, isn't it?"

"Yes, and you might want to move a safe distance away, because I have no idea what will happen once I unleash the net of wild magic."

"I'm not about to go anywhere," he replied evenly. "I was sent here to observe the wild magic and that's exactly what I intend to do. Especially when you're using it in ways that shouldn't be possible."

"You could end up being crisped."

He shrugged. "So could you."

"I have no choice. You do."

"How about you just shut up and concentrate on that fireball? Because I'm thinking it's getting a little too close for comfort."

My gaze jumped up again. Even though it was still a good distance from the ground, I could now see the twisting, churning mass of flames. The soucouyant had thrown all her anger, all her frustration, and all her energy into its creation.

The wild magic stirred in anticipation. It was almost time to unleash it... and then hope like hell I'd guessed right and that it *would* be able to contain the fireball. Otherwise, we were all in trouble.

My heart was now pounding somewhere in the vicinity of my throat, and sweat dotted my skin. I could hear voices and footsteps coming from the houses on either side, but I didn't dare look around. Every sense I had was now attuned to both the fireball above and the power that curled with ever-increasing velocity around my fingertips.

I briefly clenched my fingers around it. Felt the power of it roll through me. Imagined it forming a net around the fireball, containing it, nullifying it. Felt the pulsing response.

The connection between me and the magic of this place was strengthening, and that was absolutely terrifying.

But it was also something I could worry about later.

Then something within whispered *now*....

I raised my hand and unleashed the wild magic. It flashed skyward, a silvery streak that raced toward the twisting mass of red and gold. As the two drew closer, the net began to unravel. Silvery threads flicked out from the main mass, briefly resembling long fingers. As they spread out even further, the fireball's intensity increased; flames erupted from its surface and flashed toward the net of wild magic. The two clashed, and the silver disappeared into the red.

I briefly closed my eyes.

It hadn't worked.

Goddammit....

But even as the fear hit, the wild magic surged anew. Silver filaments crawled out of the middle of the fireball and quickly wrapped themselves around it. The flames twisted and flared, but the threads were stronger, twining around and around the fire. The heat rolling off the fireball began to ease, but it was close to the treetops now. The sharp scent of eucalyptus stung the air and the leaves were starting to curl and brown—a sure sign the tree was close to ignition point.

Monty raised a hand and began spelling, the soft words lost to the gathering roar of the approaching fireball. I doubted there was a spell strong enough to protect us against the sheer heat of it, but I wasn't about to do anything to stop him. If the wild magic failed, then a small chance was better than nothing.

The silver threads of wild magic now covered most of the fireball, but flames still shot out from various bits of the outer rim. The old gum tree was now smoldering.

It wasn't working, and we were too damn close now to run....

Energy surged again, and the fireball abruptly halted. For several seconds, it hovered just above the tree, a twisting, churning mass of red and silver.

Then, with a huge *whoomp*, it exploded.

Monty swore, cast his spell into the air, and then pushed me sideways and down, onto the ground. The tree exploded into flame and spots of silver and red scattered like ashes all around the lawn. Some caught, some didn't, but the heat and smoke from the burning tree swirled around us, briefly cutting sight down to several feet and giving little indication of what else might be on fire.

For several minutes I didn't dare move. I just hunkered down on the ground, listening to the roar of flame and waiting for the heated hammer to fall.

It didn't.

"Fuck, that was close." Monty pushed up onto his knees and looked around. "But it looks as if your net of wild magic worked. For the most part, anyway."

I sat back on my heels, wincing a little as pain slithered down my cut thigh. Not only was the old gum tree ablaze, but there were also minor spot fires all over the lawn, and both the wooden window frames and the door of the soucouyant's house showed signs of blast marks. But it could have been a whole lot worse. The net of wild magic had somehow succeeded in both containing *and* erasing most of the fireball.

"What was that spell you cast before the explosion?" I asked. "Because you seriously need to teach it to me."

He raised an eyebrow. "Sure, but why would you think you'd need it?"

"Do you really think that'll be it for retaliation?" I said. "From the little I saw of soucouyant, she's not going to take kindly to either of us getting the better of her."

"Probably not, but she's going to find it hard to sneak up on us unseen given she now has no skin." He rose and offered me a hand.

I accepted it gratefully. The world briefly spun and then settled—a sure sign I really was pushing my limits now.

"The skin on the bed wasn't the skin she was wearing when she went after tonight's victim," I said.

"Yes, but if she was able to maintain those other forms beyond a night, she wouldn't be reclaiming her 'original' skin every morning," he said. "Most spirits need to escape the daylight. The soucouyant does that by using her human skin—without it, she won't be able to hide in plain sight."

"Which gels with something Belle discovered tonight." I gave him the information, then added, "Is it possible we're dealing with two soucouyants rather than two different types of fire spirits?"

"Could be, although it's odd for them to be hunting in the same area. They're usually loners."

I hesitated. "I have no idea if fire spirits can reproduce, but is it possible there's some kind of kinship between them?"

He frowned. "There's certainly documents that state some demons are capable of reproduction, but I've never read anything that suggests spirits are."

"But they have to come from somewhere, don't they? Granted, there are some witches whose destiny it is to move into the spirit realm, but entities such as fire spirits have *always* existed alongside humanity."

"And I guess we witches have tended to hunt them down rather than study them, so we really haven't got much more than old wives' tales to go on."

Which made Belle's books even more valuable. "Surely the archive in Canberra has more than that? They've been collecting information, both here and overseas, for eons."

"You'd think so, but I'm coming up with squat so far." He thrust a hand through his hair, shaking loose random bits of inert wild magic and leaf matter. "Either way, we'd both better sleep with half an eye open."

I couldn't help smiling. "You can sleep with half an eye open; I'll be layering in additional protections in the spell network that protects the café."

"Which will only protect you from the spirit, *not* her arcane fire."

"And that's exactly why I want you to show me the shielding spell you used—it *did* protect us, and it's possible I might be able to weave it into the current layers."

"Hasn't anyone told you it's dangerous to adjust spells in such an ad hoc manner?"

"Yes." I glanced around at the sound of footsteps and saw Aiden approaching.

"You okay, Liz?" he said, stopping beside me.

"Yes, but it's mainly thanks to Monty spelling a last-minute fire ward." I leaned into Aiden's warm body; his arm immediately went around me, preventing retreat. Not that I actually wanted to go anywhere. His tender but protective touch made me feel safe. Loved, even.

Which I wasn't, of course, and never would be, but it

was nevertheless nice to believe otherwise, even if for a moment.

"I'm also okay, thanks for asking," Monty said, clearly amused.

"Good, because the last thing this reservation needs is to lose another witch," Aiden said. "Is this it from the soucouyant? Or will there be more attacks?"

"This is probably it for tonight, but she may well resume hostilities tomorrow night."

"Which gives us tomorrow to find her. Any ideas?"

Monty grimaced. "It's possible I can use a piece of her skin to track her in much the same manner as Lizzie used the ember, but I'll need Eli's guidance. I've studied the spell's basics, but never actually performed it."

"More than happy to help out with that," Eli said, as he and Ashworth strode up.

"And her skin?" I asked. "Even if it's salted, what's the chance of her trying to get it back? Or even washing the salt from it and reusing?"

"That, I don't know," Monty said. "The records I've read only go as far as saying salting prevents them from reclaiming their skin. It doesn't mention anything about the possibility of them cleaning it."

"What about keeping it in brine?" Ashworth said. "The fact salting her skin makes it physically impossible for her to move back into her flesh suggests it's her Achilles' heel, so keeping her skin in a brine mixture should make it impossible for her to reach into the jar and grab it."

"What's to stop her grabbing the jar and smashing it open?" Aiden asked.

"Spells that will contain a lovely little sting in their tail, Ranger." Ashworth's smile was wide. "And you'd better believe I have one or two of those up my sleeve."

Monty raised his eyebrows. "Care to elaborate?"

Ashworth slapped him on the back hard enough to send him staggering forward a step before he regained his balance. "One thing at a time, lad. One thing at a time."

The two of them moved into the house. Eli followed, but not before muttering a somewhat bemused, "And there goes the rest of our nice, quiet evening."

"And there goes ours," Aiden said softly. "I'll have to stay here and supervise."

He didn't actually have to, as there *were* other rangers within the reservation. But I withheld the rather snarky comment—the fact of the matter was, I had to accept his job was his life, and that would never change, whether he was with me or the love of his life.

Something within me twisted at that, and I wasn't entirely sure if it was the green-eyed demon or the prophetic part of me warning of what would be.

I rose on my toes and kissed him, long and slow. It was a promise of what might have been, and what might yet be. But not tonight. Maybe not even tomorrow night, depending on how all the aches and pains went.

Rather reluctantly, I pulled back out of his arms. "I'd better go."

"Do you want me to drive you home?"

"I'm frustrated enough. I don't need to be in the close quarters of a truck with you right now." I hesitated, a smile twitching my lips as my gaze skimmed downward. "And from the look of things, neither do you."

He chuckled softly and lightly brushed his fingers down my cheek. "Here's hoping that we catch a break with these cases and manage some time together. Otherwise, I might just explode."

I grinned. "You managed over a year flying solo, Ranger. I'm thinking a day or two extra won't do you any harm."

"Then you would be wrong." He glanced around at the sound of sirens. "That'll be the fire department and Mac. I'd better let you go."

I kissed him again—this time briefly—and then called for a cab. It only took a few minutes to get home, and I arrived to find the promised bath waiting for me. The highly scented, herb-enriched water did wonders for both my energy and pain levels, and the solid ten hours sleep that followed didn't hurt, either.

Over breakfast the next morning, I said, "Did you manage to uncover anything else about fire spirits last night?"

Belle shook her head. "It seems the spell book we need is in storage."

"Which is always the damn way," I said. "I wish we had room for them all here."

"It's probably better that we haven't." Belle picked up her coffee and leaned back in her chair. "The café has already been hit once. We were lucky it didn't cause all that much damage to our personal effects, but next time that may not be the case."

"True." I tore off a bit of toast and mopped up the left-over egg. "You know, it might be time to make preparations against that possibility."

"As in, make an e-copy of each book?" Belle grimaced. "That'll take a damn while."

"Yes, but it's better than losing any of her information." It also guarded us against the possibility of the high council discovering the existence of the library and confiscating all the books.

"It'd only be a safeguard if they're stored on a drive

that's *not*, in any way, connected to the net. But having a backup *is* a good idea." Belle briefly pursed her lips. Though her expression was thoughtful, there was an odd glint of anticipation in her eyes. "One of our regulars is an IT guy. I might talk to him and see if he can help us out."

I raised my eyebrows. "Who?"

"Kash Kennedy."

Amusement twitched my lips. "Now there's a name that must have given him hell as a kid."

"Apparently so." Her silver eyes twinkled. "And it's also probably the reason he looks so damn fit now."

"Oh, hello," I said, grinning. "Do I sense the possibility of a romance brewing?"

"Possibly." She shrugged. "We actually met at the gym —he's a part-time trainer there. He's asked me out a couple of times, but I'm playing it cool."

"Why?" I rose and reached across the table to touch her forehead. "I can't feel a temperature or anything, so you're not sick."

She laughed and knocked my hand away. "I really do like him, but I just don't want to be jumping into anything feet first. This time around, I want to be friends first, bedmates later."

Suggesting that despite her protestations, her split with Zak had affected her more than she'd let on. "I still can't remember seeing him in the café."

"Think six-five, dark hair, neat beard, and the most amazing green eyes you've ever seen."

I clicked my fingers. "The French-sounding guy with the sexy voice."

"The very one." She grinned. "I think that man could make me come just by reading the newspaper out loud."

"Experience talking there, I take it?"

She grinned again but didn't elaborate. "I'll probably see him at the gym again tomorrow night, so I'll ask him then."

"Good." I pushed away my plate and picked up my coffee. "Of course, the other major problem is the two damn spirits."

"Yes." Belle wrinkled her nose. "There must be some way to stop them outside ensnaring and banishing them with a spell."

"If there is, there's apparently no damn record of it."

"That anyone has uncovered thus far. Doesn't mean it's not there, just that it's kept in some obscure manual or note."

"Very obscure." I drank some coffee and shuddered a little at the taste. I'd forgotten to put sugar in it. "You know, Ashworth suggested we store the soucouyant's skin in brine to counter any attempt by her to regain it, which makes me wonder if it would also be a good weapon against her."

"Possibly," Belle said. "Salt's been used to both purify and sanctify places—and ward off evil—for eons."

"And if we combine it with holy water, we might just have a workable weapon."

"One that will at least weaken them even if it doesn't kill them." She clicked her coffee cup against mine. "Good thinking there, Sherlock."

"I think Sherlock would be highly offended by your gifting his name to an investigator as amateurish and haphazard as me." I stirred sugar into my coffee and took another sip. "We'll need a quick and easy means of applying the brine—"

"Water pistols," Belle said. "Easy to get and easy to use."

"I'm not sure a water pistol will hold enough water to damage a fire spirit."

"A Super Soaker, then." She paused. "Of course, there's also the problem of acquiring enough holy water to fill it."

"It might be worth talking to the local priest—if we explain the situation, he might be willing to bless a large amount."

"Worth a shot." She glanced at her watch and then downed the rest of her coffee. "If I go out early, I can be back before the brigade gets here."

"You might as well go talk to the priest while you're out. Penny and I will be able to handle things even if there is a rush." Belle had certainly held the fort down often enough —time for me to carry some of the load for a change.

"Great." She bounced up. "I'll go get ready."

I nodded and finished my coffee, then cleared the plates and got everything ready for the day's trade.

We were busy from the get-go, but Belle was back by the time the brigade came in. Mrs. Potts tried a number of times to question me not only about the murder of her neighbor but how my relationship with Aiden was going. I didn't give her much on either, but couldn't get angry at her nosiness. Not when she actually had my best interests at heart—at least when it came to my relationship with the ranger.

Aiden came in just as we'd finished cleaning up for the day. He tugged me into his arms and kissed me with all the hunger and desire a woman could want, then pulled back and licked his lips. "You've been eating brownie."

"I was just taste-testing the latest batch."

"Meaning I've timed my arrival just right?"

"It would appear so." Belle came out of the kitchen carrying a plate of brownie slices. "Would you like a coffee to go with it?"

"Please."

He walked over to our usual table and slid out a chair. I followed him across and snared the biggest piece of brownie before he could. "How goes the soucouyant hunt?"

He grimaced. "Not well."

"Couldn't Monty replicate the tracking spell?"

"He did, but it appears that by salting the soucouyant's skin, we severed her connection with it."

"Ah. Bugger." I sat down beside him, my thigh lightly brushing his. "Has he come up with anything else?"

"As yet, no. But he was talking to some professor up in Canberra when I left, so there's still hope we might yet get some definitive information on these things."

I bit into the brownie, well aware that he was watching me. Watching and enjoying. I chewed the delicious gooey slice for several seconds, then said, "Have you finished for the day?"

"No, unfortunately." There was a decided huskiness to his voice, and my hormones danced in delight. "I'm actually here for business rather than pleasure."

"That's a shame."

"Indeed." He glanced up as Belle walked over, three coffee mugs in hand. "Thanks for that."

She nodded and sat down opposite us. "What about the skinning murders? Any progress on that?"

"No, but they're why I'm here. I wanted to follow up on Liz's premonition about the Greenhill skinning." He picked up a piece of brownie and demolished it in short order.

Belle glanced at me. "You didn't tell me about that one."

I grimaced. "Because it wasn't a premonition, more a feeling that something about the timing of that particular murder was off."

"Huh." She snared a slice as Aiden went in for a second one. "In what way?"

"The fact that it was done during the day rather than night or the near morning, as all the others."

"Is it possible the farmer walked in on her?"

"That's what I'm thinking—and why I'd like you to come along," I said. "If his death wasn't destined, we might be able to question his ghost."

"He might not be able to tell us anything—it really just depends on how he died."

I nodded. "Still worth a shot."

"Yes." She licked the chocolate off her fingers then picked up her coffee and rose. "I'll go grab our gear."

As she left, Aiden said, "So, tonight?"

I raised an eyebrow, a smile teasing my lips. "What about it?"

"We need to finish our *Lord of the Rings* marathon."

"It's hardly a marathon when there's a couple of days between the two," I said. "And given the length of that movie, I find myself unable to commit to such a venture when I have to work the next morning."

"What about dinner then? Perhaps a little dancing afterward?"

My smile grew. "Only if dancing is a euphemism for hot monkey sex."

He laughed. The warm sound sent a shiver of delight down my spine. "I actually did mean dancing but more than happy to do the hot monkey sex thing as well."

I raised an eyebrow. "Considering that whole exploding possibility you were mentioning earlier, why on earth would you want to go out dancing? I didn't figure you'd be the type to enjoy a venue like Émigré."

"I'm not—I'm more your ballroom type of guy. Used to do a lot of it when I was younger."

With the wolf who'd broken his heart, if the

shadow that briefly crossed his eyes was anything to go by. "I didn't know ballroom dancing was big around these parts—or that werewolves were even into that sort of thing. It's rather old-fashioned and straitlaced, isn't it?"

"You've obviously never indulged in ballroom dancing," he said. "It can be very erotic done right."

"I think it's fairly safe to say that I've never done it right, then."

"I think it's safe to say that she has three left feet and has seriously injured the toes of anyone who has tried to teach her," Belle said, as she came out of the reading room. "And I'm speaking from experience there."

"Then I'll just have to risk bruised and battered feet," Aiden replied. "Because we can't sit around all weekend just watching movies and having hot monkey sex."

"We can't?" I let my expression fall. "Just so you know, this is my disappointed face."

He laughed, threw an arm around my shoulder, and hugged me. "It *is* possible to do all three things—or four, if we include feeding ourselves at some point."

"Good idea to add the food," Belle commented. "She gets very grumpy if she's not appropriately fed."

"'Appropriately' meaning chocolate?"

I gently patted his knee. "Keep thinking like that, and we won't ever have any problems."

Aiden snorted. "Considering the flashes of temper I've seen of late, I'm doubting that."

"You just need to stop going all macho on me." I drained my coffee then rose. "I do know what I'm doing."

Most of the time, anyway, Belle all but drawled.

I grinned and didn't deny it. Aiden picked up another piece of brownie and then stood. "In case you've forgotten,

I'm a werewolf. Macho protectiveness comes with the territory."

"Then expect a few more of those temper flashes, Ranger," Belle said, amusement evident. "Where have you parked?"

"Out the front, just down the road." He spun on his heel and led the way out of the café.

It took us just over an hour to get to Greenhill. Aiden slowed as he approached the small intersection that was basically the entirety of the town, and turned left after the pub. We drove for about a mile and then turned into a graveled, tree-lined driveway that swept up a long hill. The house—a white weatherboard with a tin roof that had seen better days—sat three-quarters of the way up the hill, but we didn't stop, driving on through a couple of farm gates until we came to a massive old barn. One half of it was open on three sides, and stacked to the brim with hay. The other half was fully enclosed.

Aiden stopped near the hay and climbed out. "We found the body in the shed."

"I couldn't imagine a soucouyant hiding out with the hay." My voice was dry. "To say that would not end well would be an understatement."

"It would have been better the hay than the man." Aiden led us around to the other side of the barn. "It was his poor wife who discovered him."

"Is she okay?" I asked.

He half shrugged. "Unknown. She had a heart attack not long after she called us in, and is currently in a coma. The docs don't know when or if she'll recover."

I didn't say anything, because there was really no point. I didn't know the family, but even if I did, I knew from experience that all the "sorries" in the world didn't make a blind bit of difference.

We turned the barn's corner and walked up to the old wooden doors that dominated the center of this section. Aiden pushed one of them open, then ducked under the police tape and disappeared inside. We followed.

Almost instantly, energy hit us.

And while some of it was simply the lingering heat of the soucouyant's presence, the majority wasn't.

There was a ghost here.

And it was in an almighty snit.

NINE

Belle sucked in a deep breath. "Well, he's not happy, is he?"

Aiden glanced around sharply. "Baker's ghost is here?"

"Hell yeah." Belle glanced at me. "A protection circle is called for, I think. I can't feel any magic here, but his anger is fierce and he might well attack."

She unzipped the backpack and handed me the spell stones. I walked past Aiden until I found a nice open area between the various farm machines and other bits of equipment, and then quickly set up a protection circle. Baker's fury continued to burn around us, and it was bad enough that sweat was now rolling down my spine.

"Why is he so angry at us?" I said. "We didn't kill him."

"I'm not sure he realizes he's dead." Belle stepped into the circle and sat down opposite me. "There have been some instances where there's a mental disconnect between the ghost and the body they see lying on the ground. And given that the body here would have been skinless, confusion is not unexpected. Especially if he also saw his body— or a replica of it—walk out the door."

I grunted and glanced across at Aiden. "I take it you want to record the session?"

He nodded. "His full name is John Baker, by the way."

As Aiden dug his phone out of his pocket, I took a deep breath to center my energy and then raised a protection circle, lightly layering the threads of the spell onto each stone, until what surrounded us was a glowing weave of red, gold, and silver.

The silver was wild magic. It wasn't anywhere near this barn and yet here it was. Uneasiness stirred yet again, but I thrust it aside, tied off the last line of the spell, and then activated it.

As the threads glowed brightly, I raised my gaze to Belle. "We're protected against fits of anger and thrown objects." Silently, I added, so that our ghost didn't hear and get ideas, *But not really heavy missiles.*

He's only a new ghost, so he shouldn't have the power to throw anything truly heavy. Most can't even interact with cutlery at this stage.

She wriggled closer. Once our knees were touching, she took a deep breath to clear her thoughts and gather her energy, and then closed her eyes and placed her fingers in mine. While some spirit talkers used personal items to make contact, or objects such an Ouija board or even a spirit pendulum, Belle had no need. According to my mom—in what had been a rather rare moment of kindness—Belle was one the strongest spirit talkers currently alive.

With our hands lightly touching, I felt the moment she silently summoned John Baker. His anger instantly intensified, but the shimmering walls of my protection spell kept most of it out.

What has happened to me? he all but shouted. *Why can't I leave this place? Where is Elsie? Is she okay?*

I'm afraid you were murdered, John—

I repeated both their comments for Aiden's sake, but kept my attention on Belle.

No, he cut in. *I can't be. I don't feel dead.*

Whether or not you feel it, you are, Belle said gently. *Your spirit lingers here not only because you were killed before your time, but also because your anger and sense of unfinished business hold you here.*

I'm not dead, he replied stubbornly. *I'm not.*

Belle didn't bother arguing. *You need to tell me what happened here yesterday.*

Yesterday? There was puzzlement in his voice. *Nothing happened. It was just a normal day.*

A statement that suggested he was blocking the memory —and *that* really wasn't surprising given how traumatic his death must have been.

If nothing happened, then why were you so concerned about Elsie? Belle asked.

His anger ebbed as concerned flowed. *She came into the barn and screamed. I don't know why, but she called emergency services and then fell down. I couldn't wake her. I couldn't help her.* He paused. *Is she all right?*

Yes. She's in hospital, but she's receiving good care.

I need to see her. Why can't I see her? Why can't I leave this place?

You can't leave because of what happened to you, Belle said. *I can help you move on, but I can't get you past the walls of this place and to the hospital. No one can now, John.*

His anger surged again; the threads of my magic burned brighter, countering and muting the emotional wave.

That is unacceptable, he growled.

And with that, his spirit moved around my protection circle and raced toward the barn's doors. He hit them, and bounced back. The interior of this barn was his prison. He couldn't move beyond the barn's walls or doors—not without Belle's help, and only then to whatever new life fate had decreed his soul be reborn into.

Damn it, let me out. I need to see her.

You can't help her, Belle said. *Not now. But you can stop what has happened to you from happening to others.*

I don't want to help, he growled. *I want to see Elsie.*

The force of Belle's magic crept into the connection. She was now compelling him—forcing him to remember what he obviously had no desire to even acknowledge. It was something very few spirit talkers could do.

Tell me what happened yesterday, John.

No. It was sullenly said.

Her pressure increased. *What brought you into this barn yesterday, John?*

I needed a tractor part. The damn thing was playing up again.

And then what happened.

Fire. He hesitated. *I saw fire.*

Where?

It was sitting in the corner, all curled up like a ball.

What did you do?

What do you think I did? I grabbed a hose and tried to put it out.

Then what happened?

His energy twisted, turned. Fighting the memories. *I don't know.*

Yes, you do, Belle said. *I need you to tell me.*

Damn it, no!

Yes. Belle's magic surged a third time. *Tell me.*

When the water hit it, John said, *the thing unfurled and damn if it didn't look like a woman. I kept spraying it with water, but it didn't seem to make any difference. She came at me and then... and then....* He stopped, a catch in his mental tones.

And afterward? Belle said gently. *What happened after her flames kissed you?*

I was standing in the same spot, but there was this red thing at my feet. He hesitated, the crack in his voice increasing. *And then I saw myself, walking out the door. But that can't be possible. How can I still be here and yet have walked out of the barn?*

"The soucouyant is wearing his skin?" came Aiden's abrupt comment.

I glanced at him and nodded. "My phone is in the backpack if you want to put out an APB. But warn your people not to go near him if they spot him."

He nodded, propped his phone on the wheel arch of the nearest tractor to keep recording, and then grabbed my phone out of the pack and started making the call.

My attention returned to Belle. Her weariness was beginning to slither down the connection between us. Angry or confrontational ghosts always took far more out of her than the peaceful ones.

The being you saw walking out of here wasn't you. It was a spirit wearing your image.

Why would it want to do that? he asked.

Because it's evil. Because it likes to kill and steal.

He was silent for a moment. *And that red thing at my feet? That was me, wasn't it? My body?*

I'm afraid so.

He didn't immediately say anything. He didn't even get angry. He just hovered near the door, emitting an odd sort of sadness.

So I really am dead? And stuck here?

You are dead, Belle said gently. *But you're not stuck here. I can help you move on, if that's what you wish.*

What's the other option? Remaining stuck in this place, unable to see or communicate with Elsie?

I'm afraid so.

He sighed. It was an unhappy sound. *Then I guess I have no choice.*

So you do wish to move on? She needed formal acknowledgment before she could help him.

Yes, I do.

Then I bid you health, happiness, and good fortune in your next life, John. And with that, she began the spell that would guide his soul onwards.

As his energy shimmered and began to fade, she finished the spell, then took a deep breath and opened her eyes. Her tiredness washed through me, and I quickly pushed a little bit of my strength through to her. She squeezed my hands and released them.

"Well, that went better than I'd initially expected."

"Yes." I swiftly pulled the protection circle down and then pushed upright and gathered my spell stones. "I'm surprised it took his skin, though, given up until now, her victims have been women."

She scrubbed a hand across her eyes, then pushed upright. I grabbed her arm, steadying her as she wobbled a little. "Maybe she had no other choice once he'd found her. Maybe she needed his skin to get out."

"Possibly," I said. "Monty did say yesterday that soucouyants use their 'human' skins as a barrier against the sun."

She nodded. "That makes sense—they're spirits rather than human, so their skins would need to be genetically different to ours."

"It also means the ones she's stealing simply aren't up to the task of containing her heat for more than a few hours," I said. "And *that* would explain the puddled piles of skin we're finding."

Aiden frowned. "If that were true, wouldn't the skins simply burn up?"

"Maybe she ditches them before it gets to that point." I shrugged. "After all, it'd be hard to get close enough to her next victim if the skin she's wearing is falling off around her. People tend to react adversely to that sort of thing."

He grunted. "If the soucouyant *has* claimed Baker's skin, how far is she likely to be able to travel, given she's had to move in daylight?"

I hesitated. "It's only a guess, but if she's stealing skins at night to get her through the day when she's in hiding, then it's likely she wouldn't be able to move far without being affected by both the external *and* internal heat." I studied him for a minute. "Do you think she might still be on the farm somewhere?"

"I doubt she'd risk staying in the immediate area, but the Pykes Creek Reservoir lies behind Baker's property. If the photos I saw in his house are anything to go by, he had a hut set up on the boundary so he and his mates could do some fishing."

"How would the soucouyant know about it, though?" Belle asked.

"Maybe when she steals their skin, she also steals some information about them," I said. "There's no other way she could have known where Mrs. Dale lived."

Unless, of course, she had access to her wallet. She certainly had access to her keys.

"True. But if she *is* there, we're going to need help, as

neither of us know a spell strong enough to contain a fire spirit."

"I'll get Tala to pick up Monty and bring him out here." Aiden glanced at his watch. "It'll be close to six thirty before they get here though—will that be pushing it, time wise?"

"It doesn't get dark until nearly eight, and I doubt she'd move before then," I said. "Not after her efforts here today."

"It might be worth going back down to the farmhouse and making up a brine mixture," Belle said. "Holy water might amplify the effect, but ordinary water should still work. It's just a shame I didn't think to bring the Super Soakers."

"Brine?" Aiden opened the barn door and ushered us both out.

"We figured if brine could stop the soucouyant from taking back her skin, then it's possible that it could also be used as a weapon against her."

"I think there were a couple of backpack pressure sprayers in one of the sheds near the house," he said. "They'd be more effective than a couple of Super Soakers."

"Possibly." I climbed into the truck and slid across the seat to allow Belle room. "We can make up the solution while we're waiting for Monty."

He turned the truck around and then made the call to Tala. Once back at the main farmhouse, he unlocked the back door and then went searching for the pressure sprays while we went inside.

Like most of these old places, the laundry led straight into the kitchen. This one was a large kitchen diner, with a pot rack hanging from the ceiling and cabinetry that looked handmade. There was also a large walk-in pantry. I headed in and discovered Mrs. Baker liked buying things in bulk, even when it came to simple things like salt. I gathered a couple of bags then retreated.

"I just googled brine," Belle said. "Apparently solutions can be anything from 3 percent to twenty-six."

"I'm thinking the stronger end of that scale would be better." I dumped the bags on the counter then spun around to get a couple more.

Aiden came in with two pressure sprays. Once we'd filled them with water, we poured in the salt and stirred it up.

"Well, that'll either stop her or piss her off," Belle said.

"Let's hope for the former rather than the latter," Aiden said evenly. "We've already crossed swords with one pissed off soucouyant. I'd really prefer to avoid a second encounter."

"I'm thinking the chances of that happening are on the wrong side of zero," I said.

"And on that cheery thought, lets head outside and wait for Tala and Monty."

We filled in time raiding Aiden's stash of chocolate and chatting about everything *other* than the case. None of us, it seemed, wanted to dwell on what might happen if we found the soucouyant in the fishing hut.

Tala and Monty arrived fifteen minutes earlier than Aiden's estimate, suggesting Tala had pushed the SUV's limits to get here quickly.

Aiden wound down his window and explained what was going on, then turned his truck around and led the way. We drove through a number of paddocks, our appearance spooking various herds of cattle and sheep. As Belle climbed out to open and then close yet another gate, I said, "How close are we to the reservoir now?"

"I smelled water when Belle opened the door, so we can't be far." He motioned toward the top of the paddock's long hill. "I'd say that building might be the one we're looking for."

I leaned forward and studied the building for several seconds. "It's certainly too small to be any sort of shelter for the cattle, but I'm not getting anything in the way of psychic twinges."

"Maybe we're too far away."

I glanced at him. "Not when it comes to evil. I've sensed its presence from miles away, remember."

"I'd rather not." He hesitated. "If the soucouyant *is* there, how close do we dare get?"

"Well, she didn't actually react to Baker's presence until he sprayed her with water, so there's a fair chance she won't notice ours until it's too late."

"And if she does?"

"Then we're in deep shit."

"Always nice to know."

Once Belle had climbed back into the truck, he continued on, taking the direct route up the hill. There was little point in doing anything else—if the soucouyant was going to sense us, she'd do so whether or not we came in straight or from a more roundabout direction.

We pulled up just shy of the building. It was indeed a hut, constructed out of a mix of tin and old timber. There was a window on the side closest to us but nothing that immediately indicated the presence of the soucouyant.

"Sensing anything?" Aiden asked.

"Nope."

"It's possible her fire is so diminished by her efforts that we won't," Belle said.

"But if that was the case, wouldn't she have fed last

night?" I glanced at Aiden. "Did you get any reports of missing persons or murders overnight?"

"No additional ones, but that doesn't mean they're not out there," he said. "Is it safe to get out?"

"Belle and I will. You'd better stay in the truck."

He snorted. "As if the truck will in any way provide a point of safety if that thing attacks. Besides, someone needs to be ready to use the pressure sprays while you three are doing your witch stuff."

A point I'd forgotten. The three of us climbed out of and moved to the front of the truck. Tala and Monty soon joined us. "The place looks empty," Tala said. "Are you sure that thing is inside?"

"It looks empty, but I assure you, it's not," Monty said.

I glanced at him sharply. "You can sense the soucouyant?"

"It's little more than a tremble of evil on the air, but yes, she's definitely in there."

"Wonder why I can't sense it?"

He raised an eyebrow, his amusement creasing the corners of his bright eyes. "You're an underpowered witch. I'm not."

I grinned. "How do you want to play this?"

He hesitated. "That depends."

"On what?"

"On whether you have your spell stones here, on just how strong this thing is, and whether or not our containment shields will actually be able to contain her."

"Shields?" I said, even as Belle said, "We do. I'll go grab them."

Monty glanced at her and nodded, but the amusement had fled his expression by the time his gaze returned to me.

"Yes. I'll run the main shield around the hut, and you and Belle run a secondary line of defense around that."

"But if she breaks past your shield, ours certainly won't—"

"Except yours will have the wild magic woven through it, and *that* is more powerful than anything I could conjure up."

"I wouldn't rely on its help, Monty." My voice was sharp. "It's not something I can control, and it's hit and miss as to whether it'll assist or not."

"You may not control it, but it's evident in every spell I've seen you perform—"

"Which hasn't been many—"

"*That* is beside the point. We both know it'll show up here, even if you don't want to admit it."

"People," Aiden said. "Argue about that sort of stuff later. Time is a wasting, and we need to contain this thing before it wakes up and either runs or attacks."

Monty returned his gaze to the building. "It'd probably be best if you and Tala station yourselves on the shorter sides of the building—that way, you'll be able to see more of it, and the pressure sprays can cover a greater area. I'll run the first spell line about five feet away from the building, and you two can run the second a couple of feet away from that."

Belle returned from the truck and handed me my spell stones. "It might be worth trying another weave spell. If it can counter the magic of a heretic witch for a few vital minutes, it can surely do the same with a fire spirit."

"Now there's a story I wouldn't mind hearing over a beer once this mess is sorted." Monty's gaze swept the two of us. "Ready, ladies?"

I took a deep breath and released it slowly. "As we'll ever be."

I tipped my stones into my hand and then walked in the opposite direction to Belle, stomping down the grass before I placed each stone down. While they were white quartz, between the long, dry grass and the sandy ground, it might be hard to find them again. I passed Belle out the front of the building, and began interweaving my stones around hers, placing one on the outside of her stone, the next on the inside, and so on.

Once that was done, we joined Monty at the front of the old building. "I suspect the next bit will be the most dangerous," he said. "If she wakes while we're raising the containment circles, there will be merry hell to pay."

"Not to mention crispy witches," Belle said.

"Something I'd rather avoid if we can," he said. "I think it's best we perform the spells at the same time. We run the risk of our magic waking her anyway, so we might as well do it in one hit. Just remember to weave an exception into your spell so that I can get past it once my spell is active."

We nodded and, as he moved through the ring of our stones, we sat down on the ground. I daresay we could have remained standing—as Monty no doubt would—but aside from the basics taught in high school, neither Belle nor I had much in the way of proper spellcraft training. We'd learned to do things our own way and for larger spells, such as this containment one, sitting was better. Especially given the pull such spells tended to have on our strength—the simple fact was, there wasn't as far to fall if you were sitting.

Once our knees were touching and we'd both taken a deep breath, I said softly, "Right, let's do this."

We psychically opened ourselves up to one another. Our energy and our auras pulsed and merged at the point where we touched and I both heard and felt her sharp intake of breath.

The wild magic really has become a part of your being now. That's rather worrying given how fast it appears to have happened.

It's also something we can worry about later—

Later may be too late.

If the soucouyant crisps us, then how much wild magic runs through my soul won't really matter. Let's take care of this bitch first.

I raised the containment spell, weaving the spell threads across each of the stones, making them as strong as I possibly could and ensuring there were no exit exceptions except for Monty. Belle's magic rose around me, a familiar touch of energy almost as strong as my own. Both her magic and the ever-present wild magic wove through mine, until a netlike structure had been formed over the hut. It was a tapestry of power that outshone Monty's, and was possibly even stronger than the spell we'd created to contain the heretic's magic.

Hopefully it would be enough.

Monty glanced across at us and raised an eyebrow. We nodded and, as one, the three of us tied off our spells and then activated them.

The soucouyant reacted. Violently.

Fire exploded to life in the cabin, and a rush of heat and flame smashed through windows and burst through the door.

Monty swore and bolted for safety—the flames chased him but were brought up short by the shimmer of his containment spell. They rose, following the line of his magic, searching for weakness and an exit point. Our net shimmered as he stepped through.

"Well, that was fucking close." He hastily patted out a few smoldering sections of shirt. "Now we've just got to tighten our magic until we have her in a manageable sphere."

I glanced at him sharply. "Um, wasn't the whole point of this exercise to contain and then destroy the bitch?"

"I don't believe I said destroy—not recently, anyway," he said.

"Monty, a soucouyant is too damn dangerous to be playing games with."

"Yes, I know, but I've had some new information that changes things."

The storm inside the two containment lines grew fiercer and the old hut disappeared in a roar of smoke and ash. I raised a hand to protect my face against a wave of the heat the containment spells couldn't quite hold. "What sort of information?"

"Apparently, soucouyant *can* reproduce. It only happens when the spirit becomes old, and it's more a splintering of its being than actual reproduction."

I blinked. "Meaning we're not dealing with separate entities but two parts of a whole?"

"Well, they *are* separate, but they remain connected. It's probably why we've two in the reservation—after the younger version lost her skin, it rejoined forces with the older part of itself as a means of protection."

"And yet the older part isn't exactly doing much to protect the younger," Belle said. "It's not like they're even sharing daytime quarters."

"I know, and I have no idea why that might be so," he said. "But the professor and I believe that, given the connection, we could use this soucouyant to track the other."

I frowned. "That's still going to be damn dangerous. If

there *is* a connection, the other one will know exactly what you're doing the minute you try it."

In fact, I was damn surprised she hadn't already sent a fireball our way, fading daylight or not.

Maybe she used too much of her strength to attack you last night, Belle said. *She might have to feed before she can counterattack.*

I wanted to hope that was the case, but it would mean someone else dying, and I really didn't want that.

"Whatever you're going to do, you'd better do it fast," Aiden said. "That thing is getting more and more pissed off, and the grass is beginning to smolder. If it erupts into flame, this entire area could go up."

I glanced around sharply; multiple patches of long brown grass were beginning to curl and darken under the continuing waves of heat. It really wouldn't take much more for it to catch.

But the grass wasn't the only thing in danger of catching fire. Monty's containment spell was now being attacked by the full force the soucouyant, and the threads of his magic were beginning to stretch and melt. It was nowhere near the breaking point, but if he didn't hurry up and do something, then it might yet get there.

And I wouldn't like to bet *our* lives on the secondary line of defense Belle and I had created....

"Right, then." Monty flexed his fingers. "Keep everything crossed that this works, people."

He took a deep breath, and then magically reached through our containment spell and picked up the closing thread of his. After gently unpicking it, he exposed the main part of the spell and carefully began to weave additional threads through his network of magic. But these new threads weren't strengthing the current ones; instead, they were constricting them. He was not only drawing the spell back in on itself, but also on the soucouyant. Her fire twisted and bubbled, a storm of unhappy energy that just wanted to kill.

Monty's spell continued to contract. Sweat poured down his face and dampened his shirt, but inch by hard-fought inch, the soucouyant was being contained in an ever-decreasing net of power. Smaller and smaller it got, until what hovered above the ashy remains of the old hut was a churning, furious conflagration of heat and fury that was little more than the size of a basketball.

Monty dropped to his knees, his breathing a harsh rasp and his skin almost gray. "Liz, can you wrap a secondary layer around mine? And if you can entwine the wild magic around the spell as well, all the better."

"I'll try."

I closed my eyes and imagined a cage of wild magic encasing Monty's sphere—one that not only contained and protected *his* spell but was also self-nourishing. The last thing I needed was it to be drawing energy directly from me. When the image was complete, I cast the spell.

The wild magic responded. I had no idea whether it came from within me or if the connection I'd formed with it simply reached out and grabbed the wilder energies that haunted this reservation, but the spell was cast exactly as I'd imagined.

Weakness washed through my limbs, and I wavered slightly. Belle grabbed my arm, holding me steady as I opened my eyes.

The two spells were now entwined around the soucouyant, containing not only her but also the rolling waves of her heat. There was no danger now of the grass catching alight, let alone any of us.

Belle and I deconstructed our shield, and then she rose to collect our spell stones. I took a deep, wavering breath. "What do we do now?"

Monty wiped the sweat from his brow and then slowly climbed to his feet. "I wove a tracer through the containment spell, but there's no way known we can use it now. It'll probably take all five of us to deal with the older soucouyant, and we'd better be in peak form before we attempt it."

"I don't know about you, but it generally takes me more than a night to recover magically."

Monty grimaced. "Yeah, though I hate the idea of leaving the hunt for too long—it only gives her the chance to kill someone else."

"I think that's a chance we'll have to take," Aiden said, as he walked up. "I'd rather one more soucouyant victim than five dead witches. I rather suspect neither the council nor the witch high council will be pleased if that happened."

"Especially given it was only a month ago that their Heretic Investigations witch was killed here," Belle said.

"Not to mention the fact that Ashworth almost lost his life as well. If anything else happens, they *will* come to investigate." My gaze returned to Monty. "So please take note and don't get dead."

His smile flashed. "I can assure you that isn't currently on my agenda—and won't be until I at least reach the ripe old age of ninety."

"Glad to hear it." But I hoped fate was listening and made it happen.

"Shall we meet at the café around four?" Monty said. "That gives us all enough time to recover, and still leaves enough daylight to deal with the soucouyant if we do find her."

"What are we going to do with that sphere in the meantime?" Aiden asked. "Is there anywhere safe to actually store it?"

"I suspect not," I replied, before Monty could. "If the two soucouyants *are* connected, then the older one is going to know what has happened to the younger, and she'll be out for blood."

And probably skin.

"Which is a very real possibility." Monty's growing weariness was evident in his voice. But then, he probably hadn't really flexed his witch "muscles" this much in years. "It'd be best if we keep it well away from both us and inhabited areas in general."

"What about the reservoir?" Belle said. "I know it's not salted, but given this soucouyant reacted so violently to Baker hosing it, it's possible *any* water will be out of bounds to them."

"Good idea," Monty said. "And it just might have the added bonus of preventing communication between the two."

"Will the water affect this one, though?" I asked. "I'd hate to have gone through all this effort only to kill the bitch before we find the other."

Monty hesitated, his gaze on the floating sphere. "It might. Ranger, have you any kind of waterproof container in your truck? One large enough to contain that sphere?"

"I've got a large jerry can in the back of the truck," Tala said, as she approached. "The lid's not large, but it is a screw top, so it should keep the water out."

"That'll do," Monty said. "Now that she's contained by the two magics and not emitting any heat, we should be able to manipulate her form and get her into the container."

Tala nodded and continued on to her truck.

"Bring a rope, too," Aiden called after her. His gaze came back to us. "It'll save either of you having to run some sort of magical leash to it."

"The only problem with a rope is the fact anyone could pick it up and draw her back to the surface," Monty said.

"We'll attach it to a buoy in the no-go section of the lake and I'll assign someone to keep a watch from the shore."

"Just make sure to tell them that at the first hint of flame, they're to jump in the water and stay there." Monty accepted the already opened container from Tala and then glanced at me. "Ready?"

I nodded then reached out magically. Once I'd snagged an outer thread of the net wrapped around Monty's sphere, I tugged it toward the container. The soucouyant twisted and churned, but her force was muted by the two spells. Every movement she made echoed through the lines around her, but all her anger and all her fire had little effect on the spells.

Monty's energy joined mine and, after a little bit of manipulation, we forced the soucouyant into the jerry can. Monty quickly did the lid up then staggered back, and would have fallen had Belle not grabbed him.

"Tala, I think you'd better get these three back—"

"Belle and Monty can leave, but I'd better stick around until the jerry can containing our flaming friend is fully submerged," I cut in, "just in case the other one does something unexpected."

Like attack.

Aiden frowned. "How likely is that, though?"

"Not very, but two sets of eyes are always better than

one, especially when one of those sets is psychically attuned to evil," I said. "We have no idea if this whole water thing will work or not, remember. I'd hate to see you or anyone else crisped."

A somewhat wicked light briefly gleamed in his eyes. "It wouldn't exactly be ideal for any future plans I have."

My pulse skipped up a notch. I licked my lips and tried to ignore the images skittering through my mind. "While I might not personally be able to counter an attack, the wild magic certainly can."

"And you're the only one who can call it." Aiden scraped a hand across his chin. "I guess that means the two of us will submerge the soucouyant while Tala runs Belle and Monty back."

He didn't look happy at the prospect, but then, he'd already admitted to having overprotective tendencies.

Which is always nice, Belle said. *Up to a point, anyway, and he's shown no signs of going over that point. Are you coming home tonight or staying at his place?*

He hasn't actually asked me to stay—

Belle snorted mentally, the sound echoing loudly through my brain. *That man will take you any which way— even if it means doing nothing more than holding you in his arms for the night while you sleep and recover.*

If he holds me in his arms, I doubt there will be much sleep happening. Tiredness does not outweigh desire. I paused. *This time, anyway.*

"Who do you want me to call up for watch duty, boss?" Tala asked.

Aiden hesitated. "Byron and Jaz. I don't want anyone flying solo out here, just in case."

"It might be wise to put in a call to Ashworth and

maybe even Eli, as well," I said. "They're both at full strength magically and looking to be in on the action."

Aiden snorted. "As I said, you're all damn mad."

But he gave clearance to give them a call, and Tala immediately hustled Belle and Monty toward her truck. Once they'd departed, Aiden picked up the jerry can, tied it into the back of his truck, and then helped me into the cabin. We drove around the blackened remains of the hut and down the other side of the hill. A six-foot wire fence divided the farm from the reservoir; to our left was a large gate.

"That's padlocked," I commented.

"And we rangers carry bolt cutters."

"Farmers must love you."

He grinned. "Some certainly do."

I looked at him, eyebrow raised. "I have a suspicion you're referring to the female of the species when you're saying that."

"Could be."

He climbed out of the truck and very quickly took care of the lock. He swung the gates open and then climbed back into the truck and headed left. The sun had now dropped below the horizon, and the shadows were beginning to creep across the landscape. There was no one out on the lake, and the water looked dark and moody.

I shivered, though why I wasn't exactly sure. Maybe it was just the fact that I wasn't the world's greatest swimmer and preferred to keep my feet firmly on the ground when it came to rivers and lakes.

"Cold?" Aiden said instantly.

I shook my head but nevertheless rubbed my arms. "It's just a delayed reaction, I think."

He grunted and turned up the heat anyway. "It'll take

Byron and Jaz an hour to get here. Why don't you nap in the truck while I borrow a boat and drop the soucouyant in the water?"

I frowned. "Did you not hear that whole thing about two sets of eyes being better than one?"

"I did indeed. But I'm also aware—having been woken a number of times by it now—that your psychic radar for evil is rather sensitive, and can–and has–woken you from a dead sleep."

"Doesn't mean it will this time."

"I'm willing to take the risk. I'd rather you not push yourself to the point of exhaustion yet again."

My lips twitched, even as his words warmed me. "There wouldn't happen to be an ulterior motive in that desire, would there?"

He rather dramatically clapped a hand against his chest. "I'm totally wounded you'd think such a thing."

I raised my eyebrows, my amusement growing. "So you don't want me to come back to your place tonight?"

"I never said *that*."

I laughed and then leaned across the seat and quickly kissed him. "Go. And be careful."

He climbed out, retrieved the soucouyant's jerry can, and then moved down to the shore. The gathering darkness meant I rather quickly lost sight of him but no fear rose, and the psychic part of me remained silent and unconcerned.

Despite my best intentions, my eyes closed and I drifted to sleep. It was the arrival of several trucks and the banging of multiple doors that woke me.

I wearily rubbed my eyes and glanced at the clock on the dash. It was nearly nine—I'd been asleep for over an hour.

Not enough by half, but more than I should have had

given the situation. I shoved the door open and walked across to join the others.

"How secure is the magic that contains this soucouyant?" Jaz asked, her expression a touch dubious. Not that anyone could blame her.

I hesitated. "As secure as Monty and the wild magic can make it. But given she's also dunked in water, I think the only problem you'll have is if the other one attempts a rescue."

"I doubt it will," Ashworth said. "But we've brought along a couple of surprises if she does."

"I hope they're damn powerful, because dealing with this one wiped me, Belle, and Monty out. The other one is far older and far stronger."

"Strength isn't always what matters." He glanced across at the two rangers. "Shall we go get set up somewhere?"

He didn't bother disguising the anticipation in his voice. Eli rolled his eyes and tagged after them.

My gaze went to Aiden. "So we're free to go now?"

"Yes. Do you want to pick up some takeaway on the way home?"

"Sure, but will anything be open at this hour? Argyle isn't exactly Melbourne when it comes to trading hours."

He touched my back, his fingers warm against my spine as he guided me back to his truck. "The burger shop will be open. They do a roaring late-night trade thanks to hungry werewolves coming back from runs."

I raised my eyebrows. "I'm betting it's not just running that makes you lot hungry."

He laughed. "I think you could be right."

It took us just over half an hour to drive across to Argyle, and another fifteen for the burgers and chips to be made. Thankfully, his home was only a few minutes away from there.

And the burgers were definitely worth the wait.

I stole the last couple of chips and then leaned back in the chair and rubbed my belly. "I'm full to the brim and have never felt better."

"I'm happy to hear that."

"The only thing that could possibly make the night more perfect is a nice hot shower."

"*Not* so happy to hear that."

I raised an eyebrow and then rose, undid my shirt, and tossed it onto the table. "Really? And here I was thinking your shower was big enough for two. Such a shame you don't feel the need to join me."

I turned and continued to strip as I headed upstairs, so that by the time I reached the bathroom, I was naked.

Aiden was only a few steps behind me, and also sans clothes.

Once the water was hot enough, I stepped under and then turned and smiled at the man behind me. "Are you coming in, or are you just going to stand there and admire the view?"

He wrinkled his nose, his expression thoughtful. "Tough question."

I laughed, grabbed his hand, and pulled him under the water. His arms went around my waist and then his lips came down on mine. We kissed, long and hard, as the water drummed our skins and slid down our bodies, tickling and teasing.

After a deliciously long while, he reached for the sponge and began washing my body. And oh, it felt good. More than good. Tortuous, even.

When I couldn't stand the teasing caress any longer, I

grabbed the sponge, soaped it up, and returned the favor. His beautiful body gleamed in the bathroom's bright light, and the water reverently caressed every muscle. I followed its lead, washing every marvelous inch, until he was quivering as badly as me.

"Enough," he growled.

He grabbed the sponge and hooked it back over the tap. I grinned and wrapped my arms around his neck, my kiss fierce and demanding. He groaned deep in his throat and pressed me back against the tiles, his body hard against mine. Desire and heat burned through us both; even the very air we breathed seemed to be boiling.

He slid his hands down my sides then cupped my butt and lifted me with little effort. I wrapped my legs around his waist and, a heartbeat later, he was in me. It was such utter heaven that neither of us immediately moved. We simply enjoyed the sensations and the heat that rose with this basic joining of flesh. Then that heat became too great to ignore and he thrust deeper—harder—into me, his body moving slowly at first and then with growing urgency. It was a dance as old as time, and it was crazy and electric and utterly perfect. Desire flooded me, consumed me, a force so strong it threatened to tear me apart.

And then it *did* tear me apart, and it was intense and violent and absolutely glorious. A heartbeat later, he followed me over that cliff.

For several seconds, neither of us moved. Then he leaned his forehead against mine, his breathing harsh against my lips. "Damn," he said. "That was certainly worth the wait."

I laughed softly. "It was indeed. But I am, unfortunately, feeling utterly content and ready for sleep now."

"Sleep is never a bad thing." He cupped his hands

either side of my cheeks and kissed me softly. "And there's always the morning."

"I'd be disappointed if there wasn't."

"Good. And I'll even make you breakfast, if you'd like."

"Done deal, Ranger."

"Good."

And it was.

After yet another busy day in the café, Belle flopped down into a chair and accepted the coffee I handed her with a weary smile. "You know, we might have to start thinking about employing extra waitresses—even if only part-time."

"The finances are certainly strong enough to handle it now." My reply was somewhat absent. Now that I had time to actually sit down and think, a deep sense that something was about to go very wrong was growing.

"Which could just be your natural tendency to worry," Belle said.

"Or it could just be a signal that everything is about to go batshit crazy."

She snorted. "Our life basically did *that* the minute we decided to settle in this reservation."

A reluctant smile tugged at my lips. "But there are various degrees of crazy, and this is feeling like the 'our life is on the line yet again' type."

"Oh, fabulous," she said. "In which case, maybe we'd better do something about strengthening the spells around the café to include the rejection of fire and fire spirits."

"Except I'm not entirely sure *how* we're going to do that." I grabbed a teaspoon and scooped up some of the froth from the top of my hot chocolate. "Monty hasn't yet got around to teaching me the shielding spell he used to protect us when the soucouyant's fireball exploded."

"Which *only* did so because *your* magic contained and then stopped it."

I grimaced. "True, but the last thing we want is an explosion here at the café, and if I replicate *that* spell, that's just what we might end up with."

Belle wrinkled her nose. "What about using parts of the containment spell from last night? It did stop her fire—"

"But not the residual heat. The grass had started to catch, remember."

"Yes, but that stopped when Monty constricted his magic and you secured her. If we try a combination of all three spells, it might just work."

I glanced at my watch and then rose. "If we're going to do it, we'd better do it now. Monty said he'd be here about four."

Belle grabbed her coffee and followed me into the reading room. We pushed back the table and chairs and then sat on the rug. There was no need for spell stones in this place—it was probably one of the best-protected rooms in all Australia.

"At least when it comes to rooms protected by inadequate witches," Belle commented.

I grinned and held out my hands. Once she'd placed hers in mine, I said, "If you weave the containment spell through the current lines of protection, I'll reverse its function and add in the fire and fire spirit exceptions."

She nodded, took a deeper breath, and then begun. I repeated the process and then followed the threads of her magic as she wove it through the network already surrounding the café. I picked up each containment line and carefully added a number of exceptions that would hopefully prevent the soucouyant or her fire affecting the café in any way. It would undoubtedly force a direct attack instead but better we come under threat than her fire not only taking out this place, but also the businesses on either side of us.

Belle finished her threading. Once I caught up with her and we'd tied off the spells, I sat back and studied the result. The magic that protected the outer shell of our building from anything and anyone intending us harm was now a net that extended up the walls and across the roofline. I couldn't see the latter, of course, but I could feel it.

"Well," Belle said, a catch of weariness in her voice. "There'll be no disguising our presence now."

Not when our protections would glow brighter than a neon light to any witch who passed by the place. "We can always dismantle it once we've dealt with the soucouyants."

"Because of course there won't be any other spirits rolling in to give us grief."

Her sarcasm had a smile tugging my lips. "We'd have to be extremely unlucky to get another couple of soucouyants though."

"Yes, but it'd also be far easier to alter the protections on *this* one than raise a new one every time some fresh evil decides to hit the reservation."

"Also true." I picked up my now lukewarm chocolate and quickly drank it. It didn't do a whole lot to ease the gathering fatigue, but it was better than nothing. "And we can always hope that fate won't be the bitch we fear she is."

"Aside from the fact your prophetic dreams have been harping on the eventuality of your dad and Clayton coming here," Belle said, "the council is *not* going to keep ignoring a reservation that keeps killing or maiming its witches."

I grimaced. "I guess the thing we need to hold on to is

the fact that neither of us are the same people that we were back then."

"Yes, and we're not as powerless, either," Belle said. "We may be little more than leaves in a storm when it comes to our magic and theirs, but we do hold one key advantage over them."

"This reservation." And, more importantly, the wild magic and my link to it.

Whether in the end it would be enough was the question neither of us could answer—especially given I had absolutely no idea what my mental state would be when I eventually came face-to-face with the man who'd tried to rape me.

"And if we can't permanently leave the reservation thanks to your tie with the wild magic," Belle said, touching my knee in compassionate understanding, "then it's *that* connection that might save us even if we can't save ourselves."

"God, I hope so," I muttered and pushed to my feet. "Want a hand up?"

"Yes." Her fingers gripped mine. "Monty and Aiden are almost at our door."

"You go answer. I'll push the furniture back and grab our gear."

She nodded, picked up the two mugs, and then headed into the café. Once I'd put everything back in place, I grabbed the backpack, loaded it up with a number of charms, potions, and our silver knives, and then followed her out.

Monty was standing in the middle of the café, his gaze on the netlike structure that now flowed up our walls. "I see you've decided not to wait for me to show you that spell."

"We couldn't afford to." I walked past him and gave Aiden a quick "hello" kiss.

"Debatable point, given it wouldn't have taken all that long to show you the basics," Monty said. "But there are some very nice variations included in your version. Whether they'll hold up against a full-on attack is now the question."

"And one I'd rather avoid getting an answer to. Are Ashworth and Eli on their way?"

"They're still camping out by the lake, keeping an eye on things," Aiden said. "There's been no sign of the soucouyant, though."

"Which hopefully means she hasn't woken yet and doesn't know what is going on." Monty's gaze swept me and then moved onto Belle. "You two ready?"

"I'm not entirely sure why I'm included in this motley crew," she replied, "but yes, I am."

"You mean aside from the fact that any sensible questing company should always involve a beautiful woman?"

"Oh dear," Aiden murmured, even as I rather mildly said, "Are you saying that I'm *not* beautiful?"

He looked at me, but instead of contriteness, I got a big grin. "Lizzie my darling, you are lovely, but aside from the fact we're related, you're also not Amazonian perfect."

"Monty my darling," Belle said, in a perfect imitation of his tone. "No amount of flattery in the world could get you anywhere near my body when we were sixteen. Let me assure you now, *that* hasn't changed."

"But you can't blame a man for trying. Shall we go?"

He spun around and headed for the door without waiting for a response. I glanced at Belle; she simply rolled her eyes and then followed him out.

"You know," Aiden mused, "those two—"

"I wouldn't finish the rest of that sentence if I were you." I grabbed my keys from under the counter. "Not if you value your life."

"I'd say Belle doesn't scare me, but we all know that's not true. Besides, I've seen her punch. She has a mean right hook."

"You were out to it at the time, so technically you didn't see anything." I locked the front door and then fell into step beside him. Belle and Monty were already climbing into the back of his truck.

"Yes, but I did see the result. He'd have needed dental surgery."

Only he never made it to a dental surgeon, let alone trial, simply because he'd chosen the wrong vampire to cross swords with.

We climbed into the front of his truck and made our way back to Greenhill. It was just after five by the time we arrived. Mac was the only ranger on duty—maybe Aiden figured the presence of two witches negated the need for an extra ranger.

Ashworth greeted us with a grumpy, "About bloody time."

"Hey," I said, "the underpowered witches in this outfit needed recovery time after last night's efforts."

He gave me the look—the one that said he didn't believe a word of it. "We've already dragged the soucouyant container closer. How do you want to play this?"

"I'll attempt to find the older soucouyant using this one," Monty said. "You four are basically backup and protection."

Ashworth's expression suggested he wasn't exactly happy about being assigned the role of backup. Monty continued on obliviously, "Liz and I will head off in Aiden's car; Belle, you'd better go with Ashworth and Eli, just to be on the safe side. We'll figure out what to do next if and when we find the soucouyant's lair."

"Nothing like being prepared beforehand, laddie," Ashworth said.

Monty raised an eyebrow. "If you've got a better suggestion, old man, I'm more than happy to hear it."

"Old man now, is it?" Ashworth's voice was deceptively mild. "If you weren't so green around the edges, I'd be tempted to teach you some manners."

"Can we cut the macho bullshit and concentrate on the task at hand," Belle said. "Because we're running out of daylight and I'd personally prefer not to be tracking this thing when it's awake and aware."

"A point we can all agree on," Aiden said. "Mac, you can head back to the station and sign off. Monty, go grab the soucouyant's container. The rest of you get to the trucks. Let's get this show on the road."

Everyone else obeyed but I remained exactly where I was. Aiden stopped and raised an eyebrow in question. I motioned toward Monty, who was now standing on the shore hauling on the long rope connected to the jerry can.

"We'll need to remove her from the container before Monty can try a tracking spell, and I'd rather do that here than in the confines of your truck."

"Good point." He crossed his arms and waited beside me.

The weighted jerry can came up out of the water; almost instantly, the soucouyant became active. I couldn't see it, but I felt it. Felt the sudden press of its energy against the threads of wild magic that bound both it and Monty's magic. I rubbed my arms and tried to ignore the stirrings of unease.

Monty untied the rope, detached the rocks, then picked up the container and ran toward us.

"Right," he said, unscrewing the lid, "let's get her out and then I can try adding a tracking spell."

The lid came off and a fierce storm of magic and heat blasted into the air. The grip of the two spells on the soucouyant was starting to fade. "And if you can't add the tracking spell?"

"Then Ashworth will be seriously pissed, and tell me so in no uncertain terms." His smile flashed. "But I've had an expert run me through what needs to be done, so it shouldn't be a problem."

"The expert being your professor friend?"

He nodded. "Ready?"

I nodded and concentrated on the magic I *couldn't* see rather than the stuff I could. Monty's energy soon joined mine and, after a second, the sphere that held the soucouyant came free. The inner edges of Monty's spell were indeed fraying, and despite the fact that I'd tried to make mine self-replenishing, there were now dull patches running through the network —an indication it wouldn't last another twenty-four hours.

"Right," Monty said. "Do you want to make a small gateway through your net? It just has to be wide enough for me to pick up the end of my spell."

I nodded and did so. Monty reached magically through the gap, untied the last line of his spell, and began twining through what I presumed was the tracer spell. I watched through slightly narrowed eyes, trying to remember the patterns and words, just in case I needed to do something along similar lines when I was head witch—

My thoughts came to a crashing halt.

Where the hell had that come from? Why in the hell would anyone appoint me head witch? Aiden might have expressed the notion somewhat wistfully, but if Ashworth wasn't strong enough to be reservation witch, why would anyone even consider me?

Possibly because of the wild magic and your connection.

That connection will never make up for the lack of skill and knowledge, Belle.

I know, and it's not like I even remotely want something like that to happen. But given the way things have been rolling for us lately, it's an eventuality that wouldn't actually surprise me.

You and I could not handle the job. Not even with the wild magic's help.

You and I might not have a choice.

I didn't comment and the prophetic part of me remained stubbornly mute.

Monty wound the tracer carefully through the network of the containment spell and then thrust it deep into the soucouyant's energy. She reacted violently, her energy churning in agitation, but it had no immediate effect on either of his spells. But the heat leaking through the small gap in my magic made me wonder just how much longer that would be the case.

He hurriedly closed off the two spells and withdrew. I quickly resealed my spell and then glanced at him. Sweat beaded his forehead, but his expression was pleased.

"I take it the spell is working?"

He nodded. "I'm currently getting strong feedback. How long it'll last if she continues to twist like that is another matter entirely. It's very possible she'll either dislodge or fry the connection."

"Then let's not stand about here," Aiden said, ever practical.

He picked up the jerry can and led the way back to the truck. I caught one of the strands of wild magic and pushed the sphere along after him. Once Monty was sitting in the front passenger seat, I gave him the soucouyant and then climbed into the rear.

"Is that thing safe?" Aiden said, as he started the truck up.

"For now," Monty said. "Head out of the farm and then back into Greenhill. I'll give more directions then."

Aiden nodded and took off. I did the seat belt up and tried to ignore the unease traipsing across my skin. As long as both sets of magic held up, we really weren't in danger, no matter what my instincts might be saying.

At Greenhill, Monty said, "Go left at the roundabout."

"Out of the reservation?" Aiden queried, even as he obeyed.

"Yes." Monty's voice was absent. He was concentrating on the signal coming from the tracer.

We continued on, eventually swinging right onto the Western Freeway and then off again once we'd hit the road to Argyle.

Monty's breathing was becoming harsher, and the sting of his sweat so strong that even I could smell it. I shifted position to look at the sphere; Monty's spell had frayed a whole lot more and the patches of deadness had grown larger along my thread lines. I caught the end of my spell and hastily wrapped a few more lines of power around the sphere, but I doubted it would hold for long. With the night growing ever closer, the soucouyant was becoming stronger.

We swept into Argyle and then turned left onto the Midland Highway. The heat in the car was increasing;

Aiden flicked on the air conditioning and the blast of cool air provided a welcome if likely too brief respite.

"Right here," Monty said abruptly.

Tires squealed as Aiden obeyed. Dust flew and the truck fishtailed on the gravel road for several seconds before Aiden got it back under control.

"A little more warning next time would be nice," he muttered.

"Sorry," Monty said, sounding anything but.

I leaned forward. "How close are we?"

"Close." He hesitated. "We've probably another mile or so."

We continued on, passing a couple of even smaller side roads before Monty said, "Slow down. I think she's in the building ahead on our right."

"That's a holiday rental house," Aiden said. "Friends of mine own it."

"But they don't live there, do they?" I asked, fearing the worst if they did.

"No, but someone has obviously rented it—there's a car parked out front." He glanced at Monty. "How do you want to play this?"

"Shouldn't the first thing we do be to get those people out of there?" I asked.

"If it isn't already too late," Monty said. "The strength of the tracer suggests that if our soucouyant isn't in the house, she's damn close to it."

I briefly studied the house. It was an old double-story red-brick building that had probably been a barn at some point in its life given the height and width of the original front door. There was a newer weatherboard building added on to the rear that more than doubled the barn's original size. There was a smaller shed to the right of the building, and what looked to be a cabin behind it.

My gaze drifted back to the small shed and that odd sense of trepidation became full-blown fear.

Something was very wrong.

"You know what?" I said abruptly. "I don't think we should be taking the younger soucouyant anywhere near that place. In fact, I think the best thing we could do right now is damn well put it back into water."

Monty twisted around to look at me, his expression confused. "Why? With five of us, she's not likely—"

"Monty," Aiden said, "trust me when I say it always pays to listen to Liz's gut, no matter what common sense might otherwise say. It'll save your life. It's saved mine."

Uncertainty flickered through the confusion, but all Monty said was, "I think it unnecessary but... is there a dam or something nearby, Ranger?"

Aiden nodded. "There's one just up the road."

"Good." I twisted around to check where Ashworth was. His truck was just pulling up behind us. "Let's force *this* soucouyant back into the jerry can, then Belle and I can take her up to the dam. If there are guests inside the house, Aiden can evacuate them while the three of you check out that small shed. If she's not there, then she'll be damn close."

Monty's eyebrows rose. "You can feel her from here?"

"Magically? No." My brief smile was tight. "It's more my psychic radar screaming to keep the hell away from that shed that leads me to believe she's there."

"Huh," he said, still looking unconvinced. "But I guess if you're right, you've saved us some time."

And time was not on our side. I shoved the thought

aside, climbed out of the truck, and then grabbed the jerry can.

"What's happening?" Ashworth said as he got out.

"Liz's gut," Aiden said, as if that explained it all.

And I guessed it did, at least to Ashworth and Belle. Eli, however, looked a little perplexed.

"When Liz's gut suggests a certain course of action," Belle explained, "the wise should listen. It tends to be right more than it's wrong."

"And in this case," I added, "it's suggesting that we don't take *this* soucouyant anywhere near *that* house."

Ashworth grunted. "That does make sense, actually. If the spells around the younger one are fading in any way, it could lead to the older one sensing her presence."

"Are we going to try and evacuate those inside the house?" Eli asked. "Or do you think it's already too late?"

"Liz," Monty said at the same time. "Attention this way."

"Sorry." I tuned the others out and then nodded. As one, Monty and I picked up the threads of our spells and once again began shaping the sphere into something that would go into the jerry can. With a bit of effort and a whole lot of sweating, we succeeded.

After the lid was screwed on tight again, I glanced at Aiden and said, "Is there more rope in your truck? We left the other one back at the reservoir."

He nodded. "In the right rear storage compartment."

"Be careful in there, all of you," I said. "I really don't like the feel of this."

"The three of us should be able to handle her," Monty said.

I couldn't help glancing at Ashworth. His expression

suggested he was thinking the same thing as me—that pride often came before a fall.

But I hoped that *wasn't* the case here.

I picked up the jerry can and moved back to Aiden's truck. Belle climbed into the driver seat, adjusted it to fit her longer legs, and then took off. We'd barely gone half a mile down the road before we spotted the dam—it was large, long, and oval in shape. At the far end of it was a jetty that looked close to collapse. The dam had obviously been a popular swimming hole at some point in its life, but if the jetty was anything to go by, hadn't been used in a very long time.

Either that, or the kids who used it had something of a death wish.

Belle let the truck roll down the hill then pulled off the road and stopped. I grabbed the jerry can and climbed out. Maybe it was simply a case of me getting weaker, but the damn thing seemed heavier than before.

I walked across to the wire fence, shoved the jerry can onto the other side, and then carefully pressed down a strand of barbed wire and climbed through. Belle grabbed the rope from the back of the truck and then followed.

"Is that dam going to be deep enough?" she said, uncertainty in her voice.

I studied the exposed banks and muddy water for a second. "If it was used as a swimming hole in the past, it has to be fairly deep. With any sort of luck, there'll be at least six feet of water in the middle section."

"Good," Belle said, "because in case you haven't noticed, there's a whole lot of heat radiating from that jerry can, and I rather suspect it means the spells are failing. Rapidly."

"I suspect you're right." My voice was grim. "That's

why the deeper that dam is, the better it'll be. The soucouyant may be agitated, but I doubt it'd be stupid enough to melt the one thing that's protecting it."

"Unless it hasn't the capacity to sense water."

"Oh, I think it has. It didn't start getting active again until Monty dragged it out of the water."

Belle frowned at me. "How do you know it wasn't active in the water, given the water would have been cooling the container as fast as the soucouyant was heating it?"

A smile twisted my lips. "Guess."

Belle grimaced. "The wild magic?"

"Yeah."

"Shit."

"Yeah."

"Sensible people would just salt this thing now and be done with it."

"Except if they *don't* find the other soucouyant on that farm, we may still need this one to track it."

We walked up the dam's bank and stopped at the top. "We're going to need something to weigh it down," I said. "Otherwise it might just float."

"Not much in the way of rocks around here." Belle paused. "What about a thick tree branch?"

"That'll do."

While Belle went to retrieve one, I walked around the bank to the jetty. Close up, it looked in even worse shape, but the water was at least darker toward the end of it, suggesting it was deep.

Belle came back with a thick tree branch. We looped the rope around it to secure it, then I carefully made my way onto the jetty. The wood creaked and groaned under my weight and at every step felt like it might just collapse. It didn't, thankfully. I knelt, dropped the soucouyant into the water and then, once it had sunk, tied the rope to one of the struts, out of the immediate sight of anyone who might wander by.

I was making my way back along the jetty when the blast of energy hit and sent me stumbling. Belle swore and lunged forward, grabbing my arm before I tipped into the water, then hauling me back to the safety of the bank.

But the blast hadn't come from our soucouyant.

It had a more distant feel than that.

I swung around, fear clawing at my gut. And saw a huge fireball erupt skyward—one that came from the area where Aiden and the others were.

TEN

"No!" The denial was torn from my throat.

Belle didn't say anything. She just grabbed my hand, forcing me into motion when my mind and my limbs seemed frozen. She lifted the barbed wire, helped me through, and all but tossed me into the truck.

As the engine roared to life, I took a deep breath and tried to think. To feel.

And what I *didn't* feel was despair.

Or the wild magic.

And surely if Aiden was dead or severely injured, Katie would have come screaming for my help.

Unless, of course, she was too far away to feel his demise.

Belle turned the truck around and then flattened the accelerator. The tires spun for several seconds and then the truck took off up the hill. We all but flew over the crest, and it was only then that the full calamity became evident.

The beautiful old house had been blown to pieces. The blast had also caught Ashworth's truck, and it was now lying on its left side in the grass on the other side of the road. But there was no sign of the vehicle that had been parked in front of the house; either it had been utterly destroyed by the blast or the people staying there had been successfully evacuated. And if that *were* the case, then surely it meant Aiden and the others were also safe.

I forced my gaze beyond the smoking ruins to the old shed where I'd sensed the soucouyant's presence. It, too, had been hit by the blast, and was little more than a blackened pile of wood and metal.

There was no sign of movement anywhere that I could see and, despite my certainty that they couldn't be dead, that I somehow would have known if they were, dread crept into my heart.

Belle touched my knee and squeezed gently. She didn't say anything. She didn't need to. Her fear ran through the back of my thoughts, as fierce as my own.

She braked when we neared the now broken gate. The truck came to a sliding halt and the resulting dust plumed around the cabin. I scrambled out and ran for the house.

"Wait," Belle yelled after me.

I didn't. But I *did* gather a repelling spell around my fingertips. I had no idea how effective it would be against the soucouyant if she was still here—and it didn't feel like she was—but given the force she'd leveled against the house would have at least partially drained her, it probably wouldn't be *in*effective, either.

I slowed as I neared the still smoking ruins. There were bricks, metal, and bits of burning wood scattered everywhere—on the ground, and in the trees. However, the bulk of debris lay in one gigantic pile in what would have been the middle of the old building. The tin roof lay on top of it, its edges looking rather like melted cheese. Underneath this, deep in the heart of that ruined pile, was the yellow-white glow of coals. The soucouyant's flames must have been sun-fierce to cause this amount of damage. If anyone had been inside, there'd be little left but scraps of charred bone.

I rubbed my arms and thrust away the images that rose. They weren't dead. I had to believe that.

Belle stopped beside me and hauled a water gun out of the backpack. She must have seen my look, because she immediately said, "It may not be much, but it just might be better than magic at this point in time."

A fair enough comment given three witches more powerful than either of us apparently hadn't been able to contain—let alone kill—the soucouyant. I looked beyond the smoking pile of rubble, but there was no immediate sign of movement. Maybe the blast had knocked them out. I crossed mental fingers, toes, and everything else I possibly could, and carefully picked my way around the building. The old shed was little more than a few burned sheets of tin roofing and a couple of blackened stumps. But as I neared it, energy stirred across my senses. The soucouyant had indeed stayed in this place—her presence still lingered despite the fact she appeared to have fled.

I skirted around the shed's remains and then stopped again to scan the area. There was a hip-height fence a hundred or so feet away and, beyond that, a field in which there were a number of buildings and water tanks. The psychic part of me remained stubbornly mute, but the four men weren't in the yard, so they obviously *had* to be in one of those other buildings.

Unless, of course, they'd literally been blown to smithereens.

"They're not dead—I can feel their thoughts now, though they're somewhat fuzzy, as if there's some sort of barrier between me and them," Belle said. "They're in the next field, somewhere behind that big shed."

Relief surged, and all I wanted to do was run into the field and find them. But we had no idea if the soucouyant was still here and the last thing I wanted was to jeopardize anyone's safety through one incautious action.

The small metal gate creaked as I opened it, but the fact that it was even standing was surprising. Perhaps most of the soucouyant's force had been directed at the house... although why would she have done that if the men were out here in the field rather than in or near the house?

I'd barely stepped through the gate when something rattled to my right. I immediately stopped and half raised my hand, the repelling spell buzzing like hornets around my fingers. The sound appeared to have come from near the shed, but the side facing me was open, and there wasn't much inside other than a few bits of machinery.

"They're definitely behind it." Belle paused and frowned. "In a large body of water, from the sound of it. You go around this side. I'll take the other."

"Be careful."

"If that bitch comes near me, her face is going to get blasted with water."

I half smiled. "That'd be one way to test our theory out, but I'd actually rather you didn't have to."

"On that, we both agree."

She moved on cautiously. As the rattle sounded again, I quickly walked to the end of the shed and then paused. The ground here was wet and there were large puddles of water everywhere—no doubt a result of the closest water tank being little more than a melted plastic mess. The backwash of the soucouyant's heat had obviously hit it. There were five others beyond it, but all of them metal and, at least at first glance, intact. There were also a couple of discarded tanks lying on their sides in the yard behind the shed, but these were so old they were little more than rusty skeletons. They certainly wouldn't have offered much in the way of protection against the sort of heat that could melt a plastic tank.

I glanced back to the tanks lining the shed and, in that instant, saw one of the sheets of tin covering the second tank move just a little.

I ran over. "Aiden? Ashworth? Are you all in there?"

"Yes," Aiden said. "And we're all okay, but it appears we're stuck."

The relief that ran through me was so fierce that I had to blink back sudden tears. Which was ridiculous given Belle had already told me they were alive. I took a deep breath, then released the repelling spell and moved around the tank, looking for the opening. There wasn't one. "How in the hell did you get in there?"

"This sheet was loosely covering the opening," Aiden said. The bit of tin rattled again as someone hit it. "But it must have fused when the backwash of heat hit the tank."

I stared up at the sheet of tin in question. It had more than fused—the ends of the tin had melted and then set against the side of the tank. They were damn lucky to have gotten inside before that happened, because if that wave had hit any of them.... I shivered.

"I'll see if we can pry it open." I silently asked Belle to see what she could find in Aiden's truck, and then added, "How come you were even close enough to climb into the tank? And why would the soucouyant hit the house rather than the shed and these tanks?"

"Eli and I concocted an illusion spell once we'd evacuated the house," Ashworth said. "It made her think we were there when we were actually out here."

"But she would have known the truth the minute you tried confining her."

I looked around for something to stand on. If I were to have any hope of prying open the sheet of metal, it would probably be better if I did it from above rather than below. Especially given the melt factor here.

"We never got that far," Monty said. "The bitch woke before Ashworth and I could finish placing our spell stones."

"It was the illusion spell that saved us," Ashworth said. "Her attack on the house gave us time to get in here."

"But she must have realized her mistake the minute she demolished the house, so why didn't she come after you?"

I found an old metal barrel and rolled it toward the tank —almost running over Aiden's phone in the process. He must have tossed it clear before he dove into the water. I shoved it into my pocket and then stood the barrel on its end and clambered up. Belle came around the corner carrying what looked like a wood splitter and one of those hooked pry bars.

"She didn't come after us because she couldn't see us," Eli said. "I cast a second illusion the minute she woke, and it provided a few brief but very vital seconds to haul our butts into this water tank."

"If she'd hit this tank, you could have all been boiled alive."

"Maybe," Monty said. "And maybe not. I think the combination of our magic might have been able to hold off a second wave of heat—especially given her destruction of the house would have left her pretty close to empty energy wise."

"Which means she'll be on the hunt again," Aiden said. "And *that* means you need to get us out of the tank."

"Working on it, Ranger." Belle stopped next to the barrel and handed me up the pry bar. "I'll see if I can break the fuse line. You tackle it from the above."

I nodded. "Guys, you might want to swim away from the opening, just in case the bar goes through the metal and hits someone on the head."

There was a snort of amusement—Ashworth, I suspected—and then the sound of splashing as they swam away.

Belle began bashing the underneath section of the metal sheet. As dust and soot danced along its length, I shoved the curved end of the bar under the side edge and, once it seemed fairly secure, pulled back in an effort to leverage one sheet from the other.

It took a fair bit of time and cursing from the two of us, but we eventually managed to break the bond between the sheet of tin and the tank. Belle jumped up onto the roof of the tank and, together, we grabbed the edge of the sheet and peeled it back to fully reveal the opening. Aiden hauled himself up onto the roof, water sluicing off his body as he turned to help the others. Ashworth was the last one out, and his cast was, rather remarkably, dry.

He must have seen my surprise, because he gave me a look and said, "I have no intention of going back into the hospital, lass, so you can bet I made damn sure not to get the thing wet."

"I would have thought it'd be the last thing on your mind given the situation and the urgency," Belle said.

"When you've confronted as many evils as I have, you learn to keep your head and never let utter panic take control." Though he didn't look at Monty, I rather suspected the comment was aimed that way. "Now what? Do we attempt to find her again tonight?"

"We've no other choice," Monty said. "We can't afford the older one to find another victim and become strong again."

Aiden jumped off the tank, then turned and helped Belle, and then me, down. "I'll need to call in someone to deal with this mess—"

"You'd better call in a tow truck, too." I handed him his phone. "Ashworth's truck is on its side."

"What?" Ashworth said. "If that bitch's actions have written her off, I'll be royally pissed."

He was a man who loved his truck, obviously. "Relax, she looks fine."

He grunted and carefully climbed down from the tank. Eli was the last one down.

"That leaves us with Aiden's truck as transport, and it only seats five," he said.

"Six," Aiden said, "If you count the small holding area in the back."

"Which I'll preemptively assign to Monty," Ashworth said. "Eli and I are too old."

Monty snorted. "I like how your age very conveniently comes into it in a situation like this, but not others."

Ashworth's grin flashed. "You're just annoyed that you didn't get in first."

"Actually no, because you're forgetting one point—I'm the only one who can trace the first soucouyant using the second, and I need to be able to communicate directions."

"Oh for God's sake, I'll get in the back," I said. "I'm the shortest anyway, so it makes sense. Can we just get moving?"

I didn't wait for an answer. I just turned and headed back to the truck.

"I guess hiding the younger soucouyant was a bit of a waste of time," Monty said as he caught up with me.

"Not necessarily." I waved a hand at the house. "I suspect you four would have ended up looking like that if you'd had her with you."

He frowned. "The force of our combined spells around the jerry can might be waning, but they still should have been enough to stop the original from sensing the other."

"My gut says otherwise." I hesitated. "I really think we need to take the time to reinforce—"

"We haven't got the time," he cut in. "Not if we want to stop her killing someone else."

"Yes, I know, but—"

"Liz, I won't have the strength to track down and kill the original soucouyant if we reinforce the contained one." His expression was grim. Determined. "If for any reason we can't find her, then we'll reinforce. The magic should hold up until that point."

If it didn't, we were all in trouble. But there was no point in saying that or arguing any further.

Ashworth squeezed my shoulder in sympathy but didn't say anything as we moved back to the truck. Once the jerry can was retrieved from the lake, Monty wrapped a tracking spell around the container—something I felt rather than saw, thanks to my rather basic perch in the back of the truck —then started spitting out directions.

Trust me, Belle said. *You're probably better off where you are. Drenched men lead to drenched seats, and my ass is getting wetter and wetter.*

I smiled. *What are the restraints around the jerry can looking like?*

She paused. *Not good. The heat is becoming quite fierce. But Monty's having no trouble tracking her?*

Not at the moment. She paused. *I've got a bad feeling this is all going to go to pot, though.*

It's usually me getting the bad feelings.

I know. Her unease drifted down the line, stirring mine to life. *But the soucouyant's actions when she saw you suggests she's not afraid of witches, and a whole lot cannier than Monty is giving her credit for.*

Most older spirits are. That's how they get old.

She chuckled softly. *My spirit guides may or may not have just said something very similar.*

I don't suppose they also offered any advice when it comes to dealing with either soucouyant?

Yeah, don't get in the way of their flames, because they'd hate to see us crisped.

Helpful. Really helpful.

Belle's amusement deepened. *They did say that the reversal spell we have wrapped around the café might be put to good use in a personal charm.*

I blinked. *I hadn't thought of that.*

So they noted. They suggest you need to up your game.

Hey, I'm not reservation witch. I don't need to up anything.

Also noted. But they also suggested it never hurts to practice such things in the eventuality the impossible happens.

I don't like the sound of that. Especially given it gelled with my own nebulous feeling that the future I didn't want was screaming toward us.

The truck slowed. I peered through the closed but not locked bars of the containment area but couldn't really see anything out of the reinforced rear window. *What's happening?*

Monty thinks we're close.

Where are we?

On the outskirts of Castle Rock, in some place called Golden Point. It's a mix of acreage properties and forest.

I grabbed the bars as the truck bounced off the road. *Which is a nice, semirural place to go hunting if she's looking for skin replacement.*

The truck came to a halt and then doors slammed. A second later, Aiden opened the rear of the truck. "You okay?"

"Yeah." I swung the containment door open. "I'd like to know how you get less-than-compliant arrestees in here though—it's not the easiest place to get in and out of."

"In the case of the less than compliant, I order in other vehicles." He caught my hand and steadied me as I jumped to the ground.

Immediately in front of us was a long gravel drive that meandered up the hill to a brick farmhouse. Lights shone through a couple of windows, but I had no sense of the soucouyant.

I *did* have a sense of death.

I glanced at Monty. "Are you sure she's here?"

"Yes." He hesitated. "Though I can't be 100 percent certain she's in that house. The tracer spell is becoming spotty."

No surprise there, given the heat radiating from the jerry can. "I don't think she's there. Not now."

He frowned and motioned toward the still-bound soucouyant. "The tracer spell says otherwise."

I glanced at the container. The connection between the wild magic and me allowed to see what otherwise wouldn't be visible. The spell binding and immobilizing the soucouyant had frayed even further, and the dead spots in the wild magic now accounted for at least half of the spell. That it was still holding together and active was rather amazing, but that didn't mean the faltering state of either spell remained capable of preventing contact between the two soucouyants. And the long tracking thread that had been inserted into this soucouyant's energy was now little more than half its size. It obviously *was* still working, but the loss of length would have altered the spell's reliability.

I rubbed my arms and returned my gaze to the house. "I'm not liking the feel of this, Monty."

"Neither am I, but we really have no choice if we want to stop this thing." He hesitated. "But just in case, maybe Belle needs to go back to that lake we passed, and shove the jerry can into it. At the very least, she'll still be confined by the water if our spells fail."

Plus it keeps me out of harm's way and more able to help you if the soucouyant attacks. I like this plan. Belle retrieved one of the water pistols and then handed me the backpack and her phone. At my raised eyebrows, she added, *The phone is new. I'm not risking it slipping into the water when I'm trying to drown the soucouyant.*

Aiden tossed the keys to her and then said, "I'd rather we approach the house from different angles. That way, if she *is* there, she'll have to split her attack."

Monty handed Belle the jerry can. As she jumped into the truck and took off, he added, "Splitting her energy isn't going to be a problem if she *has* fed, but it's worth a shot."

"Eli and I will head right," Ashworth said. "You three go right up the center to the front of the house. If she's in there, we'll all feel her before we get too close."

"And have that fire spell of yours ready, Monty," Eli said. "It's your tracer spell that led us here, and she's likely to have some sense of your presence because of it."

He nodded and immediately began weaving the spell around his fingers. Ashworth and Eli walked through the old wooden farm gate and then quickly disappeared through a grove of olive trees. The three of us jogged down the gravel drive until it started a sweeping curve around the hill and then cut straight up it.

The closer we got to the old farmhouse, the more convinced I became that the soucouyant wasn't there. But that didn't mean she'd fled the area.

She hadn't.

I began twining a repelling spell around my fingers, and almost ran straight into Monty as he stopped abruptly.

"Can you feel that?" He wasn't looking at the house. He was looking at the hill that rose steeply on the other side of the road.

"Define that." My gaze swept across the dark gully and the trees that lined the hill beyond it. There was no light, and no fire, and yet... and yet energy was gathering.

Dark energy.

"I think she's—"

The rest of my comment died as a huge ball of flame erupted from the earth itself and thrust skywards. Monty swore and immediately cast his spell. It fell around us like a cloak, a fierce net of energy that neither looked nor felt strong enough to protect us from the sheer force of that fireball.

But it didn't turn. It didn't come at us.

Instead, with an inhuman scream, it spun and raced away, trailing flames behind her like a comet.

Dread surged as I realized where it was going. I had no way of getting there, no way of helping her.

Belle, get out of the truck and run like hell. Out loud, I added, "Monty, it's going after Belle and the jerry can!"

He hastily cast a second spell and then threw it after the soucouyant. The glowing threads of red and gold spun through the night, an arrow that lodged deep in the tail end of her flames. She screamed again and began to barrel roll, obviously trying to dislodge the spell. It didn't work but she didn't retaliate. She just continued to flame away from us.

Belle?

Running as fast as I can.

How far away from the truck are you? Because the older soucouyant is coming in fast.

Probably because I killed the other one.

What?

Had no choice—the spells containing it utterly broke down. It's just lucky I had the water gun handy or I would have been toast.

Shit, Belle—

Oh, I said a few harsher words than that, I can assure you.

But you're okay?

A little singed around the edges, but yes. She paused. *Not sure the same can be said about the truck's cabin though. The water may have killed the soucouyant but boy, did she go out with a bang.*

My gaze rose to the skyline. The soucouyant had dipped below the hill line. *Are you in the water yet?*

Diving in now. And I still have the water pistol with me.

Keep under as much as you can. I pushed through Monty's net and began to race down the hill. *I'm coming.*

Don't—

It's a witch's duty to keep her familiar safe, I bit back. *So just keep your head down until I get there.*

Nothing like having your own words used against you,

she muttered, with a slight edge in her mental tone. *Just be careful, okay?*

I ran across the road and up the hill, slipping and sliding on the rubble in my haste. A hand grabbed mine, at first steadying me and then sweeping me up into his arms and racing on.

"Aiden—"

"Shut up and let me concentrate."

I did. Even with my weight, he was getting up the hill far faster than I could.

But as we neared the top, there was a huge whoosh of energy and a fireball of heat lit up the night sky.

Belle? I silently screamed, my heart going a million miles an hour.

Safe, still safe, she said quickly. *But the bitch is now hunting me.*

Keep under the water as long as you can. We're not far away.

I'm a familiar, not a goddamn fish.

We reached the top of the hill. The valley below rolled out before us, a dark expanse lit by two fires—one the burning wreckage of Aiden's truck, the other, less bright fire the soucouyant.

Over the water and hunting Belle.

"Quick, put me down, Aiden."

Even as he obeyed, I began adding to the spell already twined around my fingers. I threw in everything I could think of, making it a combination of the fire spell that protected the café, wild magic, and the repelling spell. Then I took a deep breath and cast it, with as much force as I could muster, at the soucouyant.

The effort had my knees buckling, and I would have fallen had Aiden not grabbed me. I didn't say anything; I just watched, my heart beating so fiercely it felt ready to tear out of my chest. The fierce, pulsing ball of red, gold, and silver rocketed toward the soucouyant, but at the very last moment, she seemed to sense it and spun around. The ball hit the middle of her fiery form and then exploded. The force tore a scream from her body and sent her spiraling at speed away from the lake, away from Castle Rock.

It wasn't until her flames winked from sight that I in any way relaxed. *Belle, she's gone.*

That was some fucking spell you hit her with, she said. *Where'd you drag that one from?*

Desperation is the mother of invention. I glanced at Aiden. "The soucouyant is down for the night, but not dead."

"And Belle?"

"Safe."

"Does she want me to arrange someone to come pick her up?"

I silently asked the question and then shook my head. "She said it'll be quicker and easier if she simply walks back."

"Good." His gaze went to his burning truck for a second and then he touched my back lightly. "We'd better return to the house and see what sort of mess the soucouyant has left behind."

I turned and headed down the hill. Aiden called in his troops but kept close, touching my elbow and holding me steady the few times I slipped on the stony ground.

"We tried knocking front and back, but got no response," Monty said, as we neared. "Is Belle okay?"

"Yes, but the second soucouyant is no more."

His eyebrows rose. "The explosion destroyed her? I wouldn't have thought that possible."

"It wasn't. Our spells gave way and Belle super-soaked the soucouyant before it could crisp her."

"Shit." Monty thrust a hand through his hair. "How are we going to find the other one now?"

"That's your problem, not ours," I bit back. "And I'm sure Belle will appreciate your concern over her safety."

Surprise, and perhaps a bit of contriteness, crossed his expression. "That's not what I meant, and you know it."

"Argue about that on your own time," Aiden said. "We've a crime scene to investigate. Ashworth, Eli, can you two keep watch out here? Just in case that bitch comes back?" He glanced at Monty and me. "Ready?"

I flexed my fingers to ease some of the gathering tension and then nodded. Aiden pulled a set of gloves from the apparently endless supply in his pocket and then spun and walked to the door. Monty and I followed.

The door wasn't locked. Aiden pressed it open but didn't immediately enter. The short, somewhat dark entrance hall beyond intersected with a second hall that ran at right angles to it. Light glimmered from the left end while a TV blasted away to the right.

The sense of death I'd felt earlier hit like a hammer. I rubbed my arms and said, "There's someone dead to our left."

"Yeah, I can smell it. Follow me, and try not to touch anything."

He moved cautiously into the house, his footsteps making little noise on the old floorboards. We walked to the end of the hall and swung left, through a wide doorway that opened into a large kitchen-diner.

Lying in the middle of the floor was an elderly couple. They were both half naked and bore the love-bite-like bruising that had been evident in the very first murder, but neither of them had been stripped of their skin.

Aiden squatted next to the man and felt for a pulse. He grimaced and then moved across to the woman. "Both dead," he said, looking up.

"That's not what's so surprising here," Monty said. "But rather the fact they're both intact."

"Maybe she didn't have the time to strip either of them," I commented.

"She had time to feed," he replied. "And she wasn't in the house when we rocked up, remember. That suggests she had no intention of skinning either of these two."

I frowned. "But why not? It would have been a whole lot easier to steal a skin and then head out into the unknowing population."

Monty hesitated. "Maybe it has something to do with her skin."

I glanced at him. "But she can't reclaim her skin—it's been salted."

"Yes, but maybe the fact her skin is still out there rather than destroyed means she can't claim another, however temporary."

"Which means she might try to either reclaim or destroy it." I glanced at Aiden. "Where's that skin being kept?"

"I had it moved to the tank around the back of the station, just in case she decided to retrieve it." He grimaced. "Of course, given her willingness to blow things up, that might not help."

"I doubt she has the same sort of connection to her skin as she did the other soucouyant," Monty said. "If she did, she would have hit it by now."

"At least that's one bit of good news in an evening filled

with bad." He rose as the sound of sirens began to approach. "I'll get Jaz to take you both home."

Monty frowned. "The possibility of the soucouyant returning tonight is low, I know, but I'd rather stay, just in case."

Aiden shrugged and touched my arm lightly. "I'll see you tomorrow sometime."

I nodded and left. Belle had returned and was now standing next to Ashworth and Eli under an old eucalypt tree. The left leg of her jeans had a handful of burned patches, and there were a couple more on her T-shirt. The skin underneath was red but didn't appear to be blistering—probably because she'd jumped into the water not long after the soucouyant had escaped. I tugged some of the holy water out of the backpack and handed it to her. It had stopped Anna's more serious burns from causing permanent damage, so it would certainly take care of Belle's.

"You know," I said, as she started dousing the burns, "considering the explodability of gum trees and the fact we're dealing with a fire spirit, standing under this tree isn't the brightest of moves."

Ashworth's grin flashed. "Nothing like a bit of danger to spice up life. What's it like inside?"

"Two dead people with skins intact. Monty's theory is the soucouyant can't claim another until hers has been destroyed."

"That's more than possible," Eli said. "What's being done to protect her original skin?"

"It remains in salt water."

Ashworth grunted. "It should be safe enough, then."

"I hope so." The noise from the sirens sharpened; I glanced around and saw three ranger vehicles crest the hill and race toward us. "Aiden's asked Jaz to take us all home."

"Do you think that's wise?" Eli asked. "The soucouyant might return to finish what she—"

"Which is why Monty is staying."

Ashworth snorted. I raised an eyebrow and added, "I get this feeling that you're not overly impressed with Monty."

"I'm not overly impressed with his lack of experience," Ashworth said. "He certainly has the power, but he hasn't anything more than basic knowledge when it comes to the dark forces in this world, and *that* could be dangerous for us all."

"All?" I raised my eyebrows. "You've definitely decided to settle here then?"

"It's your fault," he said. "You and Belle are too damn interesting."

"And our cakes too damn delicious," Belle said dryly. She handed me the empty bottles, and I tossed them back into the pack.

"That could also be a factor."

I grinned and glanced around as the three ranger trucks switched off their sirens and pulled up in front of the house. Jaz motioned us to get in and then whisked us back to Castle Rock. I was pretty relieved to be home, but it wasn't like my day—or rather, my night—was over just yet.

"Wouldn't it be better to worry about the charms tomorrow, when you're well rested?" Belle locked the front door and then followed me through the main room.

"Probably." I tossed the backpack on the counter and moved around to flick on the kettle. "But I feel the need to do it now."

She grunted. "The timing of your psychic radar sometimes leaves a lot to be desired. Do you need some help?"

"No. You go rest—and make sure you put salve on those burns."

"I've already used the holy water, and they're only minor—"

"And they're the ones that often present the most danger when it comes to infection."

She raised her hands, a smile touching her lips. "Okay, okay, salve will be applied, but only after a shower. That water was filled with things that moved, and I want to make sure no leeches—or anything else, for that matter—have hitched a lift on this bod."

"Before you go, I'll grab your charm—it'll be easier to attach the fire repelling spell to that than start all over again."

She nodded and tugged the charm from her neck. The magic within it caressed my fingers, a wash of energy that was possibly the strongest we'd ever created—at least until I'd woven the fire spell into the café's protections, anyway. Both our charms were made from multiple strands of leather and copper, with each strand representing a different type of protection. Silver would have been the ulti- mate choice when it came to spell conduits, but that wasn't really practical in a werewolf reservation. Or when I was dating a werewolf.

Belle went upstairs. I made myself a hot chocolate, grabbed a large piece of banana cake to boost my energy, and then headed into the reading room. I shifted the furni- ture, then sat cross-legged on the floor. The spells protecting the room swirled around me—an energy I could now see as strongly as I could feel. The wild magic seemed to be strengthening my "other" senses, and I couldn't help but wonder again just how far it would go.

And whether it would be enough to stop my father and Clayton when they got here.

Trepidation and fear shivered through me. I shoved

them both aside and pulled my charm over my head, placing it on the floor beside Belle's.

But I didn't immediately begin. Instead, I ate the cake and drank my chocolate, knowing I'd need the sugar rush to get me through the next half hour or so. Then, with a deep breath to center my energy, I picked up Belle's charm, first deactivating it and then undoing the sealing thread. With the spell lines exposed, I carefully picked my way through them until I'd reached the two at the heart of the charm—the ones that repelled specific demons and spirits. I gently recrafted the spells to include both the soucouyant and other beings of fire. The wild magic once again stirred through my spell, adding to its power. Whether in the end it would be enough, I really couldn't say, but it was certainly better than nothing. I locked the fire spell down and then retreated, strengthening and then closing the other layers as I did. Once that was complete, I activated the charm once again. A niggling ache flared in my head, a warning that I was pushing my limits. I briefly closed my eyes then got to my feet and headed out to grab some painkillers and make myself another cup of hot chocolate. The task was only half done—I still had one charm to go.

By the time I'd finished, that niggling headache was full-blown. I rubbed my temples wearily and then picked up the two charms, putting them both over my head before shoving the furniture back into place.

I was halfway to the kitchen when the prophetic part of my soul kicked into gear, swamping my vision and my senses with heat and fire.

I swore and grabbed at the wall in an effort to steady myself, but my senses were swimming and the visions flickering so fast through my brain that it was disorientating. I slid to the floor before I fell and closed my eyes, trying to concentrate on slowing the images down, on trying to see what my psychic senses wanted to show me.

After a dizzying couple of seconds, the fiery reel slowed. I didn't immediately see anything other than fire—a huge ball of it, rising from beyond the buildings that lined the other side of our street. Then it spun and a building formed —a brick double-story townhouse.

Monty's place.

Fear had my heart tripping into a higher gear, but the vision wasn't finished with me yet. Even as the building became clear, it exploded into flames. And then I saw Monty—unhurt, unburned—coming out of the building. But not under his own steam.

He was in the arms of the soucouyant.

The fear increased, but the dream flicked direction. A sky emblazoned with the rich colors of sunset. A deep, dark forest. Aiden in a ranger SUV.

The latter two were on fire.

No, I thought. *No.*

A sob tore up my throat and the dream shattered. I dropped the cup, scrambled to the backpack, and grabbed my phone.

Aiden answered on the second ring. "Liz—"

"Where are you?" I said.

"Still at the house—why?"

"And Monty?"

"Also here." The concern in his tone grew. "Again, why?"

"Because I just had a vision, and I saw the soucouyant attacking you both."

Saw you die....

I swallowed heavily against the tears that rose. Just because I saw it doesn't mean it was meant to be.

"Did she attack us here?" he asked quickly. "Because we'll evacuate immediately—"

"No, it didn't happen there." I took a deep breath and tried to calm down. "It just scared me enough that I had to ring and make sure you were both okay."

His grunt sounded rather relieved. "Thankfully, we're almost finished."

"Good." I hesitated. "If Monty's near, can I speak to him?"

"Sure." The sound of footsteps echoed down the line, and then Monty said, his tone surprised, "Liz? What can I do for you?"

"I just had one hell of a vision about you and the soucouyant." I quickly told him what I'd seen and then said, "It might be best if you come here tonight rather than to your own place. You can sleep on the sofa—"

"Liz, the mere fact it was dusk when the attack happened suggests it'll be safe enough to go home tonight."

"Yes, but—"

"I'll boost the protections around the townhouse and weave the fire net through it," he continued evenly. "It should hold her off long enough for me to get somewhere safe."

"I'm not worried about her fire," I bit back. "I'm worried about *her*. About what she plans to do with you."

"Given she hasn't an actual body, she can't do much more than throw firebombs at me. I doubt she'd actually risk coming into town in her true form—especially at sunset, when there's so much traffic and people moving about."

"You're wrong." *So* wrong.

"I'll tell you what," he said. "I'll pack a bag and head over to your place tomorrow evening. If I'm not at my house, the vision can't come true, right?"

"Prophetic dreams deal in possibilities not absolutes—"

"Yes, but that doesn't alter the fact that if I'm not there she can't get me."

I took a deep breath and hoped with all I had that he was right. "Fine. I'll see you tomorrow then."

"Yes you will," he said, and hung up.

I looked at the screen for a second, then swore and rang Aiden back. There was nothing more I could do when it came to Monty. I'd warned him, and if he chose not to take it seriously, then on his head be it.

Aiden was an entirely different matter.

"Liz," Aiden said, "I take it the talk with Monty didn't achieve the desired results."

"How'd you guess?"

"Monty made a comment along the lines of you and Belle being worrywarts. I informed him you had good reason, and that he was better off to listen than not."

"And his reaction?"

"I suspect he thinks I'm defending you because I'm sweet on you."

I snorted softly. "Just shows how little he knows either of us."

"Indeed. We're about five minutes away from packing up—do you need something?"

"Yeah—that charm I made for you. I want to add another spell to it that'll hopefully protect you from the soucouyant and fire, the latter if only briefly."

"Briefly might just save my life." His voice was somber. "I'll be there in about twenty minutes."

He was there in eighteen. I locked the door behind him and then said, "How'd things go up at the farmhouse?"

He grimaced. "As well as can be expected. But the council will probably have to release a statement tomorrow

—we've too many kills now for them to expect the press to sit on it."

"Not to mention the efforts of the gossip brigade."

"Yeah." He pulled out a chair at our usual table and sat down. "The council is also unhappy about the prospect of replacing so many vehicles."

"That suggests you've already talked to them."

"The weekly council meeting is on tonight and I'm usually there to make a report. When I didn't show up, they rang me—and that's when I mentioned the two trucks and the car."

I moved behind the counter to make him a coffee. "The soucouyant might have destroyed your truck, but Ashworth's didn't look that damaged. And what car?"

He raised his eyebrow. "Have you forgotten you're currently without a vehicle?"

"Well no, but why would they replace ours?"

"Because you were in pursuit of the soucouyant on our behalf at the time, and *that* makes it their responsibility. Besides, it's the *least* they can do, given how much help you've been to this reservation."

"Well, I can't say that it wouldn't be appreciated. We do have insurance, but the car was so old, we won't get much in the way of replacement value." I dragged out a mug and tossed some instant coffee into it. "And Ashworth's truck?"

"The whole undercarriage and all the wiring was basically burned out by the blast of heat. It'd be more cost-effective for the council to replace it than try and repair it."

"I can't see Ashworth arguing about that."

"Then you'd be wrong. He apparently has a soft spot for the truck—he rebuilt it with his brother."

Which totally explained his surge of anger when he'd heard it had been overturned. "So what's going to happen?"

"The council will probably replace it. If the insurance company decides to wreck it—as we suspect they will—then Ashworth will buy it back and start the repair process."

"Huh." I made his coffee, then plated up several pieces of brownie and carried them over. I exchanged them for his charm and then said, "This will take about half an hour—can you wait? I don't want you going home without it."

You could ask him to stay the night, Belle said. *We can bend the "no booty call in the home" rule this once.*

And if I do, I'll be forever plagued by memories of his presence in my bed when we break up.

Ah, she said. *Good point.*

"If it's going to save my life," Aiden was saying, "then I have all the time in the world."

"Good." I kissed him quickly and then hurried into the reading room before my suddenly awake hormones were tempted to do anything more.

I shoved all the furniture aside yet again and then sat on the floor. I'd designed his charm to mimic the neck-cords I'd seen many younger wolves wearing, so it had three different-colored leathers as well as a copper strand. It protected him from ill-intent, evil spirits, and most curses *except* for those created by blood witches, but it wouldn't protect him from something as strong as this soucouyant. And it certainly wouldn't protect him against any sort of arcane fire —and that's what was needed right now.

I took a deep breath and carefully deactivated the charm. Then I undid the sealing thread and began to weave the new protections through the various other spells. It took more energy than I really had, and by the time I'd finished, my eyes were watering with the pain in my head and all I wanted to do was sleep. I didn't bother pushing the furniture back. I just headed out and handed Aiden the charm.

He accepted it with a frown. "Are you okay?"

I waved a hand. "I will be. I've just woven new spells through three charms in the space of a couple of hours, and it takes a toll."

"You'd best go upstairs and grab some sleep then. I'd rather not be relying on just Monty tomorrow if your vision does come true."

"If my vision comes true, Monty will be the actual problem." I scrubbed a hand through my hair. "Let's just hope that I'm wrong."

"Indeed."

He caught my hand and tugged me into his arms. He didn't kiss me, didn't do anything more than simply hold me, and once again, it made me feel safer than I'd ever felt before.

"I'd better go. Otherwise you won't be the only one in no fit state to cope with problems tomorrow."

He kissed the top of my head and pulled away. I stopped him, then wrapped my arms around his neck and kissed him with all the fire and passion bubbling inside.

"That," I said, after a long while, "is how we say goodnight where I come from."

"A method I highly approve of." Amusement creased the corners of his bright eyes. "Only trouble is, it's one that inevitably leads to a restless night."

My gaze skimmed down his body and a grin split my lips. "I'm sure you're quite capable of taking *that* problem in hand."

"I think I'd rather wait until *you* can take the problem in hand."

"Which is a distinct possibility, but only after the soucouyant is caught."

"I can wait." He bent and kissed me again. Then, with a

soft curse that spoke of frustration, he turned and stalked toward the door. I watched until he'd climbed safely into the SUV and driven away, and then locked the door and headed upstairs. Where I collapsed into a deep, unbroken sleep.

I was late waking the next morning, but the headache had at least disappeared. After a quick shower to freshen up, I clattered down the stairs to help with the café. We had a steady flow of customers all day, and there was a whole lot of discussion and nervousness about the recent spate of murders—and most of it *didn't* come from the brigade. Aiden was right—if the council didn't release a statement, there was going to be trouble. It would be interesting to see what they actually said, though, because I very much doubted telling everyone there was a murderous fire spirit loose in the reservation would in any way ease the nervousness.

Monty appeared near six, a backpack slung over his shoulder and his expression suggesting he was simply humoring me. Not that it mattered. Not if doing so kept him safe.

After we'd eaten dinner, I made us all a cappuccino and brought them over to the table. "How are we going to track this thing now that we haven't got the other one?"

Monty accepted his coffee with a nod of thanks. "I'm not really sure. The only thing Jamie—my mate in Canberra —could come up with was doing some sort of heat-seeking spell. But that would only work outside Castle Rock, simply because there're too many points of heat within the city center."

Belle took a sip of her coffee and then leaned back in the chair. "What if you set a specific heat level within the spell? That would cut out much of the heat chatter from the city itself."

"Good idea, but there's one problem—I've never come across a heat-seeking spell. Jamie is still going through the archives to see what he can find."

I frowned. "There surely has to be something somewhere. Soucouyants and fire spirits have been around for as long as witches—if not longer."

"Maybe so, but that doesn't alter the fact there's nothing in the everyday databanks." Monty picked up a teaspoon and scooped up some of the froth on the top of the coffee. "I've asked him to instigate a European search. We might have greater luck in more ancient archives."

I frowned. "How long is that likely to take though?"

"He'll make it as a priority one request, so it could take a couple of hours or it could take a couple of days." He shrugged. "So unless we can fudge a spell—and I'm not really certain that's the best option right now—then we've no other choice but to wait."

"I don't think we can afford to." Especially when any sort of delay might lead to someone else dying. *Belle, what's the likelihood of us finding something in your books?*

Who knows? I did pull a couple of spell books from the boxes, but they're not indexed so we'll have to go through them.

And that will have to be done tonight if we're to have any hope of catching this thing before it kills again. I paused. *It also means we'll have to let Monty know about your gran's books.*

We don't actually have to mention or even show him the entire the library, she said. *The three spells books are sitting on the coffee table upstairs. He won't see the others—they're either in my room or in the storage unit.*

"I get the feeling you two are having a whole conversation without me," Monty said.

"That's because we are." My tone was bland. "But the upshot is, we might have a couple of books that could help our search."

He raised his eyebrows. "Really?"

I smiled at the doubt in his voice. "Do you remember Belle's gran?"

"No—should I?"

"Hell, yes." Belle's tone was indignant. "She was a rather famous cataloger, and not only had a huge library of all things supernatural, but a rather large collection of spell books."

"If that were the case, why isn't her collection in the national library?" he asked. "It should be, if it was that important."

Belle shrugged. "I'm actually not sure why it was never gifted to the national library or even where the vast majority of her books went, but Mom did give me a couple of her old spell books on my thirteenth birthday. I still have them upstairs."

Monty frowned. "And you think we'll find something in one of them?"

"Look at the spells surrounding this place," I said. "You commented on our unconventional mode of magic—where do you think we learned it, given we both left school so early?"

"We should go upstairs and start reading, then."

He immediately picked up his coffee and strode for the stairs. We scrambled after him.

"Wow," he commented. "Not a whole lot of room up here, is there?"

"No, and you can either sit on the floor or drag one of the chairs in from the balcony outside."

He gave me the look. "I hope you're not expecting me to sleep on the floor, because I'm telling you now, it ain't going to happen."

I grinned. "Don't worry, I'm well aware you're far too soft to be sleeping rough. The sofa pulls out into a double bed."

He gave the sofa a somewhat dubious look, then walked over to the coffee table and picked up the first of the three leather-bound books sitting there.

"Wow." He turned the book over almost reverently. "These really *are* old."

"Yes, so I'll ask you to be careful with them when you're reading," Belle said.

He nodded, grabbed a couple of cushions from the sofa, and then propped on the floor. Belle and I grabbed a book each, then plopped down on the sofa and began reading.

It was a long and rather unfruitful night.

Eventually, Monty snapped his book shut and yawned hugely. "The spells in here are quite fascinating, but in this one, at least, there doesn't appear to be anything resembling a heat or spirit tracker."

"Ditto, but that doesn't mean it's not possible to make one up."

He frowned again. "It's never wise to be fiddling with the nature of spells. It can lead to unforeseen consequences."

"It might also lead to the soucouyant." I glanced at him. "What have we got to lose?"

"You mean other than our lives?"

"A heat-seeking spell isn't likely to backfire badly enough to kill us," I bit back.

Monty's been in cataloguing for a very long time, Belle said. *This is all very new to him, and we need to give him time to adjust.*

Except we don't have time, Belle. And neither did Monty.

"I'll ignore that statement simply because you didn't go to university and haven't witnessed the consequences of someone not spelling as it was written."

"I've been *not* following spells as they were written for most of my adult life, Monty. Sometimes you have to step outside norms and procedures to get anywhere."

"I'd wager most of your spells have never been either major or dangerous." It was impatiently said, with just the slightest edge of annoyance. "Please give me the benefit of knowing what I'm talking about when it comes to higher-level spells."

Don't, Belle said, before I even opened my mouth. *There's no point in antagonizing him any further right now. It won't get us anywhere.*

Neither will sitting here doing nothing. I snapped my book shut, then rose and walked over to the sliding door. The night was quiet, and I had no sense of anything untoward happening. Which was odd, given my earlier vision. I took a deep breath to calm the frustration and then said, as calmly as I could, "The soucouyant is out there somewhere, and it's more than possible she's preying on someone new."

"That may be the case, but until we find another means of tracking her, there's *nothing* we can do," Monty said. "Besides, it's also very possible that after the events of the last few days *and* losing her offspring, she's lying low."

I glanced down at him. "I'd have thought losing her offspring would have made her even more determined to seek revenge."

"But as you've said a couple of times, we're dealing with a very old spirit. She won't act irrationally."

"Acting rationally *and* acting fast are not mutually exclusive."

"Yes, but she's expended a lot of energy over the last couple of days and that'll take time to replenish."

I crossed my arms and returned my gaze to the night and the stars. I couldn't escape the feeling that we needed to find her before the events in my vision had the chance to come true. I needed—we needed—to be doing something, even if that something amounted to nothing.

"That fire protection net you use," I said eventually. "Why can't we tweak that and make it seek heat rather than protect against it?"

I'd already used elements of that spell in both the protections around this place and in the three charms, but I'd also added my own embellishments because I didn't know the entire spell. Monty did—and that meant he should be able to reverse the spell's usage. It might not be easy, but it should be possible.

Monty frowned. "I wouldn't know where to start something like that."

"We could try casting aside the protection threads and weave in a heat finding spell instead. Finders are easy enough to create."

"Only because we generally have something personal to work off, and we can't use her skin because it's been salted. It'll foul whatever spell we try." His frown deepened. "Most spirits are notoriously hard to find—that's probably why there's minimal information when it comes to tracking them."

"We've nothing to lose by trying, Monty."

He studied me for several seconds and then shrugged. "I guess we don't."

"We'll need to use your vehicle if the spell succeeds," I said. "Ours is in bits."

"If mine ends up the same way, I *will* be pissed. It's a classic." He pushed to his feet. "I'll attempt the reversal in that spell room of yours. If it works, we'll head out for a few hours. Okay?"

A few hours would probably not be enough given the size of the reservation, but it was better than nothing. I glanced at Belle. "You'd better stay here and grab some sleep. One of us needs to be fit to serve customers tomorrow."

She nodded. "Just be careful out there, both of you."

I couldn't help smiling. "Careful is my middle name, remember?"

She snorted. *If you keep saying that often enough, fate might just believe you. But I certainly won't.*

My smile grew, but I didn't say anything as I followed Monty down the stairs and into the reading room.

"Nice range of spells," he said, his gaze on the ceiling. "It's tending a little toward overkill though, isn't it?"

"Wait until you're attacked by heretic witches and magic-capable vampires." I shoved the table aside and then rolled up the rug. "We'll see if you think its overkill then."

He grunted and sat down. I sat opposite him—not because I had any intention of interfering, but because I wanted to see the spell in its entirety so I could use or adjust it at a later date.

Monty took a deep breath and then began his spell. I watched intently, filing away the words he spoke as much as the look and feel of each thread. Once the spell was complete, he began unpicking various threads, reversing the polarity of them so that they would seek heat rather than protect from it. It was very cleverly done, and whatever I thought about Monty's over-cautious ways, when push came to shove, he was far superior in *every* way when it came to spelling, be it traditional or ad hoc.

Once he'd finished rearranging the threads, he fashioned the spell into an easy-to-handle orb and then activated it. "Right," he said. "Though it's not showing much at the moment, energy should pulse through the threads as we get closer to arcane heat. It's the best I could do."

"It's great, Monty. And thanks for trying."

He grimaced. "I still think it's a fool's errand but you're right—we have to at least try."

He pushed to his feet and dug his keys out of his pocket. "Drive her gently, and don't crunch the gears."

"I'll try not to—but I drive automatics for a reason, I'm afraid."

He winced but didn't say anything else. We both grabbed our backpacks and headed out. Once I'd locked the door, he said, "It's down the street on the right."

I looked across the road. "The old red Mustang?"

"It's a classic 1967 V8 Mustang, thank you very much." His voice held a hint of censure. "You're obviously a heathen when it comes to cars."

"Undoubtedly, because as long as they get me from point A to point B, I'm really not fussed."

He shook his head. "Driving should *never* just be about getting from one point to another. It should be about the experience, the power, and the feel."

I glanced at him, eyebrow raised. "Seriously?"

He grinned. "Tell me you don't understand *after* you've driven her."

I snorted but nevertheless walked over to it. "How'd you get it down here so fast?"

"I arranged for it to be transported down the minute it was confirmed I had the position. It arrived yesterday."

"What is it with you men and your cars?"

He grinned. "They don't take as much time and effort as women. And they don't talk back." He paused. "Not that often, anyway."

I smiled and shook my head. Once we were both in his car, I started her up. I had to admit, the heavy rumble of the big engine was a rather awesome sound. I took off gently, getting used to the car and the gears, but growing more confident as we began a circuit first around the main section of town and then around the outskirts.

Monty's spell remained stubbornly mute.

I pulled to a halt at an intersection and looked right and left. "Where next? Up towards Hank's Mill or down to Rayburn Springs?"

He hesitated, his gaze narrowed as he studied the orb sitting in his hand. "Left."

I put on the blinker and went that way. As the street-lights faded and the stars grew brighter, energy began to flicker across the orb's surface. But it was faint. Very faint.

We continued on. The pulsing through the orb didn't alter, which really didn't make a whole lot of sense. Unless the soucouyant was somehow aware of our movements and tracking from a distance, of course, but I doubted that was the case. If she'd been close enough to see us leave the café, she'd have been close enough to kill us.

The signal didn't alter as we entered the outskirts of Argyle and then drove through the center of town.

"This isn't working." Monty's voice was weary. "The

spell is detecting *something*, but I'm not convinced it's the soucouyant."

Which was more than a little frustrating. "Shall we go back a different way, just in case?"

He shrugged. "We've got nothing to lose."

I swung left at the roundabout and headed out of Argyle. As we left the lights behind us, the orb began to glow again, but it remained faint. As we neared Castle Rock again, the orb—and its magic—began to disintegrate.

"Sorry," Monty said. "But it would have taken too much energy to create a spell to last much longer than a couple of hours."

"At least we tried." Which didn't ease the niggling feeling that the soucouyant was waiting to pounce the minute we had our backs turned.

As I pulled up in front of the café, Monty said, "Leave the engine running. I think I'll head home."

"Monty—"

"I know what you saw," he said. "And I believe it. But we're a long way from dusk right now, and I'd rather sleep in my own bed than on your couch."

"Yes, but—"

"You can make me dinner again tomorrow night," he said. "Hopefully by that time, Jamie will have come through with a better means of tracking and killing the bitch."

I hesitated, but his set expression said there was no way I was ever going to talk him out of this course of action.

I blew out a breath in frustration—a common affliction tonight, it seemed—and then reached around and grabbed my backpack from the rear seat. "Just make sure you set your protections—"

"Liz," he said gently. "I may be new to this whole spirit-hunting thing, but I'm *not* stupid."

"I'm not saying you are, but—"

"Stop worrying," he cut in again. "I'll see you tomorrow, and we can plot our next course of action. Okay?"

"Okay." I shoved the door open and clambered out.

He jumped into the driver side, slammed the door shut and, with a quick wave, drove off. Leaving me standing in the middle of the road, staring after him and feeling even uneasier.

I grimaced and headed for the front door. Monty was a grown man and a strong witch besides. I had to trust he knew what he was doing, even if my gut was saying he was doing the wrong thing.

Once I'd grabbed my phone, I placed the backpack in the reading room and then headed upstairs. I took a quick shower in a vague effort to wash away the unease and frustration and then finally climbed into bed. But my dreams were filled with fiery dread, and I woke with a start some hours later.

For several seconds, I didn't move. I just stared into the darkness, listening to the creaks and groans of the old building, wondering what had woken me. Wondering why my body was bathed in sweat and my heart beat so fiercely.

Nothing stirred through the darkness. There was no hint that anything—or anyone—was testing the magic that protected this place.

But something was happening. Not here, perhaps, but out there in the deeper darkness. I frowned and reached for my phone—it was four forty-five. Dawn was still a good half an hour or more away. Plenty of time yet for the soucouyant to be active without the sunlight pulling on her strength.

I tossed the covers aside and hastily pulled on a T-shirt as I padded through the living room to the sliding door. It squealed slightly as I pushed it open, the sound reverberating through the silence as sharply as fingernails down a blackboard. I hesitated, glancing over my shoulder, wondering if I'd disturbed Belle. Relief stirred when she didn't appear. I didn't want to be waking her if the trepidation stirring through me was nothing more than unwarranted fear.

The predawn darkness held a cool edge, but the sky was clear and the stars still bright. I stepped out onto the balcony and walked over to the edge. There was little noise to be heard other than the occasional rumble of a car from the nearby Midland Highway, and nothing moving on the street below.

Castle Rock was at peace.

And that, for some reason, only tightened the strands of unease.

I hesitated and then walked across to one of the chairs, dragging it around and then carefully standing on top of it. It didn't really help me see over the rooftops of the buildings opposite, but I nevertheless looked in the direction of Monty's street and scanned the skyline. No hint of heat. No flicker of fire to suggest either the soucouyant or one of her fireballs was about to attack Monty.

And yet I feared that was exactly what was about to happen.

I jumped off my chair and strode toward the sliding door. But just as I stepped inside, energy hit. It was a fleeting wash of power and heat that nevertheless promised death. I swung around, my heart pounding violently somewhere in the vicinity of my tonsils.

And saw a huge whoosh of flame erupt from the area where Monty lived.

My vision, come to life.

ELEVEN

My vision *hadn't* been wrong; I'd just interpreted it incorrectly. I locked the sliding door and ran for my bedroom, barely avoiding Belle as she came out of hers.

"What's the problem?"

"Monty's being attacked. Get dressed."

She swore and disappeared again. I quickly got dressed then grabbed my phone and ran downstairs for the backpack.

And only *then* remembered we didn't have a car.

I cursed, but I wasn't about to hang around waiting for a cab—not when Monty's place was only a couple of streets away. I dug out my keys and, as Belle came clattering down the stairs, opened the front door.

"You want me to call Ashworth?" she said.

I nodded and locked up once we were both out. "I'll call Aiden."

I tugged my phone from my back pocket and bolted down the street after Belle. The phone rang a couple of times, then Aiden's sleep-laden voice said, "What's happened?"

"Monty's being attacked."

"I'll be there in ten."

"You're up at the O'Connor compound?"

"Yeah." He paused. "You're obviously running to Monty's but be careful, Liz. She could be out to grab you both."

"That's not what I saw, Aiden. Something else is going on—something *other* than the immediate need for revenge."

"That may be so, but I'd still appreciate it if you're careful."

"Oh, trust me, the only thing I intend to get burned by is your body heat."

"Good," he said, and hung up.

I shoved the phone back into my pocket and picked up my pace to catch up with Belle—a hard task given her longer legs.

"Ashworth and Eli felt the explosion and are on their way," she said. "They should be there the same time as us."

I studied the flames shooting skyward and hoped like hell the soucouyant hadn't taken out the houses—and the people—on either side of Monty's place. "I guess if this *is* a trap, we'll find out pretty quickly if my alterations to the charms worked."

We continued to pound down the footpath, our footsteps echoing across the night. There were lots of people standing in the middle of Monty's street, most of them in pajamas or with dressing gowns wrapped tightly around their bodies. A few had hoses out in an attempt to keep the flames from consuming the houses on either side of Monty's.

His place was just a fire pit. I could feel the force and the heat of it long before we got anywhere near it, and it made me wonder if the soucouyant had simply decided to obliterate him.

If that were the case, then there was very little chance of us ever finding his remains. The flames were white-hot and the house little more than ashy piles that were being picked up and spread in the vortex of the fire.

We stopped out the front of his place; the air practically sizzled, and sweat instantly broke out across my body. I threw up an arm to protect my face from the heat and desperately scanned the front yard.

There was no sign of the soucouyant, but the faintest sliver of her energy lingered in the air. She'd been here, all right. I guessed the question we desperately needed an answer to now was, had she taken Monty as I'd seen? I hoped so, if only because it gave us a chance, however faint, to find and save him. I really *didn't* want to lose one of the few relatives I didn't actually hate.

"There's absolutely nothing left," Belle said, shock in her voice. "She's obliterated everything."

A finger of fire flicked toward us. We both took a quick step back, but its speed and reach died little more than a dozen feet away from the main blast. But it was warning enough—get too close, and the fire *would* hit us.

The squeal of tires rose above the babble of noise behind us, and I looked around to see Eli's truck race toward us. It slid to a halt, then the two men climbed out and ran toward us.

"Oh, fuck," Ashworth said. "How likely is it that he's in there?"

I hesitated. "That depends."

He glanced at me sharply. "On what?"

"On whether what I saw in my vision is true or not. This part of it certainly is."

"Meaning she's taken him?"

"Possibly, yes."

"Which means you could find him if we found something bearing his life force?" Eli asked. "I rather suspect that even if he *is* alive, time is of the essence."

"I'm well aware of that point, trust me." My gaze swept the disintegrating ashes of the house again. "Where's his car? There's no carport or garage here, and I doubt he'd keep his precious Mustang in the street."

"He keeps it in a storage facility several streets away." Aiden came running up. "I'll ring the facility's owner now, and get him over there to open it up."

"His car keys won't be there, though, and believe me when I say he will not be impressed if you break into it."

"There's no spell to magic car doors open?" Aiden asked. "I find that surprising."

"There is," Eli said. "But there are also quicker ways to get into a car—especially the older ones."

Aiden's eyebrows rose. "Indeed there are, but I'm surprised you know them."

Ashworth's grin flashed. "He doesn't. I do. I'm a car nut who broke the occasional rule when I was a down-on-my-luck teenager needing parts."

"You're an Ashworth," I said dryly. "None of them could ever be classified as poor."

"Except my father did *not* approve of my car habit and cut my allowance." He shrugged. "Let's just say I played in the shade for a few years before sense reasserted itself."

"Don't you get more and more interesting," Belle said, amusement evident.

"I'm old, but I'm certainly not boring, lass."

"That's the one thing no one will ever accuse you of being."

The fire brigade and a couple of ranger vehicles appeared in the street, their lights flashing as they screamed toward us.

"I'll go update Tala," Aiden said, "and then we'll head over to the storage unit."

I nodded and returned my gaze to the fire. "We know salted water works on soucouyants—Belle used it to destroy the younger one. What we need is a better means of applying it than the water pistols and weed killer dispenser we currently have."

"A couple of high-pressure backpack sprayers will give us wiggle room when it comes to distance," Ashworth said, "but that bitch will burn us all the minute she sees or hears any of us."

"The thing I don't get," Eli said, "is her taking Monty. Why not just kill him straight away?"

"What if she wants revenge first?" Belle's voice was grim. "I killed her offspring, remember?"

I scrubbed a hand through my tangled hair. "That's more than possible."

"It still doesn't explain why she went after Monty," Eli said.

"Monty lodged the tail of his tracking spell into the younger soucouyant's fire, so it's possible the older one got a feel for his magic once our containment spells started breaking down," I said. "And Belle was in the water by the time the older one blew up Aiden's truck. She might be aware Monty *didn't* kill her offspring, but not really sure who did."

"Which means she'll either have to steal another skin," Belle said, "or find a means of contacting us."

I rubbed my arms, cold despite the heat still rolling from the fireball. "I have a bad feeling it's going to be the latter."

Ashworth grunted and gently squeezed my shoulder. "There's four of us, lass. We'll figure out a way to beat this bitch—believe that if nothing else."

A smile tugged my lips; it very much seemed that in becoming a person of interest to Ashworth, I'd also gained something of a pseudo-grandfather. Which, considering my real grandfather was long gone, was all right by me.

Jaz stopped beside us, her expression grim as she studied the house remains. "Aiden wants you to head down to the rear ranger's SUV, and he'll meet you all there." She hesitated and then added, "How safe is it for anyone to approach the house?"

"I wouldn't be going anywhere near it until the fire dies down," Ashworth said. "I'm afraid it's not a natural fire and will attack anyone who approaches."

Jaz nodded. "I'll tell Tala and we'll set up a perimeter. Good luck out there."

We headed for the SUV. Belle and I climbed into it while Ashworth and Eli continued on to their own truck. Aiden got in a few minutes later and, after a quick check in the rearview mirror to ensure Ashworth and Eli were ready, led the way across town to the storage facility. He stopped beside the old Toyota truck parked in the driveway and, as we all climbed out, a gray-haired, somewhat paunchy man in his midfifties came around the corner and strode toward us.

"I've opened the unit." His tone was matter-of-fact. "But I'll have to be present when you enter, and the cameras will be recording what happens."

"That's fine," Aiden said, and motioned the man to lead the way.

Monty's unit was one of the larger ones to the rear of

the facility, and was double-door—no doubt to avoid any possible risk of scratches when reversing out.

The Mustang sat in the middle of the large unit; to the left, there were multiple stacks of full packing boxes— meaning at least he hadn't lost everything he owned in the explosion—and, on the other side, shelves stacked with car bits and pieces.

I moved to the right and ran my hand over the various items, looking for something that contained enough of Monty's vibes to find him. A slight tingle of energy came from the polishing cloth sitting on top of the wax container, but it wasn't strong enough to be of much use.

I moved around the car and ran my fingers along the front of the boxes. Again, nothing. I swore and then glanced at Aiden. "We're going to have to break in."

"Hang on while I go grab a coat hanger," Ashworth said.

He was back within seconds, a screwdriver and an elongated coat hanger in one hand. He carefully levered the window away from the weather strip with the screwdriver and then stuck a hanger down in the gap between the window and the door. After a couple of seconds, the door popped open.

"Impressive." Aiden's voice was dry. "And your proficiency suggests you did more than dabble."

Ashworth didn't deny it. He simply opened the door and then motioned me to get in. I slipped inside the car and skimmed my hand over everything. It wasn't until I neared the glove compartment that I got a reaction. I quickly opened it; the top layer consisted of the car's service books and packets of spare fuses and globes—none of which held his resonance. I pulled them out and then leaned over the center console for a better look at the back of the compartment. And there, in the rear, was a gold ring. Even before I grabbed it, my fingers began to burn.

It wasn't a reaction caused by my psychometry flaring to life.

It was a reflection of what Monty was currently feeling.

But the fact I was getting *that* so strongly, without going too deep, not only suggested his connection with this ring was strong, but also said he was very much alive.

I wrapped my fingers around the ring and then climbed out of the car. But before I could say anything, my phone rang, the sharp sound making me jump.

I frowned and dragged it from my pocket. Monty. My mouth went dry, and I swore again.

"What?" Aiden said immediately.

I turned the phone around so he could see the screen. "It can't be him. He's in the hands of the soucouyant."

"Answer it," Ashworth said. "It's just possible he's escaped and needs help."

I didn't think that would be the case, but I nevertheless hit the answer button and said, "Monty, are you okay?"

"No," he said, his voice etched with weariness and pain. "But I *am* alive. And I want to remain that way."

"Where are you and what does she want?"

"Her skin, in exchange for me. I think I'm in the clearing where we found the second body."

Which wasn't all that far away. "She'll kill us all the minute she gets her skin."

"More than likely, but you've more in your arsenal than just—"

He was cut off by a harsh, "Bring it. Tonight. Or he pay."

The broken statement *hadn't* come from a human throat.

The phone went dead.

I took a deep breath in an effort to contain the surging fear and said, "This *will* be a trap. How are we going to deal with it?"

"I'm guessing bullets won't do anything against this thing, so that's basically me out of the picture," Aiden said.

"Not if you're armed with a high-pressure backpack sprayer," Eli said.

"And if the five of us hit her with salted water from different angles, there's a fair chance we'll be able to destroy her," Belle said. "The problem is getting close enough before she senses us."

I took another of those useless deep breaths. "She wants her skin, so I'll deliver it. It should provide enough of a distraction for the rest of you to get close."

"And if she hits us first?" Aiden said.

"Then pray like hell that fire-repelling spell I placed on your charm works." I glanced at Ashworth. "Did Monty give you that fire screen spell he used when the soucouyant attacked the house that held her skin?"

"Yes." He glanced at Aiden. "Where are we going to get pressure sprayers at this hour?"

"We've some up at the compound. I'll go grab them and the skin, and meet the four of you back at the café." He glanced at the facility's portly owner. "Thanks for helping us out, Charles."

"I'm just glad you didn't damage the car," he said. "*That* would have made for one unhappy customer, let me tell you."

Aiden clapped him on the shoulder, then the five us quickly returned to the trucks and drove out. As Eli parked out the front of the café, Belle said, "Why would Monty point you toward the wild magic? Because I gather that's what he was going to say before he was cut off."

"I don't know." And I wasn't entirely sure it was safe to be relying on a power that seemed to be gaining some form of sentience—one beyond Katie's presence within it. I dragged my keys out of the pack and opened the door.

"Wild magic is a force of nature." Eli said, "and, as such, can only be used by—and directed against—the living. Spirits technically aren't, even if they can take on human form."

"So why were we able to use it to contain the younger soucouyant?" I tossed the backpack onto the table and continued to the reading room. "And why would he mention it?"

"Perhaps he wasn't suggesting you use it *against* the soucouyant," Ashworth said. "But rather as a means of protecting yourself—like you did when the bitch flung the fireball at us."

I skirted the reading room's furniture and pressed my hand against one of the many panels that lined the back of the bookcase—which was basically little more than front for the multiple storage compartments we'd built behind each shelf. Magic stirred across my fingertips, then the compartment clicked open.

I grabbed the box of holy water, then collected my silver knife and its rarely used harness, and headed out. "The wild magic might have stopped the fireball, but it was Monty's spell that actually saved us."

He waved a hand. "Perhaps, but you've woven it successfully enough through the protections around this place."

"Yes, but they haven't exactly been tested yet."

I placed the box on the table and opened it up. Inside

were a dozen small bottles—our entire remaining collection of holy water. "Use these if you get burned. I used holy water on Anna Kang when she took the brunt of an explosion that had been meant for me, and it saved her from extensive scarring."

And it would no doubt do the same for them if the soucouyant didn't simply cinder them straight out. Whether four bottles would be enough to help Monty was another matter entirely.

I strapped the knife to my leg, then pulled the ring out of my pocket just to make sure Monty was still alive. He was, but the pulsating heat was getting worse. He was running out of time.

The bell above the door chimed as Aiden stepped through. "Everyone ready?"

I grabbed our backpack and followed everyone across to the door, locking up before striding over to the ranger SUV.

Aiden didn't speak, but his tension filled the air and his aura was dark with fear and worry. We sped through the night and quickly reached the area where we'd found the second body.

Aiden stopped and, as Eli and Ashworth pulled up beside us, climbed out. We met at the front of his SUV.

"I'll have to lead Ashworth and Eli in, as they weren't here when we found the second victim. We can spread out a little once we get close." He glanced at Belle. "Are you two going to be able to find the clearing again?"

I nodded and glanced at Belle. "Hopefully she'll be so focused on me she won't notice you behind me."

"And if she does, I'll soak her ass."

"What's the plan once we all get close?" Ashworth said. "She'll undoubtedly hear us approaching—Aiden may be able to walk through the scrub without making much sound, but the rest of us won't."

I hesitated. "It might be best if you let me enter the clearing first. That way, she'll be focused on me and hopefully won't hear the rest of you. Belle can let you know when to run in and soak the bitch."

"Sounds like a game plan." Aiden touched my arm, squeezing it lightly. "I feel like a broken record right now, but be careful."

"As long as you promise the same, Ranger." I quickly kissed him and then glanced across at Ashworth and Eli. "Same thing with you two."

"I have a truck to rebuild thanks to that bitch," Ashworth grumbled. "Trust me when I say she's not going to get the chance to write off anything else I care about."

He glanced at Eli as he said that, and there was such an obvious depth of love between the two that it made my heart melt. I wanted to find a love like that. I really did.

The four of them collected the high-pressure sprayers from the back of the SUV, and then Aiden handed me the backpack that held the large jar containing the soucouyant's skin. It was surprisingly heavy. He touched my cheek lightly, briefly, and then turned and led Ashworth and Eli into the scrub.

I took a deep breath and glanced at Belle. "Ready?"

"As I'll ever be. Let's do this."

I grabbed my phone, flicked on the flashlight app, and retraced our initial path. And as before, we'd barely entered the forest when Katie's energy spun around me, leading me away from the main track. The path gradually grew steeper and rockier, forcing us to slow down even further. Neither of us bothered curtailing our noise, however. Right now, we needed the soucouyant focused on our approach rather than the men trying to sneak up behind her.

We reached the point where we had to leave the track and make our way through the trees, and my pulse rate went up several notches. The brightness of the soucouyant's fiery form was very visible, despite the thickness of the scrub dividing her and us.

I took a deep breath and called the wild magic to me. It answered, a rush of power that was both intoxicating and euphoric. My senses immediately expanded, and suddenly I could hear the soucouyant as easily as I saw her—heard the rustle of the flames, the shudder of the earth under her fiery feet. Smelled Monty's fear and agony, but *not* his burned flesh. She might have him trapped, but she hadn't yet set her flame on him.

I turned, took Belle's hands, and said, "Right, we need to cast a couple of fire nets. Raise your magic and repeat everything I say."

I didn't bother with mind speech. There was a risk of the soucouyant hearing us, but better her attention was on us rather than the men.

Belle frowned, but didn't object. I started the spell; Belle's words echoed mine, and the air around began to burn as twin nets formed around each of her hands. The wild magic wove its way through each thread, toughening and empowering our magic.

Once we'd both closed and activated the spell, Belle said, "Two nets?"

"One for the soucouyant, one for you."

"Fuck my protection—what about you?"

"The wild magic is with me. I'll be fine."

Her gaze scanned mine briefly. The concern so evident in her thoughts and in her expression didn't change. "And if

Eli is right? If the wild magic does prove to be useless against spirits?"

"It won't be. These spells are a mix of both our magic and the wild magic, and it was a similar combination that successfully contained the other soucouyant. Once her attention is on me, you should be able to cast the net over her. It won't kill her—it wasn't designed for that." And I certainly didn't want to stain the wild magic by making it party to murder. "It'll just contain both her and her flames long enough for us to hit her with water."

"And what if she hits you with fire the minute you appear? I'm betting she doesn't want to reclaim her skin but simply wants it destroyed so she can start stealing the skin of others."

"Undoubtedly, which is why I'm about to weave another net."

She studied me, her concern increasing. "Your weariness is already pulsing through me, and you'll need a whole lot more strength—"

"Which I can pull from the wild magic rather than you at this point. Relax Belle, it'll be fine." I smiled as I said it, even though I didn't personally believe it. There were too many things that could go wrong. "Ready?"

She took a deep breath and then nodded. I began weaving another fire net around my fingers as I continued on through the trees. With Katie's presence enhancing my senses, it didn't take very long to reach the clearing. I paused before I stepped through the last of the trees, scanning the clearing, looking for Monty. After a moment, I saw him. He was on the ground to the right and there were threads of disintegrating magic roiling around his body. That's why he hadn't yet been burned—he must have sensed her approach and cast the spell before he and the house had been hit. But the relief that surged was very quickly extinguished when my gaze slipped down to his legs. The bottom half of his left leg lay at right angles to his body. How he was still even conscious I had no idea.

The soucouyant sat on a chair fashioned out of fire in the center of the clearing; a queen on her throne, ready to meet her subjects. I took another of those deep breaths that didn't really do a lot and then said, *Belle, contact the others. Tell them I'm about to enter the clearing.*

Done, she said. *Be careful.*

Stay in the shadows directly behind me. I'll step aside once I've got Monty clear.

Wait... what?

No time to explain.

And with that, I flung the fire net around the container holding her skin and raised it high as I stepped into the clearing.

"Kill me," I said, even as her flames began to stir and hiss. "And you will never regain possession of your flesh."

"You die, spell dies," she said.

I stopped halfway between Belle and the soucouyant. "Except it's not just my magic. Look closer, spirit. You're old enough to know the caress of wild magic."

And hopefully *didn't* know enough about it to understand that wild magic could fade just as easily as any other.

The hissing of her flames grew louder. "What you want?"

I motioned toward Monty. "I want him released and out of this clearing first."

Her mirth was evident in the roll of the flames. "He free. Make no difference in end."

I glanced at him. "Monty, hate to ask this, but can you move?"

"Just fucking watch me."

And with that, he began a slow, torturous crab crawl toward the forest. His breaths were little more than pants of pain, and his sweat and determination stung the air. But inch by agonizing inch, he was getting there.

In the forest behind him, a twig snapped. My nostrils flared as Katie's senses once again flooded mine. Aiden, attempting to get close enough to help drag him clear.

I cleared my throat, dragged the soucouyant's attention back to me, and stepped closer. Fingers of flame reached toward me; the charm at my neck flared to life and though I could feel the heat of those fingers, none of them came within touching distance.

I kept moving toward her, the container held in front of me like an offering. Out of the corner of my eye, I saw Aiden grab Monty's arms and drag him into the trees. At the same time, I caught Ashworth and Eli's scents to the left and behind the soucouyant.

Tell them to move at my signal, Belle.

And your signal is?

You'll know it.

You and I are going to have a serious chat when all this is over, she growled, frustration in her mental tone.

Look forward to it.

The soucouyant's flaming fingers were now moving all around me, seeking a means to touch and burn. The pulsing in the charm at my neck grew stronger and began to match the pulsing in my head. I ignored both and continued to approach the soucouyant.

"Witch clear." She rose from the throne and stepped toward me. "Release skin."

I stopped and smiled. "Sure thing."

And with that, I threw the container, with all of my

might, into her fiery form and then dropped and curled into the smallest target possible. She exploded, and her fury and her flames washed over me. But she didn't immediately attack, instead reaching within herself to pull out the container.

Belle spun the net through the air, but the soucouyant must have sensed it and, at the last moment, flamed away. The net settled over the ground and part of her form, grabbing her, pinning her, but not entirely containing her.

She screamed, the sound earsplitting, and turned on me. Fire hit me, a furnace of heat that felt like it was boiling me alive. My skin turned red and my sweat dried in an instant, but I remained alive and breathing thanks to the charm at my neck.

Screams rose, but they weren't mine. I didn't dare waste the breath when the air in my small bubble of protection was becoming scarcer. My heart pounded so fast it felt like it was going to tear out of my chest and fear was so thick, so strong, it closed the back of my throat.

Hurry, Belle.

Trying.

Try harder, I wanted to say, but restrained the urge. Katie was still with me, so I closed my eyes and listened instead. Heard the whoosh of flames, the grunts that were elicited every time a fireball hit. Heard Ashworth shout, then Eli, and Aiden, and finally Belle—around and around it went, each one snaring her attention as she attacked the other. Rising above all that was the scent of smoke, of desperation, of fire being quenched. The pressure sprays were slowly but surely erasing her fire.

The pulsing in the charm became more frantic and smoke began to fill my small bubble. I twisted around, saw the ends of my jacket begin to curl and light. I swore and hastily pulled it off, but the T-shirt underneath didn't fare any better. In fact, it almost immediately began to brown. I waited until a line of red appeared in the fabric and then tore it off too. But that left me in nothing more than a bra....

Then, with a gigantic *whoomp*, the soucouyant exploded. Fire and heat briefly boiled over me, forcing a gasp from my throat as fingers of flames speared through the disintegrating barrier of my magic and eagerly caressed my skin.

Then they died, the energy died, the heat began to dissipate, and there was nothing but silence around me.

Belle? I said, then more urgently, *Belle!*

Here. The explosion sent me tumbling.

I blew out a relieved breath, then thanked and released Katie and the wild magic. And instantly felt a whole lot weaker. I took a deep, shuddering breath, and then carefully unrolled and pushed up onto my knees. Saw Belle behind me, climbing to hers. Saw the three men in various stages of doing the same.

Aiden twisted around, spotted me, and then scrambled up and ran at me. He dropped to the ground, his knees inches from mine, and reached out for—but didn't quite touch—me.

"Are you okay?"

"I've a mother of a headache and am a little singed around the edges, but yeah, I'm okay."

"Thank God." And with that, he gently wrapped his arms around me and hugged me like he never intended to let go.

I closed my eyes and just enjoyed the sensation.

Against all the odds, the soucouyant was dead and we were all alive.

Life didn't get much better than that.

EPILOGUE

Belle glanced up from the newspaper she was reading as I stepped through the café's front door. "How's Monty?"

"Extremely pissed off."

"Well, that's to be expected. He's got two shattered legs, after all, which means he's uncomfortable, in pain, and has a fair chunk of rehabilitation ahead of him."

"None of which is what he's grumpy about." I walked around the counter and flicked on the kettle. "You want a coffee?"

"Thanks. So what is he grumpy about if not for the long road that lies ahead?"

"The fact that the long road will be happening in Melbourne rather than here."

Belle grunted and got back to her reading. "That makes sense. They probably haven't got the full range of rehabilitation facilities here."

"That's exactly what he was told. He doesn't care."

Belle snorted. "I'm betting it has something to do with that car of his."

"Yes—apparently it can't survive a week without being polished. I got the impression he thinks she'll fall apart if he's not there to cosset her for months."

"I'm sure the owner of the facility would be all too happy to polish and cosset her. For a fee, of course."

I grinned and carried two instant coffees over. "Apparently he doesn't trust her in anyone else's hands."

"And yet he let you drive her." Belle raised her eyebrows. "If that isn't cousinly love, I'm not sure what is."

"That was nothing more than the simple fact he couldn't spell and drive at the same time. It won't happen again, I'm sure of that." I glanced around as the door chime sounded. Aiden stepped through and a delighted grin split my lips. He was wearing black jeans and a deep blue shirt that enhanced the color of his eyes while emphasizing the lean strength of his arms.

"Hey, Ranger, isn't it a little early for you to be arriving?" I said. "I thought you were working until seven?"

"I was, but the council called me to a meeting, so I gave myself the rest of the afternoon off." He bent to kiss me and then pulled out the chair and sat down.

"You want a coffee? Or a brownie?" I asked.

"No to the coffee, as I had one at the meeting, but I'll never say no to a brownie."

I smiled and rose to grab him a couple of slices. "What did the council want? Just an update on events?"

"Yes, but they also needed to discuss their options, given that Monty is going to be out of action for between three to six months."

I grimaced. "I have to be honest, the last thing I want is another damn witch coming down from Canberra, however temporarily."

"Oh, trust me, it's the last thing they want as well. Monty was the best of the remaining applicants."

"What about their first choice?" Belle said. "The one that missed the plane?"

"He accepted another position elsewhere." Aiden shrugged. "Anyway, they're thinking of asking Ashworth and Eli if they'd step in again on a temporary basis."

"Ashworth will more than likely say yes," I said.

Aiden picked up a brownie and bit into it. "That's their thinking—especially given he's spent a good chunk of time since Monty's arrival bitching about being bored and having nothing to do."

I grinned. "Yes, but I actually think he's also enjoying spending more time with Eli."

"Not sure Eli is so pleased about it," Belle murmured.

I chuckled. "True, but only because Ashworth is bored."

"They'll probably make an official approach tomorrow."

"And if for some weird reason Ashworth defies expectations and doesn't take the job?" I asked. "What's their plan then."

He shrugged. "Start the application process again and hope for a better result this time."

"Unlikely, from what Monty said."

"Perhaps, but our council has little choice. The witch council is aware there's a wellspring here that needs protection, so they'll no doubt force the issue if necessary."

"At least the wellspring is still protected by both Ashworth's magic and mine."

"I suspect the witch council will not leave the safety of such a large wellspring to an RWA witch and an unregistered, unvetted one," Belle said, voice dry. "Remember, they don't know the wild magic itself strengthens your spells and protects the wellspring."

"And long may that continue." I raised my mug and clicked it against Belle's, then returned my gaze to Aiden. "So what are we doing tonight, Ranger? Heading back to your place?"

"No. Not immediately, anyway. I thought we'd grab some dinner and then head over to Bendigo. Their annual charity dance is on, and I bought a couple of tickets."

Belle leaned sideways and looked under the table. "You're not wearing steel-capped shoes, Ranger. Bad move."

I leaned across the table and tried to whack her. She avoided it with a laugh. "Hey, I've tried to teach you proper dancing. I still bear the scars."

"You lie."

She grinned. "Maybe a little."

I snorted and glanced at Aiden. "How fancy is this shindig?"

"Not that fancy. I'm going as I am."

"Cool. I'll just race upstairs and get ready."

"Don't take forever. We've a dinner booking for six thirty."

I gave him the look—the one that said "don't be daft." "I *never* take forever to get ready."

He grinned. "Just in case this is the one occasion you do—don't."

"Huh." I picked up my coffee and headed upstairs.

After a quick shower, I got dressed, gussied my face up a little, found some heels comfortable enough to wear dancing, and then clattered back down the stairs.

His gaze slid slowly down my length and came up heated. "Very nice."

"See you tomorrow," Belle said. "And don't be complaining about your feet, Ranger. You were warned."

"Aside from being a very good dancer," he said, as he

tucked an arm around my waist. "I'm a very good teacher. We'll be fine."

With that, we headed out.

He was a great dancer and a very patient teacher, and we had an absolutely brilliant time.

But I wasn't entirely sure his feet would ever be same.

ABOUT THE AUTHOR

Keri Arthur, author of the New York Times bestselling Riley Jenson Guardian series, has now written more than forty-four novels. She's received several nominations in the Best Contemporary Paranormal category of the Romantic Times Reviewers Choice Awards and has won two Australian Romance Writers Awards for Scifi, Fantasy or Futuristic Romance. She was also given a Romantic Times Career Achievement Award for urban fantasy. Keri's something of a wanna-be photographer, so when she's not at her computer writing the next book, she can be found somewhere in the Australian countryside taking random photos.

for more information:
www.keriarthur.com
kez@keriarthur.com

ALSO BY KERI ARTHUR

Kingdoms of Earth & Air

Unlit (May 2018)

Cursed (Nov 2018)

Burn (June 2019)

Lizzie Grace series

Blood Kissed (May 2017)

Hell's Bell (Feb 2018)

Hunter Hunted (Aug 2018)

Demon's Dance (Feb 2019)

Wicked Wings (Oct 2019)

The Outcast series

City of Light (Jan 2016)

Winter Halo (Nov 2016)

The Black Tide (Dec 2017)

Souls of Fire series

Fireborn (July 2014)

Wicked Embers (July 2015)

Flameout (July 2016)

Ashes Reborn (Sept 2017)

Dark Angels series

Darkness Unbound (Sept 27th 2011)

Darkness Rising (Oct 26th 2011)

Darkness Devours (July 5th 2012)

Darkness Hunts (Nov 6th 2012)

Darkness Unmasked (June 4 2013)

Darkness Splintered (Nov 2013)

Darkness Falls (Dec 2014)

Riley Jenson Guardian Series

Full Moon Rising (Dec 2006)

Kissing Sin (Jan 2007)

Tempting Evil (Feb 2007)

Dangerous Games (March 2007)

Embraced by Darkness (July 2007)

The Darkest Kiss (April 2008)

Deadly Desire (March 2009)

Bound to Shadows (Oct 2009)

Moon Sworn (May 2010)

Myth and Magic series

Destiny Kills (Oct 2008)

Mercy Burns (March 2011)

Nikki & Micheal series

Dancing with the Devil (March 2001 / Aug 2013)

Hearts in Darkness Dec (2001/ Sept 2013)

Chasing the Shadows Nov (2002/Oct 2013)

Kiss the Night Goodbye (March 2004/Nov 2013)

Damask Circle series

Circle of Fire (Aug 2010 / Feb 2014)

Circle of Death (July 2002/March 2014)

Circle of Desire (July 2003/April 2014)

Ripple Creek series

Beneath a Rising Moon (June 2003/July 2012)

Beneath a Darkening Moon (Dec 2004/Oct 2012)

Spook Squad series

Memory Zero (June 2004/26 Aug 2014)

Generation 18 (Sept 2004/30 Sept 2014)

Penumbra (Nov 2005/29 Oct 2014)

Stand Alone Novels

Who Needs Enemies (E-book only, Sept 1 2013)

Novella

Lifemate Connections (March 2007)

Anthology Short Stories

The Mammoth Book of Vampire Romance (2008)

Wolfbane and Mistletoe--2008

Hotter than Hell--2008

CPSIA information can be obtained
at www.ICGtesting.com
Printed in the USA
BVHW070221240122
627003BV00005B/53